Kingz of the Game 7

Playa Ray

Lock Down Publications and Ca$h
Presents

Kingz of the Game 7

A Novel by *Playa Ray*

Playa Ray

Lock Down Publications
P.O. Box 944
Stockbridge, Ga 30281

Visit our website @
www.lockdownpublications.com

Copyright 2023 by Playa Ray
Kingz of the Game 7

First Edition February 2023
Printed in the United States of America

This is a work of fiction. Names, characters, places, and incidents either are products of the author's imagination or are used fictitiously. Any similarity to actual events or locales or persons, living or dead, is entirely coincidental.

Lock Down Publications
Like our page on Facebook: Lock Down Publications @
www.facebook.com/lockdownpublications.ldp

Book interior design by: **Shawn Walker**
Edited by: **Sunny Giovanni**

Stay Connected with Us!

Text **LOCKDOWN** to 22828 to stay up-to-date with new releases, sneak peaks, contests and more…
Thank you.

Submission Guideline.

Submit the first three chapters of your completed manuscript to ldpsubmissions@gmail.com, subject line: Your book's title. The manuscript must be in a .doc file and sent as an attachment. Document should be in Times New Roman, double spaced and in size 12 font. Also, provide your synopsis and full contact information. If sending multiple submissions, they must each be in a separate email.

Have a story but no way to send it electronically? You can still submit to LDP/Ca$h Presents. Send in the first three chapters, written or typed, of your completed manuscript to:

LDP: Submissions Dept
P.O. Box 944
Stockbridge, Ga 30281

DO NOT send original manuscript. Must be a duplicate.

Provide your synopsis and a cover letter containing your full contact information.

Thanks for considering LDP and Ca$h Presents.

Acknowledgements

Well, we have finally reached the last installment of this series. I'd like to thank all of my readers for tuning in, and giving me a chance to entertain you with my art of storytelling. Just make sure that you tune into the Crime Boss series as well.

Other people I'd like to acknowledge are: Mary B. McCoy, Mary Robinson, Alicia 'Twin' Flemister, Rayquan Nunn, Latasha M. Brooks, Osric 'Big O' Williams, Michale 'Trip James' Pullins, Christopher 'Mr. Situation' Pullins, Randal 'Big Ru' Jones, Moerise 'Major Gramz' Williams, Jesse 'Pistol Pete' Askew, Kionte 'Savali Kilumm' Glover, Kasim 'Young Cap' Gandy, Eric 'Perk' Perkinson, Yasmin Perkinson, Che 'Six-Nine' Clemons, Susan Dadzie, Abigail Dadzie, Leslie 'Sean P' Pruitt, Tavares 'Zero' Atwell, Franklin 'Drew' Andrews, Tommy 'Usher' Wright, Cameron 'Cam' Wright, tobbie 'Mankey' Dantzler, Cedric 'Monty' Salley, Ronnie 'Double R' Rucker, George Richardson, Brandon 'Houston' Connes, Rodney 'IceMan' Culver, Sharese 'Say No More' McCowan, Tellis 'West Side' Clark, Carlie Esco, South Phila, Kimmia 'Toot' Webb, Loquez 'Queail' Bell, Kimberly Davidson, Anthony 'Quick Ru' Whipple, and last, but not least, the whole staff of Lockdown Publications.

"Blessed is the King who comes in the name of the Lord"
-Luke 19:38a

Playa Ray

Chapter 1
Monday

"I'm going back. The streets owe me!"

Ray's words echoed in Sheila's mind for the duration of their ride home. The only reason these words bothered her is because she knew that he meant them which infused her body with a chill she'd never known.

Of course, money was a little tight as they fought to keep up with the bills, car note, and take care of two children, but it wasn't to the point where they had to result to any kind of illegal activities in order to make ends meet. Especially the kind of activities that Ray was considering pulling himself back into.

She also felt that someone could still be watching them, and it hurt her to her heart to know that Ray wasn't thinking the same way. Maybe she'd try to talk some sense into him later. Right now, he was beyond angry. She drew this conclusion from the remark he made about her and their manager, Jerry, as if intimating that something was going on between the two of them. She was definitely going to have to talk with him about that, also.

As always, after punching in the code to the electrical gate of Regal Park Apartments, and waiting for it to slide open, Ray drove up to the mailbox unit. The moment that Sheila was out of the car, he stomped down on the gas pedal, causing the vehicle to jerk forward as he sped towards their apartment.

All Sheila could do was shake her head as she zipped up her Checkers windbreaker and moved towards the mailboxes. After retrieving the mail, she made off in the direction of Shatera's apartment to pick up the kids.

While sifting through the mail, Sheila tried her best not to look in the direction of the group of men who always seemed to be gathered around the same white Dodge Magnum in the same spot every time she came home from work, as if they were waiting on her.

"Girl, when are you gonna get rid of that scrub, and let a real nigga slide up in that fat ass?" One of the men voiced, initiating the impudent rant that Sheila had become accustomed to.

"Yeah," another chimed. "Why settle for a nigga who flips burgers when you can have a nigga that flip bricks?"

Yeah, right! Sheila thought as she passed them. *If these niggas were playing with anything close to a brick, they wouldn't be staying in these cheap, raggedy-ass apartments.* This brought her mind back to Ray, whose birthday was in two more days, which seemed to sadden her, being that she had no money to buy, or either do something nice for him.

"Hey, girl!" Shateria greeted upon opening the door for Sheila. She was dark-complexioned, 5'6", and 143 pounds, clad in a pair of blue jeans, and a black sweater with the word 'SHAWTY' on the front, in bold, gray letters.

"Hey, Shatera!" Sheila returned, with less enthusiasm than usual.

"They must've worked you like a slave, today?" Her friend inquired, apparently noticing her mood.

"Girl, you don't know the half!"

"Hey, Momma Sheila!" Nine-year-old Rachel beamed, upon rounding the corner.

"Hey, baby!" Sheila replied, duly noting that she didn't have on her coat, nor her bookbag, as if she wasn't ready to go home. "Where's your brother?"

"Still playing video games with Tyrique," she answered. "Can we stay for chicken tenders?"

Sheila looked to Shantera. "Chicken tenders?"

"Momma wanted me to ask you if they could stay for dinner," she explained. "She should be almost done. I'll walk them over after they eat."

"Will this—"

"You won't owe me anything extra," Shatera cut her off. "Besides, Momma asked Prince Ray what he wanted to eat, and he said chicken tenders, which is why she's slaving over the stove, now."

"Okay." Sheila looked down at Rachel who was still a bit too small for her age. "Y'all can stay for chicken tenders," she told her stepdaughter. "Just remember that y'all gotta shower and do homework."

"Yes, ma'am!"

As Sheila made the short walk to their apartment, she figured it was good that the children were having dinner at the babysitter's, because she could have this impending conversation with Ray without them getting a whiff of it, just in case things got heated, which was highly expected.

Entering the quiet apartment, Sheila locked the front door, then made for their bedroom, although she could hear the shower running, which indicated that her man was in the bathroom.

Thankful that Ray wasn't upset enough to forget to cut the heating system on, Sheila shed her coat and hat, then made for the bathroom where she took it upon herself to enter, surprised that the door was unlocked. However, she did lock the door. Ray stuck his head out of the shower as she was letting the lid on the toilet down to sit on.

"The kids are eating dinner at Shatera's," Sheila offered, as if to answer Ray's inquisitive look. "She'll walk them home when they're done."

"So, what the hell are you doing?" He asked.

"I came in here to talk to you."

"About what?"

"About what you said in the car."

Ray seemed to study her for a few seconds before snatching the shower curtain closed, apparently to get back to his washing.

"Are you serious about going back to the streets?" Sheila went on, now regarding his silhouette through the curtain.

Ray didn't answer.

"Did you, at least, consider the fact that you have children now?" She persisted. "What about the fact that somebody could still be watching us? We could still be under investigation."

"You don't think I thought about all that shit?" Ray finally voiced. "Look at us! We're living in a cheap-ass apartment, working at a sorry-ass job, and can barely keep the utilities up, or afford to buy our children some decent clothes. They walk around, looking like the Adams family children, and you haven't had your hair fixed since Jesus graduated from high school."

Sheila wanted to laugh but she knew that he was being serious. However, at the mentioning of her hair, she absently ran a hand over her disheveled ponytail, though she wasn't at all disconcerted.

"Keeping a roof over our children's heads is way more important than worrying about how I look," Sheila went into defense mode, although she was, also, fed up with living the low life.

"See?" Ray responded. "You just gave up on life. Or, maybe you're in denial. You know this shit ain't what's happening. We both came from broken homes, and we vowed, right after you found out that you were pregnant that we'd never let our children experience that shit. What happened to that promise?"

"Don't give me that bullshit, Ray!" Sheila spat, figuring it was time to put him in his place. "You know what the hell happened! Or, did you forget that you barely escaped the death penalty?"

"I understand that you're scared," he offered, coolly. "That's a good thing. In fact, I'd rather you stick close to the kids, while I do what I feel I need to do, as a man, to take care of y'all."

"You're already doing that, baby," she tried to reason. "The kids and I are not complaining. Money means nothing to us— we're just glad to have you in our lives."

"I won't always be here, Sheila," Ray admitted. "I don't have life insurance, so I won't be leaving my children a damn thing! Do I have to paint the rest of the picture for you?"

Sheila didn't respond. No, she did not need for him to explain to her how the kids' lives may turn out, if they had nothing to fall back on. Honestly, that reality bothered her, also. She didn't want to die, leaving the little ones to fend for themselves, and she definitely didn't want to get hauled off to prison, which would bring about the same result.

"What if I take on a second job?" She finally asked, remembering that her grandmother had to work two jobs in order to take care of she and Shonda when they were young.

"That won't be necessary, Sheila'," Ray said, exasperation lacing his tone. "I understand everything you're saying, but my mind is already made. I just have to be extremely careful, this time, which is why I don't want you involved. That way if something happens to me, the children will still have you."

Playa Ray

Chapter 2

The following day, Ray struggled with fatigue while operating the grill with extreme caution. Especially after burning himself, twice. After having the talk with Sheila in their bathroom yesterday, he could not bring himself to fall asleep, for having to cope with disturbing images of him being murdered or hauled off to prison, as a result of returning to the drug game, which could've very well been an omen.

However, he wasn't the only one suffering from temporary insomnia. While he was being tortured by his unwelcomed thoughts, he couldn't help but notice that Sheila was tossing and turning and mumbling in her sleep, perhaps hashing it out with her own demons, induced by the same conversation.

At the thought of his girlfriend, Ray flipped the twelve beef patties over on their uncooked sides before moving over to the registers where he could see the dining area, where Sheila was assigned the sanitation detail. She didn't notice him watching her as she tended to the trash, looking as though she hadn't slept in days.

"Ray?"

Ray turned to see Leela, one of the three cashiers who also happened to be Calvin's girlfriend. She was light- complexioned, 5'6", with a slender build. At that moment, she was regarding him with that knowing glint in her eyes, and one hand posed on her hip.

"What's up?" Ray asked, purposely displaying disinterest in his voice.

"I have two grills," she informed, nodding towards the grill order monitor.

Quickly prying his eyes away from her, he looked to the monitor and saw the two special-made burgers ordered by one of her customers. There was also one for a customer in drive-thru, so Calvin was also waiting on him.

"Coming right up," Ray told Leela, then spun on his heels to see Calvin giving him an expecting look. "Shut up, Calvin! I'm on it."

"Hell, his ass can wait!" Calvin replied, laughing. "I told him to park over there— it may take ten minutes."

"Did you really tell him ten minutes?" Inquired Ray.

"Hell, yeah!" Calvin answered. "This ain't no damn Chinese restaurant! Do I look like Jackie Chan?"

All Ray could do was laugh and shake his head as he pulled the patties off the grill and fixed the two burgers for Leela, first. After fixing the one for Calvin, Ray checked his order monitor, saw there were no more special orders, then began scraping the grill off, preparing it for more meat.

"Sheila, could you take this out to that red car?" Ray heard Calvin ask.

Whenever a customer has to pullover from the drive-thru window to await their order, the employee working the dining area is responsible for taking their order out to them, so Ray thought nothing of it. Once the fresh meat was laid on the grill, he pressed the timer button, then took his two empty boxes to the trash buggy at the back door.

"Do you need more patties?" asked Toni, the assistant manager, who was exiting the office as Ray was passing it on his way back to his station.

"Not right now," he told her. "I still have three more boxes."

"Well, let me know."

"Yeah," Ray mumbled, moving on.

"Yo, check this out, Ray!" Calvin stopped Ray in his tracks, indicating something outside his window.

Giving it no thought, Ray moved over to the window. There were a few people exiting their vehicles and moving towards the building, but Ray doubted that this was what Calvin was trying to show him. Therefore, he shifted his gaze until he spotted Sheila, standing at the driver side of a red Audi with chrome wheels, talking to its occupant, who he couldn't see for the tinted windows.

"That's Major Gramz," Calvin offered, as if Ray inquired. "He's over every IF Gang nigga in Georgia."

"IF gang?" Ray asked, still watching Sheila, who was giggling like a schoolgirl.

"Inglewood Family," answered Calvin. "He's from Summer Hill, but he got his sect stamped in California by some high-powered Bloods."

"I guess he deals drugs too, huh?"

"He's not one of the major plugs, but he supplies niggas in Summer Hill, and a few more spots. He's getting up there, though. Especially since Drop Squad fell off the face of the earth. Hell, a lot of them niggas became Blood. We got some of them niggas in our sect."

That's when Ray turned to Calvin just as the timer on the grill went off. "You're Blood, too?"

"I'm Folk," he said, as if insulted. "Perk G is my O.G."

For the remainder of the day, Ray racked his brain about the drug game, wondering how he was going to get back into it without having to start over at the bottom, because standing on a corner, or operating a drug house was totally out of the question.

He was used to men trying to court Sheila's fine ass, so losing her to a nigga with money was the last thing on Ray's mind, though he was well aware that it could happen. Despite all that bullshit she said about money not meaning a thing, he knows his girlfriend misses the life she was living, prior to the Feds taking them down and confiscating everything. He knew that she meant well, but reality is reality.

After getting home from work, Ray showered, ate dinner with Sheila and the kids, then excused himself. Of course, she didn't ask where he was off to. "Be careful!" was all she said when he was leaving out the door. Plus, there was that worried expression on her face in which he very well expected but ignored altogether. She knew how he was when he had his mind made up.

The house in Marietta, Georgia looked the same as it did the last time he'd seen it six years ago. Plus, the white, four-door BMW and the red BMW coupe sitting in the driveway gave him confirmation that the person he was seeking out still resides there, although the older BMW that used to sit off in the grass with the tarp over it wasn't there.

After furtively taking a look around to see if he was being watched, Ray grabbed his cellular then exited the car, tugging at his coat for the sake of the cold wind. As he moved up the driveway, his eyes darted from window to window, searching for any sign of movement, but before he reached the front door, it came open. Ray didn't slow his momentum, and his friend's expression remained unreadable.

"I thought only cats had nine lives," Eric asserted in a mirthless tone.

"Trust me," Ray replied, stopping five feet in front of Eric, "I'm already tired of playing the ghost of Christmas past, for the second time."

Laughing, Eric stepped forward and embraced his little homie. "It's good to see you, again!"

"You, too." Ray returned the affection.

"Come on in!"

Ray entered and immediately noticed that the entire living room suite had been changed. Even the plasma television had been replaced with a much larger one, though it hung in the same place as its predecessor. Though the tube was on, there was rap music playing at a low volume from a system he couldn't see.

"I just sent the kids to bed," Eric informed upon closing the door back. "Sharonda's at work. She went back to working at the hospital when the Feds shut down the dealership. Can I get you anything?"

"I'm good," Ray answered. "Just came to talk to you about some business."

"Well, have a seat!" Eric gestured toward the sofa as he moved to the recliner. Once they were both seated across from each other, with the coffee table between them, he asked, "So, what's on your mind?"

"I'm trying to get back in," Ray told him. "Right now, I'm working at Checkers, and this shit ain't cutting it!"

"Where's Sheila?"

"At home with the kids."

Eric looked surprised. "Y'all got kids?"

"We have a son together," he explained, unzipping his coat. "Rachel came from Sylvia."

"Not the Sylvia that was murdered, right?"

"It's a long story, E." Ray was reluctant to talk about Sylvia.

"But, the baby survived, though."

"I'm glad to hear that," said Eric. "Isn't today your birthday?"

"Tomorrow."

"What're you doing for it?"

"Not a damn thing," Ray told him. "Sheila plans on taking me out to dinner on Saturday."

"That's what's up," Eric replied, leaning in the chair. "You know I got you, if you need a lil' paper to keep the bills up, or whatever."

"I can make my own money, E," Ray expressed, feeling like his friend was being evasive. "All I need is the product to do it with. Can you help me, or not?"

"Not personally," Eric told him. "I'm not pushing the kind of weight that I was pushing back in the day, and I know you're not trying to stand on no corner, or sling nickels and dimes out of a crack house."

Ray had to cogitate this for a moment. His mind was so preoccupied with getting back into the drug game that not once did he think about how he was going to go about it. He didn't want to start off peddling crumbs, but in order to move weight, he would need someone to sell the weight to, which was a standing problem at the moment because he didn't have contact with any of his old clientele.

"What's the market looking like, now?" Ray finally inquired.

"Shit, we're still recovering from a seven-month drought," Eric told him, just as his cell phone vibrated atop the coffee table. "I was affected, but not to the point where I couldn't keep up the bills, car notes, and mortgage. Hold on!" He retrieved his phone, answering it. "I'ma have to call you back, Pauline," he told his caller. "Because I'm talking to one of my homies. Just answer the phone when I call your ass!" Disconnecting the call, he looked over to Ray. "I fucked around and got another bitch pregnant."

"Does Sharonda know about it?"

"Hell no!" Eric let out. "It's one of her best friends, too."

"Ouch!" Ray sympathized.

"Don't remind me," Eric replied, slowly shaking his head. "I already feel like the bitch is on some extortion shit, always asking for money."

"How old is the baby?"

"Going on three."

There was a pregnant pause before Ray said, "I need your help. Standing on a corner is out of the question, so I need something to work with."

"Do you still have links to your old clients?"

"Some of 'em," Ray lied. "So, it shouldn't take long for me to get off of whatever I get."

Eric seemed to study his comrade for a moment before saying, "Give me some time to relay this to my connect. Once he lets me know what's up, I'll get back at you."

Chapter 3
Saturday

"It doesn't look that bad, baby," Sheila offered when Ray re-entered their bedroom, clad in the three-piece gray suit she'd bought for him at a local Men's Warehouse. "You can't even tell it's not tailored."

Draped in a light-blue, snug-fitted dress, Sheila was seated on the bed, browsing her Facebook page while awaiting her man to get ready so they could head on out to the event she had planned for his birthday, although it was three days ago. Being that Ray wasn't a fan of social media sites, and frowned whenever she indulges herself in it, Sheila immediately logged out of her account, then placed the phone on the bed, beside her.

"A blind man can spot this cheap-ass suite from a mile away," Ray responded, moving over to the dresser where he began putting on his burgundy tie.

"I'll do it." Sheila got off the bed and assisted him. "You'll mess around and be late for your own funeral."

"Yeah, whatever!"

Ray hadn't told her, but Sheila was looking extremely good in her dress and the red, braided synthetic hair in her head. He had no clue as to where she attained the money to pay Shatera for doing it, nor to take him out to a birthday dinner that he was quite sure they couldn't afford, but he didn't pry. Yes, Ray was under the impression that his woman may have another man on the side, but he held his peace. At least, until he could prove it.

"There you go, baby!" Sheila said once she was done, regarding him with those big, brown eyes and wonderful smile of hers. "You look great!"

"I always look great." Ray replied, turning to gander at himself in the vanity mirror.

Sheila gripped one of his buttocks. "I'll never deny that, with your sexy ass!"

"Momma?"

Sheila quickly removed her hand as they both turned to see their six-year-old son, Prince Ray, standing in the doorway, buttoning up his coat. "What, baby?" Sheila answered.

"I thought we were going over Shatera's and Tyrique's house," he said, accusingly.

"You are," she told him. "Is your sister ready?"

He shrugged. "I don't know. She won't let me in her room."

"Because you be tearing up her toys," Ray joined in, staring down at his son whose cornrows were in dire need of re-doing.

"Should I go ahead and walk them over there?" Sheila intervened.

"You can."

"How long will it take for you to pick me up?" She questioned.

"However long it'll take for the car to warm up," Ray shot back.

Sheila regarded her son. "Knock on your sister's door and tell her to come on!"

"Okay."

When their son left, Sheila gripped Ray's buttocks, again. "I'll see your fine ass in a minute. Just don't have me waiting. We have to make our reservations."

Ray didn't respond, and Sheila didn't expect him to. She donned her coat that was on the bed, grabbed her pocketbook, then exited the bedroom just as Prince Ray and Rachel were approaching. For some reason, Sheila could not get over the fact that the both of them were the same height, though Rachel was three years older than Prince Ray.

"Come on, y'all!" She told them.

Sheila didn't bother with locking the door back upon exiting the apartment. At 7:12PM, the remainder of daylight was slowly fading away as the goings-on of the community resumed as usual.

Approaching Shatera's apartment, they saw Shatera standing on the porch in conversation with a man who was standing against a white Lexus coupe that was still running. Knowing Shatera, Sheila figured the man at the bottom of the steps was one of her new play things.

"I was wondering where y'all were," Shatera said when she saw Sheila and the kids approaching.

"Girl, no comment," Sheila offered, refusing to place the blame on Ray in front of the children. "However, we're here. And I appreciate you for doing this!"

"Girl, you know you can count on me," her friend replied. "Would I have enough time to braid Prince Ray's hair?"

Sheila looked down at her son who definitely needed it.

"I'll be doing it for free," Shatera added. "Hell, I'm bored and have no customers for tonight."

"Okay." Sheila pulled fifty dollars from her pocketbook, handing it to Shatera. "Here's what we owe you."

"Shawty, you look familiar," the guy standing by the steps said to Sheila. He was brown complexioned, 6'1", and about 230 pounds, but he wasn't at all familiar to her.

"Is that one of your pick-up lines?" Sheila asked, eyeing him from head to toe.

The man laughed. "Naw, baby. I don't use those. But, we did meet back in two thousand and eight."

"How?" Sheila was hoping like hell that he wasn't one of their old clients, because Shatera knew nothing about 'Queen' Sheila.

"You owned The Warehouse," he told her. "My group, Southern Comfort, was set to perform on the night the Feds stormed the spot."

"What's your name?" Sheila asked, feeling disconcerted that Shatera had to hear this.

"I'm Trez," he said, jerking his thumb in the direction of the guy leaning against the Lexus. "That's my man, Lavish, our engineer. We actually had a sit-down with you in your office."

"I remember that," Sheila admitted, just as Ray brought the car around. "Are y'all still doing music?"

"Yeah, we're still trying to get up through there," he answered. "I see you know my sister."

This came as a surprise. "Um, yeah, I do."

"We need to get going, Trez," Lavish finally spoke. He was brown complexioned and stood about 6' 5".

"I need to get going myself," Sheila said, kissing the kids on their foreheads. "Y'all be good. I'll see y'all later."

"You can see me later, too, beautiful!" Trez took his shot.

"Boy, leave my friend alone!" Shatera intervened. "Don't make me tell Nikki on your ass! You know she don't play!"

"Ooh, shit!" Lavish let out, laughing.

"You're a real hater, sis!" Trez expressed, a disappointing look on his face.

"Whatever!" Shatera regarded Sheila. "Girl, I got the babies. Y'all enjoy yourselves."

"Thanks, Shatera!"

When Sheila turned to head to the car, she immediately noticed that Ray had already made the transition from the driver's seat to the front-passenger seat. He did this because it was agreed upon that Sheila would drive, being that Ray knew nothing of the place he was being treated to.

However, upon climbing behind the wheel, she was hoping like hell that he didn't go into a conniption and accuse her of one of those men, but he remained silent. In fact, he continued doing whatever he was doing on his phone as if he hadn't noticed she'd joined him.

"Shatera said she'll braid Prince Ray's hair for free," Sheila offered, testing the water.

"Mm-hmm," he let out, still absorbed in his device.

***

Ray had never heard of The Marshmallow. As Sheila pulled into the lot of the nondescript building, he eyed it with contempt, wondering what kind of 'special' dinner they would have at such a place. Seeing that the parking lot was partially filled, he assumed they had to be doing something right. So, with that in mind, and considering the fact that his woman had gone to whatever trouble she'd went to in order to celebrate his birthday, he figured that he'd retain his critiques, no matter what.

It didn't take long for Sheila to find a place to park. They hadn't swapped one word for the whole ride, and the crickets were definitely chirping as Sheila and Ray climbed from the car, only to be assailed by the cold wind that felt like it was doing at least fifty-five miles per hour.

As they approached the small building, Ray tried his best to see through its large, tinted windows. Either the windows were extremely dark, or the interior lights were extremely low, because he couldn't see not one silhouette.

For some reason, as they neared the entrance, it seemed like Sheila put a little more pep in her step, pretty much leaving him in her wake. The moment she made it to the door, she yanked it open, and entered, without even looking back to see if he was behind her. Ray had to quicken his steps in order to catch the handle. Just as he did, he immediately realized that it was actually dark inside the place. Out of instinct, he wanted to stop in his tracks, but his legs kept moving as if by some magnetic force. Then, the lights came on.

"Surprise!"

The place wasn't as small as it looked from the outside, but it was jamb-packed with a bunch of familiar faces. Mostly of faces Ray hadn't seen in years. As they all clapped their hands and moved towards him with genuinely happy faces, Ray noticed that Sheila was nowhere to be found. That's when it dawned on him that she didn't have to stay and greet their old friend, because, obviously, she's been keeping in touch with them, which was why they were all there.

"Hey, Ray!" Nikki was the first to greet him with a hug. "Happy birthday!"

"Thanks, Nikki!" He replied, embracing her back. "How are the kids?"

"They're fine. When will you get the chance to visit them?"

"Hopefully, soon."

"What's up, Ray!" This was Nikki's husband, Ace. The last time Ray laid eyes on him was at the hospital, when Nikki pulled her selfish suicide attempt.

"How's it going, pimpin'!" Ray slapped hands and embraced him.

"Man, I can't call it," Ace answered, smiling. "It's good to see you!"

Ray found himself smiling back at the man that he felt comfortable with entrusting the welfare of Nikki and the kids to, although the glint in his eyes was a little off. It definitely didn't match the smile he was giving Ray at that moment. Or, was he imagining this?

Also in attendance were Kim, Poppo, Joe, Precious, Connie, and Star. Even Osric, AKA Big-O was a sight to see, right along with Eric, whom Ray felt was already aware of this surprise party, even while Ray was visiting him at his home this past Tuesday. The mischievous grin he had on his face while he wished Ray a happy birthday confirmed it.

"Enjoy yourself," Eric told him. "We'll talk business later."

With that, Eric moved on through the crowd, bobbing his head to the rap music pumping from large speakers that sat in two of the four corners. That's when Ray finally took stock of the place. It was, indeed, a restaurant, considering the tables, chairs, and service counter. Not to mention the aroma of different spices of various cooked foods. However, for the occasion, he figured the table and chairs had been rearranged to form something of a dance floor. Plus, the DJ had his turntables propped up on one of the dining tables.

While taking in the atmosphere, Ray finally spotted Sheila, who was seated at a table with her grandmother, Dorothy, and Elaine Davis, mother of deceased daughters Ebony and Erica. These women were not strangers. In fact, the last time Ray had seen them was last Sunday, when he and Sheila picked up the kids from spending the weekend at their home in Riverdale. He set out in their direction.

"Happy birthday, my boy!"

He'd only taken two steps when his path was blocked by Calvin, who was accompanied by his girlfriend Leela, three other men, and another woman. Like everyone else, they weren't dressed casually, but everything they had on was black, including their bandannas.

"Thanks!" Ray said, only bumping fists with the man that he didn't really consider a friend.

26

"This is Perk G," Calvin introduced, gesturing to the guy who was dark-brown and stood about 5' 9". "That's his wife, Yasmine, and two of our bros, Blade and Savali."

"I hope we're not intruding," Perk offered. "I don't like to show up at people's parties, unannounced, unless it's on official business."

"It's all good," Ray told him. "Enjoy yourselves."

Finally, Ray was able to set his feet back into motion. As he moved about, he casually scanned the crowd for other known and unknown faces he hadn't greeted yet. That's when he spotted their manager, Jerry, and his wife Toni, who were both leaning against a far wall, clearly watching him. It angered him to know that Sheila invited them when she knew how much he hated Jerry.

"Hello, ladies!" Ray greeted Dorothy and Elaine, once he reached their table.

"Hey, Ray!" They replied in unison.

After hugging the older women, he leaned over and whispered in Sheila's ear. "Why is Jerry here?"

"He and Toni pitched in on this," she said with attitude. "Just like most of these other people. If it'll make you feel any better, I can ask him to leave."

Ray was highly tempted to call her bluff, but it wasn't in him to be spiteful just for the hell of it. Therefore, after kissing his woman on the forehead, he took a seat beside her, and cast another glance across the room at Jerry and Toni, who were looking back in their direction.

"So, what am I getting for dinner?" Ray asked Sheila, taking his mind off of Jerry and his wife. "Or, is it a surprise?"

"Everything's a surprise," she replied with a playful smirk on her face.

Playa Ray

Chapter 4
Monday

After cleaning the grill and putting on fresh meat for the second shift grillman, Ray retrieved his coat, then entered the manager's office to clock out. As always, Toni was present, but she said nothing to him as he logged himself out, which was surprising to him.

In fact, it seemed like Jerry and Toni had been treating Ray and Sheila a little different today. They were being nice. Maybe, a bit 'too' nice. Well, the two of them did have a good time at Ray's party.

Instead of making critiques, Jerry was periodically complimenting Ray on how he handled the grill, and Toni seemed to have become buddy-buddy with Sheila, chatting her up whenever she came to the front of the store, where Sheila was working one of the registers.

Exiting the office, Ray made for the rear of the store where Calvin was angrily tossing trash into the trash cart, and pretty much talking to himself, although Ray knew that he was cursing Jerry out for putting him on trash duty.

"You need some help?" Ray asked upon approaching.

"Naw, I got it," he answered, not even looking in Ray's direction.

"You're being stubborn," Ray told him as he began helping out. "Two pairs of hands are always better than one."

Calvin gave no further argument. Instead, after loading the cart for the first round, he disarmed the alarm, then pushed the back door open. Ray trailed behind the cart as Calvin pulled it towards the dumpster.

"My folks enjoyed the party," Calvin offered once they began unloading the cart.

"Yeah, I saw that," Ray replied, glad that he brought the subject up. "Your boy, Perk, got a little tipsy."

Calvin chuckled. "Yeah, he drinks like a faucet, but he handles business."

"I can dig that." Ray decided to plunge right in. "Do you think he'll front me some work?"

His co-worker stopped what he was doing to regard him. "You can't be serious!"

"That's who you get your work from, right?"

"Yeah," answered Calvin. "So, you really want some work?"

"I'm quite sure you know our story," Ray said, knowing everybody at the job were aware of his and Sheila's past lives.

Calvin shrugged. "Of course, I mean, who doesn't know about the notorious King Ray and Queen Sheila?"

Ray just looked at him.

"My bad!" Calvin offered with a grin on his face. "I'll call him later and see what he says. That's all I can do."

"I'd appreciate it," said Ray. "And, let him know that it's only me— Sheila's not involved."

***

Upon making it home, Ray showered then placed a call to Joe and Poppo, while Sheila was taking her shower and the kids were doing their homework. Before the surprise birthday party, he hadn't seen nor heard anything from his friends since that day in trial. He also found it strange that Sheila had been keeping up with everyone on social media and didn't tell him. He didn't question her about it, though.

However, the two of them agreed to meet with Ray at the Varsity restaurant in Atlanta, which is why Ray was now pulling into its lot, not knowing what kind of vehicles his friends were in. It didn't matter because the moment he found a spot and parked, he looked up to see them both approaching. He was glad to see them, but his main focus was on Poppo who was draped in a trench coat that was open to a three-piece suit that he was wearing. He'd never thought his friend would become an ordained minister, although it didn't come as a great surprise.

"Thanks for coming, fellas!" Ray said, when Joe slid in beside him, and Poppo climbed in the rear, behind Joe.

"It's all good," Joe told him. "You know we got you, if you need anything."

Ray caught on to the statement, instantly. It seems that everyone felt he and Sheila needed some kind of hand-out. Yes, times were hard, but, clearly, they'd forgotten that he was known to get out and get his own.

"I'm not looking for a hand-out, bro," Ray replied, taking umbrage. "You know that's not me."

"Don't look at it like that, babe," Poppo offered from behind them. "We're just letting you know that we're still here for you, like brothers are supposed to be."

In response, Ray directed his attention out his side window and took a deep breath.

"I have a service tonight, brother," Poppo resumed. "What is it that you need to speak to us about?"

"I'm getting back into the drug game," he answered, now facing his friends.

"You're what!" Poppo let out.

"Did you forget that we barely escaped that last ordeal?" Joe voiced with a serious look on his face.

"Of course, I didn't forget," said Ray. "Hell, the shit still haunts me."

"God gave us another chance, Ray," Poppo told him. "Think about all the people we lost to the streets. We could've easily been one of them, but God had better plans for us."

"We kinda figured that's what this meeting was about," Joe said, holding some kind of folded documents out to Ray.

"What's that?" Ray asked, making no effort to reach for the papers.

"I opened another customs shop in Dekalb County," Joe said. "I'm willing to sign it over to you."

"That's a hand-out," Ray reminded.

"It's not," Joe begged to differ. "You helped build RJP Customs. Poppo sold me his shop, and I'm giving you the one in Dekalb. I don't need three of 'em."

Ray turned to Poppo. "You sold your shop?"

"It was started with drug money," Poppo replied. "Whatever the Feds didn't take, I got rid of. Right now, I just hustle for the Lord."

"I respect that." Ray turned to Joe. "Keep your shop, bro. My mind is already made. The streets owe me, and I'm 'bout to sweep through those bitches like the Grim Reaper!"

Chapter 5

"Why are you working there?" Asked Ray, who was seated in the front-passenger seat of Calvin's black Jeep Cherokee.

It was Saturday, and the both of them were on their way to Perk G's home out in Decatur, Georgia. Well, that's what was told to Ray by Calvin, who'd called in sick from work just to make sure that Ray made his appointment with the guy.

The ride worked out, because Sheila needed the car to go grocery shopping, although they always went together. After receiving the call from Calvin about the meeting, Ray relayed this to Sheila who didn't bother to protest, which wouldn't have done her any good, by the way. Plus, she already knew that Ray was on a mission, and that it would take the hand of God to stop him.

"I'm on parole," Calvin answered Ray's question. "It's either work or go back to prison. If I go back to prison, it'll be for burning a nigga, or slinging this dope. Hell, I just might hold court in the streets."

"Yeah, I hear that," Ray replied. "Your boy Perk seems like a decent dude, but what's up with those other two kats?"

"Who?" Calvin shot him a glance. "Blade and Savali?"

Ray said nothing.

"Those are Perk's shooters," Calvin explained with the shrug of his shoulders. "He keeps them around because those are some ruthless-ass niggas! They don't spare shit!"

"I kinda sensed that about them."

At that time, Calvin turned onto a residential street lined with modern-style houses on each side. The one he parked in front of had a black Range Rover and a burgundy convertible Chevy Camaro sitting in its driveway. They didn't hesitate to get out and travel the driveway up to the front door. Before they could reach the door, it swung open, and Yasmine, Perk's wife, stood there in a gray jean suit with a lit blunt in her hand.

"What's up, y'all!" She greeted with a broad smile, prominently displaying the gap in her teeth. "Come on in! Perk's in the living room."

Giving her a peck on the cheek, Calvin entered the house, followed by Ray, who immediately took stock of the place that was pretty much mediocre, but very today. As Yasmine asserted, her husband was seated on the living room sofa with his eyes affixed to the screen of the large plasma television hanging on the wall.

"Welcome to my castle, Ray!" Perk greeted when they entered. "Please, have a seat! Can I get y'all boys anything?"

"I'm good," Ray said, copping a seat in the sole recliner.

"Where that weed at?" Calvin wanted to know as he took a seat beside his O.G.

"Yasmine's blunt-hogging ass got the dope," Perk complained.

"I heard that shit, nigga!" Yasmine finally entered the room.

"I was hoping you heard it," he shot back. "You and Shamari are supposed to be already gone, anyway!"

"I'm waiting on his slow ass," she replied, taking an extremely long pull on the blunt.

"Look at this vacuum cleaner!" Perk said of his woman. "She'll fuck around and make me tie her black ass up!"

"Boy, I'm about to give you this damn blunt!" She huffed. "Don't make me kick your ass in front of your company!"

Ray found himself smiling at the two, who put him in the mind of how James and Kim used to go at it.

Just then, a young boy entered the living room, buttoning up his coat. "I'm ready, Momma," he announced.

"It's about time!" Yasmine responded, walking over and handing the blunt over to Perk. "I'm about to go upside your daddy's head."

Shamari giggled.

"Don't believe that, Shamari!" Perk told his son. "Your mom'll end up in one of those cold case files."

"Whatever!" Yasmine grabbed her cellular and purse off the table. "Do you still need me to pick that up?"

"Yeah," Perk answered. "If it don't look right, don't take it. I'll send the boys to pay him a visit."

Yasmine shrugged. "Okay. Come on, Shamari!"

"What'd y'all boys know about this movie?" Perk asked, when his wife and son left out.

Ray glanced up at the television. "That's Equilibrium."

"You know your movies!" Perk marveled, flicking his lighter to re-light the blunt.

"I know this one," Ray let on. "It's one of my favorite action movies."

"Mine, too." He took a long drag on the blunt, then passed it over to Calvin. "So, how much work are you looking for?"

"How much can you front me?"

"Personally, I don't think I have enough to satisfy *your* appetite," Perk admitted. "I know your story. You went from King Ray, to the Last Kind standing. I wasn't hustling then, but I heard of the Kingz and LKS. Like I said, I don't have the quantity of product you may be looking for, but I'm willing to turn you on to my connect."

"Who's your connect?" Ray inquired when he paused to hit the blunt, again.

"Big Ru," Perk answered at a length.

"He's Blood," Ray pointed out. "Doesn't that make y'all rivals?"

Calvin and Perk exchanged a glance before bursting into laugher.

"Not necessarily, Ray," Calvin took the initiative. "That's the bullshit they portray in movies and shit. We bang what we bang, but, at the end of the day, it's all about that paper. Ain't no discrimination when it comes to that green."

"I already told Big Ru about you," said Perk. "He's already ready to put you on. All I have to do is make the phone call."

***

Being that the kids were spending the weekend with Elaine and Dorothy, and Ray was probably out meeting with some drug cartel, Sheila was determined not to go grocery shopping, alone. Therefore, she called upon her friend, Precious, who'd dated Ray way before Sheila came into the picture, and asked her to meet her at the local grocer, being that Precious didn't live too far from them.

"Girl, I'll never get my hair done by her again!" Precious was saying as she trailed Sheila, who was pushing a shopping cart down one aisle. "She had me looking like Aunt Esther from the Fred Sanford Show."

Sheila laughed. "You mean, Sanford and Son?"

"Hell, that one, too!" Precious let on, giggling. "All I know is that I had a weave falling out of my hair before I even left the shop."

"Girl, that's why you should've waited for your stylist to finish," Sheila told her, stopping to view the selection of cereal. "Just because a woman owns a salon, that doesn't mean she's good at the profession."

"I know that's right!"

Then, after a moment's pause, Precious asked, "So, when will I be able to come by and see the kids?"

"I haven't figured that part out yet," Sheila answered, although she was highly aware that Precious could be using the children as a pretext to get close to Ray. "I'm still trying to ease you all back into Ray's life. Right now, he's agitated and fed up with the way we're living, so I really don't think it's a great idea to invite anyone to our *humble* abode."

"That's understandable," Precious sympathized. "I mean, he's used to people seeing him in the light of a boss. A fall like that could really damage a person mentally."

"Yeah, I know," Sheila replied, placing a box of Honey Nut Cheerios into her cart. She knew exactly what her friend was talking about, because she was experiencing that same mental shift.

"I sensed that about him at the party," Precious went on, as Sheila chose more cereal. "He seemed, like, dejected, and his smile was forced. But, the eyes … the eyes never lie."

"Hi, Sheila!"

Sheila looked to see Andrew approaching, pushing his own cart. The last time she'd laid eyes on him was in 2005 at her birthday bash, although the most memorable moment was her catching him in her bed, performing fallatio on another woman, who just so happened to be her supervisor at the time.

"How are you?" He asked.

Sheila just glared at him.

Andrew let out a sigh. "I know what I did was wrong, but that was a long time ago. Do I regret it? Yes, I do. Every day of my life."

"You were always good with words," Sheila let on. "Have you ever thought about running for President?"

"Come on, Sheila!" he tried to reason. "I mean, what do I have to do to prove to you that I'm sorry for what I did?"

"You can jump into an ocean full of sharks," Sheila answered, pushing her cart on past him with Precious at her heels.

***

Ray couldn't remember the last time he'd been anywhere near Gresham Road. However, memories began filling his mind as he took in the surrounding community from the passenger side of Calvin's SUV.

Right after getting off the phone with Big Ru, Perk informed Ray that the supplier wanted to meet with him today, which came as a surprise. Plus, Ray was kind of skeptical about this, being that he could still have enemies lingering from his past life who would just love to settle an old score. He was packing his Glock .40 just in case.

Now, Calvin was turning onto Settle Circle which really brought back memories to Ray, whose late-grandmother resided in this neighborhood for as long as he could remember, although he'd only visited her whenever he was living with his dad. Of course, his eyes were locked on the gray and white house that she once occupied as they neared it. He just didn't expect for Calvin to park directly across the street from it.

Re-directing his attention, Ray took to analyzing the red brick house they were parked in front of. There wasn't anything particularly outstanding about it, except for the burgundy GMC Denali, and the blue, boxed Chevy Caprice with its yellow, checkered flag design on the front-end of it, sitting in its driveway. The car that Calvin parked behind was a gray Audi.

"Another thing," Calvin spoke, killing the engine and getting Ray's attention. "Big Ru has a personal shooter by the name of Quick Ru. As soon as we enter, he'll pat us down for our straps."

"So, I have to leave my gun out here?" Ray asked.

"Not really, but—"

"Well, let's get this over with!"

Ray pushed his door open and climbed down from the jeep but didn't take a step towards the house until Calvin joined him. As they passed the vehicles, Ray found himself marveling at the yellow up-holstery of the Caprice that was in sync with its checkered flag design. Calvin rang the doorbell.

Seconds later, without an answer, the door was opened up, and Ray figured the guy that was regarding them with a menacing look was Quick Ru. On top of looking like he'd never had a good day in his life, he was brown-complexioned with deep waves in his head and light-brown eyes. His jewelry wasn't much to wow at, but the handle of a chrome .45 sticking from the waistband of his pants could not go unnoticed. After seconds of notably sizing Ray up, he stepped aside, allowing them entrance.

"You know the procedure, Cal," Quick Ru reminded Calvin, upon closing the door back.

"I left mine in the car," Calvin told him.

The man looked to Ray who wasn't a fan of being frisked, let alone having his weapon lifted off him, which is considered taking. Therefore, not giving dude the pleasure, Ray pulled the pistol from the waistband of his pants and handed it to him.

"Lift your shirts!" Quick Ru ordered.

Once they did this, he ordered them to do a full spin before gesturing for Calvin to lead the way to the kitchen, where Big Ru was seated at the table, running bills through a counter. He was dark-complexioned with a temp fade, and looked to be 320 pounds. He almost put Ray in the mind of deceased rap artist Biggie Smalls.

"The famous King Ray!" Big Ru acknowledged, getting to his feet. "It's good to finally meet you!"

"Likewise," Ray replied, shaking the man's out-stretched hand.

Big Ru gestured to the other chairs. "Y'all boys have a seat! I got some beer in the fridge, if y'all want any."

"I just wanna get down to business," Ray told him.

He looked to Calvin.

"I'm driving," Calvin offered.

Besides the money counter and a few stacks of bills, there were a scale and several zip-loc bags containing marijuana, cocaine, and ecstasy pills on the table. Ray and Calvin chose chairs and sat down, just as the big guy re-took his seat.

Big Ru regarded his shooter. "Puff and Mankey should be on the way," he told him. "If they pull up while I'm dealing with these guys, you can let them in."

With a slight nod, Quick Ru left the kitchen with Ray's gun still in his hand.

"I like you already," Big Ru told Ray. "A man who likes to get straight to the business. So, how much work are we talking 'bout?"

Playa Ray

Chapter 6

The following Monday, Sheila was assigned to drive-thru window two, where she was responsible for preparing the orders of the drive-thru customers.

All morning, while doing her best to keep the order line from being congested, Sheila could not stop thinking about how different Ray had been acting ever since coming home from his *meeting* on Saturday. Though she didn't see him with anything, she knew that he'd made some kind of progress, because his foul mood seemed to have lifted a bit.

He'd even sexed her in a way that he hadn't done since they'd first started officially dating. Sunday was even better. He cooked breakfast, fed her, then sexed her, again. He'd even taken time to comically entertain Elaine and Dorothy when they went to pick the kids up.

"We meet again, beautiful!"

The red Audi planted a seed of *maybe* in her mind, but the red Range Rover left no doubt in Sheila's mind that this guy was a member of the Bloods gang. On their last encounter, he was trying to court her. She hoped like hell that he wasn't thinking about pursuing her at the moment, because Ray was about seven feet away from her, working the grill, and would definitely be able to hear the exchange.

"How are you, sir?" Sheila said, for the sake of her man. "We're still holding on fries which shouldn't take lone."

"I know it wouldn't take long for me to log your number into my phone," the guy, who introduced himself as Major Gramz, shot back. "What is it?"

"I can't give you my number," she told him. "I already have a man."

Major Gramz tilted his head to look past her. "I hope that's not him, right there, showing me his ugly face, because I can straighten that shit out!"

"Real quick!" added the man in the passenger seat.

As if hearing the timer on the fries go off, Sheila moved over to the frier, re-set the timer, and lifted one of the baskets out. She didn't have to look directly at Ray to know that he'd stopped what he was doing, and was frowning up at the two occupants of the truck.

After placing two large fries into the bag with the two burgers they ordered, Sheila bumped the sensor for the drive-thru window to open up, and handed the bag to Major Gramz, hoping that they would be on their way. "Have a nice day!" Sheila pressed.

"We can't have a nice day without our drinks," replied Major Gramz as he handed the bag over to his friend.

"Oh! I'm sorry!" Again, Sheila had to pass Ray in order to reach the soda machine. From her periphery, she could tell that he went back to minding the grill. Remembering that one drink was a Pepsi and the other a Mountain Dew, she filled the cups, stuffed them into a cardboard cup holder, then returned to the window. "Here you go, sir!" Sheila handed the drinks out. "I apologize for the delay!"

"It's all good," Major Gramz offered, accepting the drinks and rubbing her hands in the process, which sent a tingle up her spine.

Sheila snatched her hands back but kept her eyes on the dark-complexioned man who was smiling from ear to ear, displaying the sole gold tooth in his mouth. Finally, he drove on, and Sheila regarded her monitor before fetching the next order for the next customer.

Ray was boiling over with rage but did his best to hide it. Of course, he heard the exchange between Sheila and the guy in the truck, but that was beneath him. However, when he chose to disrespect Ray in the process, that's when it became a problem. And he was determined to find out who the nigga was. The threat was still ringing in his mind, but so was the first thing he said when he pulled up to the window: 'We meet again, beautiful!'

Maybe, Sheila didn't know his name, but his statement indicated that they've encountered each other before and, for some reason, he was thinking about Major Gramz, whom Calvin was telling him about. Thinking of Calvin, Ray looked over his left shoulder to see him hustling to fill the orders rung up by the three cashiers.

Figuring he'll question Calvin later, Ray flipped the burgers on the grill over, collected the empty boxes, then made for the trash cart. Sheila didn't look in his direction as he passed. Leela, Calvin's girlfriend, was working drive-thru window one but, at that time, she was accompanied by Jerry, who was standing extremely close to her. Of course, they were secretly flirting with each other, and just before passing them, Ray saw Jerry pinch her on the behind.

"Do you need more meat, Ray?" Jerry asked, once he passed.

"Yeah," Ray answered, not looking back.

After disposing of the boxes, Ray returned, expecting for Jerry to take him into the cooler, but Toni, as if she appeared out of thin air, was already standing at the cooler, holding the door open, with a grin on her face.

"After you," she gestured.

Ray looked over at Jerry and Leela, who were both giving him parallel expecting looks, which seemed a bit awkward to him, though he didn't dwell on it for too long. He preceded Toni into the cooler, where he heard the door slam shut behind them.

With the intent to grab the meat patties, and be out of there as quick as possible, Ray grabbed the four, awaiting boxes, but the moment he turned around, he almost bumped into the assistant manager, who was blocking his path. Plus, he noticed that she had unbuttoned the top three buttons of her shirt, leaving her cleavage on display, as well as the top lining of her purple bra.

"Why are you in such a rush, Ray?" She asked, seductively, drilling her dark eyes into his. "You act like you're scared of me."

"Maybe, I am," he replied, casting a glance at the door of the cooler, as if expecting Jerry to burst through it at any moment.

"Nobody's coming to your rescue," Toni told him, gripping his dick through his pants. "And, you can't be too scared of me. Not with your dick getting hard like that."

"I have meat on the grill, Toni."

"Fuck that meat!" She replied. "I want this meat in my mouth. If you're good, I might even let you come by the house and put it in my ass."

Ray was fully erect, now, but he knew he couldn't give into her sexual advance with both of his hands full. He had to side-step in order to break away from her grasp, and to get around her.

"I don't mind paying for what I want, Ray," she said to his back as he made for the door.

That's good to know, Ray thought to himself as he used his back to push the door open and made his exit. He was half expecting for Leela and Jerry to be standing in their same spots, regarding him with the same expressions, but Jerry was nowhere to be found, and Leela was talking into her headset, taking a customer's order. However, Sheila was definitely giving him an accusing look as he passed her. Or, was he imagining this?

"Are you okay, baby?" She inquired.

"Yeah, I'm good," he answered, putting the boxes down, just as the timer on the grill went off.

"We have three grills, Ray," Calvin informed him.

"I have two," Sheila chimed in.

"I'm on it," he told the both of them.

For the rest of the day, Ray did his best to avoid Toni at all costs. Even the couple of times she came out of her office and chose to chat Sheila up about nothing in particular.

Once again, at the end of the shift, Calvin was placed on trash duty. Seeing it as the chance he'd been waiting on, Ray cleaned the grill, dropped his utensils off to the dishwasher, then exited the rear door, joining Calvin at the dumpster where he was unloading his first load of trash.

"I don't wanna hear that shit about you not needing help," Ray told him as he began helping.

"Jerry thinks he's slick," Calvin mumbled.

"What do you mean?"

"Nothing." Calvin shook his head. "So, how's it going with the work?"

"I got in touch with a few a my old customers," Ray lied. "They shopped with me out of loyalty."

"That's what's up!" said Calvin. "It's hard to find loyalty like that these days."

"I know." Ray paused before diving right in. "I wanna ask you about that kat, Major Gramz."

"What about him?"

"What's he look like?"

"He's dark-skinned," Calvin offered with a shrug. "Average height. Average weight. One gold tooth. Why?"

"I was just asking."

Calvin narrowed his eyes at Ray. "The nigga's dangerous, Ray. He's not the one you wanna get caught up with. Big Ru does good business, but he's not to be one hundred percent trusted, either."

***

Calvin's words played over in Ray's head during his drive home, and even while he was taking his shower. It's not that he was incredulous to Calvin's warnings— hell, he didn't trust either of them. In fact, he hated having to deal with gang members, or someone he knew nothing about, but he had to start somewhere. At least, until he was able to do for himself.

While Sheila was taking her shower, Ray summoned Rachel and Prince Ray to the kitchen table to help them with their homework before dinner. He'd already placed a call to Joe to see what kind of progress he's made. Reluctant to speak over the phone, Joe decided that he would stop by after leaving the shop.

"What's the next question?" Ray asked his daughter.

"Um…" She referred to the textbook in front of her. "Which President proclaimed the last Thursday of November to be Thanksgiving Day?"

"You've just read the passage," he told her. "If you don't know the answer, skim back through it." While she did that, Ray looked over at his son. "Have you figured it out, Ray?"

"Is it six?" Asked Prince Ray, who was a spitting image of his father.

"We'll do it this way," Ray said, holding up four fingers on one hand, and three on the other. "This is four plus three. Count them."

He counted out loud, "One, two, three, four, five, six, seven. Seven!" He exclaimed, smiling from ear to ear.

"Are you sure?" Ray tested.

His son's smile faltered.

"Did you count seven?"

He nodded.

"If that's what you counted, write it down." He looked back over at his daughter. "Have you found it yet?"

"I think it was Abraham Lincoln," she offered.

"You think?"

"I mean, that's what it says."

"Well, write it down!" Ray said, just as his cell phone vibrated atop the table. Seeing the name and number on the screen, he answered immediately. "Talk to me!"

"I'm outside," Joe said through the device.

"Alright," Ray said, before hanging up. To his children, he said, "I have to step outside for a minute; keep going, though!"

Sheila was still in the shower when Ray journeyed off to the bedroom to retrieve his coat, donning it. With only his phone in hand, Ray exited the apartment and climbed into the front passenger side of Joes' gray Chevy Silverado, where the engine was still running, and the heater had the console all nice and toasty. Joe still had on his work uniform, which indicated that he'd actually driven right over upon leaving his workplace.

"Tell me something good!" Ray said.

***

While toweling off, Sheila thought she'd heard the sound of the front door closing, although she didn't hear anyone knock on it. After getting dressed in one of her pajama sets, she exited the bathroom and went to their bedroom. Seeing that Ray wasn't there, she made for the kitchen where the children were seated at the table, doing their homework.

After a quick glance at the closed front door, Sheila asked, "Where's y'all dad?"

"He went outside," Prince Ray answered. "He said he'll be back."

"Momma, can we have fried chicken tonight?" Asked Rachel.

"I already have the ground beef out," Sheila answered, noticing she said 'Momma', and not 'Momma Sheila'. "We're having Hamburger Helper."

Entering the living room, Sheila peered out of the window and saw two male figures sitting in a pick-up truck. She couldn't make out the one in the driver's seat, but she knew that the other occupant was her man.

It was time for her to go ahead and get dinner started but, instead, Sheila headed back to the bedroom where she grabbed her cell phone off the dresser and flopped down on the edge of the bed. After typing in her passcode, she went to the messenger app and logged in, seeing there were several messages awaiting her. Knowing she would hear the door, when Ray re-enters the apartment, Sheila started messaging people back.

***

"Everybody's always wanting something extra," Ray was now saying, shaking his head.

"If you look at it," Joe replied, "it really makes sense."

Ray looked over at his friend. "How?"

"They're already dealing with somebody," Joe told him. "If you want them to break ties, you gotta make it worthwhile."

"True." Ray understood, now. "So, I guess I'll be revealing LKS, huh?"

"Or, you can parade around as one of his lieutenants," replied Joe. "Going as LKS could only subject you to much more danger."

"I've already considered that," Ray said. "Go ahead and make those calls. Let them know that they have a deal, and I'll compensate them for every customer they refer to me."

Playa Ray

Chapter 7
Two months later

Things weren't moving as fast as Ray needed them to move, but they were moving, nevertheless. Thanks to Joe, who still wouldn't have any personal dealings with the handling of any drugs, Ray had won over three of LKS's old customers, although he had to sacrifice a great chunk of his profit by reducing the prices as agreed. Plus, he kept his promise to compensate them for every client they referred to him.

At Big Ru's deadline, Ray was only able to pay back seventy percent of what he owed the big guy. Sympathetic to what Ray had been through and respecting the fact that he was trying to get himself back together, Big Ru baded him more time, claiming that it was the only time he would do it.

On the home front, everything was pretty much the same, financially. He and Sheila stuck to their regular routine, and still weren't able to do anything extra, being that Ray didn't really have anything to show for his first run. However, he planned to change that on his next run, which was all he could think about as he rode silently on the passenger side of the black Chevy Caprice that Calvin picked them up in.

Finally, they pulled up to Big Ru's house, docking behind an orange Chevy Tahoe on chrome wheels. Quick Ru's Audi was parked in the same spot as before.

"I guess we'll have to wait, huh?" Ray asked, indicating the truck.

"Not really," Calvin answered, shutting off the engine. "Puff don't usually stay long. He'll kick the shit for a couple of minutes, but he's all about his paper."

"He's Blood, too, huh?"

"An O.G. like Big Ru," replied Calvin. "He's well-respected in these streets. Plus, he got his main shooter, Mankey, whose just as worst as Quick Ru. For him to be a young nigga, he has a mean body count."

"So, every head figure has, at least, one good shooter on their sides?"

"It's good to roll like that," Calvin told Ray. "You gotta hand-pick a nigga who don't give a fuck about nothing. Somebody who'll jump in front of a tank for you. So, when some shit jump off, you don't have to worry about getting your hands dirty, or taking the charge." Looking past Ray, he said, "There's Puff and Mankey, right there!"

Ray looked over to the house to see two men exiting. The man that stood about 6' 4", with a temp 'fro, Ray took to be Puff, because his protege seemed a bit younger, at about 6' 1", with naturally curly hair that could very well be ascribed to his ethnic background, which was probably Black and Caucasian.

As they moved towards the Tahoe, their eyes were affixed on the Caprice sitting behind their vehicle. Puff was carrying a large paper bag, and Mankey had one hand stuffed inside one of his coat's pockets, clearly clutching a weapon. Plus, he had a menacing look on his face.

"Let's do it, bro!" Calvin said, exiting the car.

Already deciding he was going to leave his gun in the car, Ray moved it from his lap to the glove compartment before getting out, zipping up his windbreaker. The sun was shining bright, but the cold wind was a force to be reckoned with.

"What's up, fellas!" Calvin greeted the two men who were about to climb into the truck.

"I can't call it, Cal," answered Puff, nodding at the Caprice. "I see you got another one."

"Not really," Calvin said. "You need to let me buy that truck."

The man scoffed. "You'll have to step your check up if you want my baby."

The two men shared a laugh as Puff climbed into the SUV. The whole time, Ray was watching Mankey just as Mankey was watching him. What Calvin said about the guy had to reign true because he was looking like he wanted to smoke Ray right on the spot.

As the men rode off, Ray and Calvin moved toward the house where Quick Ru was already waiting with the door open. Sticking to the routine, he checked them for weapons, then marched them to the kitchen where Big Ru was awaiting.

"Have a seat, fellas!" Big Ru said as he pulled bills from a money counter, wrapping a rubber band around them before adding them to a stack of other bills on the table.

Ray and Calvin did as they were told. Ray handed a wad of bills across the table to Big Ru.

"My man!" He said, looking the bills over before placing them on the table. "I assume you're ready for your next project, huh?"

"Of course," Ray answered.

"I like that!" The man looked to his shooter. "Grab the next project for me, Quick!" Once Quick left, Big Ru regarded Ray. "I still don't know how you did it, Ray."

"Did what?"

"Survive the shooting," answered Big Ru. "I remembered watching the news. Not only did they mention it, but they showed four bodies covered in white sheets. Unless there were five Kingz—"

"It was only four," Ray cut him off. "I was sick that night. My sister's boyfriend was supposed to take my place as a judge for the Battle of the DJs event. He died on my behalf."

"Damn!" Big Ru let out, just as Quick returned with a large paper bag akin to the one Puff had. "Talk about being in the wrong place at the wrong time."

"Yeah, I know," Ray replied, accepting the bag from Quick Ru and peering inside of it.

"Well, I'm glad you're here," the big guy told him. "Now, I can brag about doing business with one of the legendary Kingz. In fact, you should know how to get here on your own, now. You should swing by sometime and powwow with me. We can talk politics, or whatnot."

***

"This may take longer than I expected," complained Shatera as she added extensions to the head of Sheila, who was seated on the living room floor, between her legs. "Angie should be here any minute, and she's gonna have a fit when she realizes she has to wait."

"That's life," Sheila offered, caring nothing for Angie, who's definitely a natural-born bitch.

"I know," Shatera said. "I put up with her crazy ass because she's a good customer, and I've been doing her hair for almost five years."

At that time, they heard keys jingling outside the front door. Sheila knew it wasn't Shatera's mother because she was already in her room, just as Prince Ray and Rachel were in another room with Shatera's son. Just then, the door came open, and in walked Shatera's brother, Trez, and his in-house producer, Lavish.

"I don't know why momma haven't changed that lock, yet," Shatera voiced.

"She will once she kick you out," he shot back, switching his gaze to Sheila. "What's up, beautiful!"

"I can't call it, Trez," Sheila answered, smiling. "What're y'all up to?"

"Not too much," he said, shedding his coat and draping it over the sofa, before taking a seat on it, with Lavish following suit. "Just stopping through, checking on the fam."

"Well, go in there and check on your momma and your nephew!" Shatera intervened.

"Ain't nobody talking to you, Shatera!" Trez fixed her with a stern look.

"Ain't no need of talking to my friend!" She shot back. "She already has a man."

"You act like you're trying to save her for yourself," her brother accused. "You don't have to do that. Hell, Lavish has been trying to give you some dick for a minute, now."

"I ain't never heard him say that."

"That's because you're too busy cock-blocking on me," he told her.

***

After leaving Big Ru's house, Calvin was headed to pick up two of his G's, and asked Ray if he was okay to take the ride. Ray wasn't in a rush to get home, and he for damn sure didn't want to be riding around with the drugs he just scored, but he went along, anyway, though he had a bad vibe about it.

Calvin ended up collecting Blade and Savali, then they made it back to Forest Park, although when they exited the expressway, Calvin went in the opposite direction of where Ray lived.

It was bad enough that, when the men climbed into the back, there was no exchange between them and Calvin. Not even for the duration of the ride. There was no radio, so the only sounds that could be heard were the natural sounds outside the car, partially muffled by its closed windows.

The whole time, all Ray could think about was the kilos between his feet on the floorboard and the gun in his lap. He'd even foolishly told himself that, if they tried anything, he would come out on top, by any means necessary.

Moments later, Calvin pulled the Chevy into the lot of a plaza, and parked further away from the other vehicles, but kept the engine running. He checked his watch, prompting Ray to do the same. It was only 2:18PM, but Ray wanted to return home, so he could go ahead and prep the cocaine to be cooked, although he'd only start once the children were in bed. Sheila knew what he was doing, but didn't intervene.

After about nine minutes of sitting in silence, Calvin threw the gear into drive, and eased out of his spot. Following Calvin's gaze, Ray spotted a man in a blue jogging suit, and ballcap. Carrying a gym bag, he looked as though he'd exited the gym. Considering the color he had on, Ray quickly discerned that he was about to witness one of the many gang-on-gang fatalities.

At this time, the man had his head down, engrossed in his phone— probably informing his lover that he was on his way home— and unaware of the imminent danger he was in. Calvin sped the car up a notch, to match the guy's stride, turning into the aisle he was walking along. Considering the drugs and everything he had to lose, Ray looked around to see if any patrol cars were in the vicinity.

Just then, Calvin bared down on the gas pedal, then brought the car to a screeching halt alongside him. Savali, who was seated behind Ray, lunged from the rear. By the time Ray could look up to see who the guy was, Savali slapped the man across the head with his gun, and shoved him into the back seat, wedging him between him and Blade.

As if nothing happened, Calvin moved on, casually, leaving the man's gym bag in the spot he was snatched from. Upon hearing the man grunting from pain, Ray looked back, and immediately felt like his heart had dropped to his stomach. The first image that popped into his mind was Special Agent Brian Bishop being gunned down in the courtroom, years ago.

"What's up with this shit, Calvin!" Ray demanded.

"Just chill!" Calvin responded, exiting the lot. "Make sure y'all get that nigga's phone!"

"Already got it," Blade told him. "He was texting somebody, but I shut the whole phone off."

Once again, it was quiet inside the car, with the exception of the kidnapped man's moaning. Ray didn't need a psychic to tell him how this was going to end for the man, who was highly familiar with both he and Calvin. He just couldn't perceive how things would end with himself if these guys thought for a millisecond that he was a loose end that shouldn't be left untied. Therefore, he chose not to say another word.

"What's going on, Calvin?" The man finally inquired.

"Shut the fuck up, Jerry!" Calvin chided. "We're about to get to the bottom of this bullshit, in just a minute."

This was one of those times when Ray wished he was invisible, because he could just feel Jerry's eyes burning through him from the back seat. They weren't friends, but Ray didn't hate the nigga to the point where he'd orchestrate, or participate in whatever Calvin and his friends had planned for him.

Momentarily, Calvin pulled into the lot of a shut-down Dollar General store building and drove around to the rear of it. Once he backed up to the steel door, he put the car into park, and donned a pair of black gloves before pressing the trunk-release button in the glove compartment and getting out.

Seconds later, there was the sound of loud pounding on steel. It was still daybreak, though no one could see them. However, they were sitting in a blind spot and couldn't see anyone approaching from the front of the building. Ray didn't like this one bit.

"Let's go, y'all!" They heard Calvin say, followed by some kind of tool dropping into the trunk, and the trunk slamming.

The men in the back didn't hesitate. Blade basically pulled Jerry from the car by his garment, as Savali rounded the rear of the car to help usher him into the building. Ray was thinking about the drugs, his life, and the car that was still running. Something was telling him to take the car and get the hell away from there, but he didn't want to look like a coward to Calvin or the other men.

Reluctantly leaving the drugs on the floorboard, Ray got out and entered the barren store. There was broken glass on the floor as a result of the boarded-up windows and damaged light fixtures. Several of the front windows were still intact, which is where the sunlight spewed in from. The place wasn't completely trashed, but a lot of the shelves were displaced. At first, while looking around, Ray didn't   see   any   of   them.

"Shut the fuck up!" He heard Calvin's voice, followed by a loud smacking sound. "Open this shit!"

"Okay, man!" This was Jerry's voice.

Following the voices, Ray found them in the middle of an aisle, where the three gang members were standing over Jerry, who was sitting on the floor, typing something into his cellular. Once he was done, he handed the phone to Calvin, then looked up, locking eyes with Ray, who'd just joined them.

"Let's see what you and Leela have been chatting about," Calvin said, as his fingers danced along the screen of the device.

While he was searching for whatever it is he was searching for, Ray noticed that Blade and Savali were also wearing gloves, and Blade was holding a gasoline can. Of course, Jerry had to know that things were not going to end well for him. Hell, the dejected look on his face revealed that, which made Ray feel a little sympathy for the man, though he dared to show.

"Ah!" Calvin let out. "Here we are. She has a fake account under the name of Foxy Brown. I know this, because I created my own fake account, and viewed the profile of every friend you have on Facebook." He turned to his boys. "Could y'all believe that the dumb bitch actually used her real picture?"

The two men just shook their heads.

"I know, right?" He went back to scrolling through the messages. "Damn! Y'all be talking some real freaky shit in these texts, Jerry! She said that she'll suck your dick from the back. The bitch ain't never sucked *my* dick from the back. How's that shit feel?"

Jerry only stared at the man.

"I asked you a question, nigga!" Calvin spat, raising his voice a few decibels. "You're man enough to fuck my bitch, and smile in my face like everything's good, but you can't answer one simple question? How was that shit?"

"It never happened," Jerry answered. "We were just talking."

Calvin scoffed. "She probably ain't never sucked you from the back, but the bitch gave you some head. That's what y'all be doing in the cooler when you send me to take out the trash. Don't try to play me like I'm fucking stupid!" He scrolled some more. "Oh! Look! She sent you pictures of her pussy. I can spot that pretty pussy anywhere. See, I already knew you were fucking Leela." Calvin was looking down at Jerry, again. "I just needed this confirmation. Now, what about Sheila?"

"Huh!" Jerry let out, casting a frantic glance at Ray.

"Don't 'huh' me, nigga!" Calvin voiced, kicking him in the thigh. "What's the name that Sheila uses for her fake page?"

"I wouldn't know," he purported. "I don't talk to her on messenger. I swear to God!"

Calvin looked back at Ray. "You know he's lying, right? Whenever you took out the trash, I'll see him and Sheila sneak into the cooler."

"Ray, I ain't never fucked Sheila," Jerry pleaded. "I said what's up to her on messenger, one time, and she blocked me."

"What's her name on there?" Ray asked, feeling there was a little truth to what Jerry was saying.

"She uses her real name."

"Show me!" Ray told him.

"The nigga is lying, Ray!" Calvin intervened. "Why the fuck would he—"

"Give him the phone, Calvin!" Ray cut him off, garnering disapproving looks from the others.

After a few seconds of giving Ray the same look, Calvin relinquished the phone to Jerry, who immediately put his fingers to work. It took a moment to find what he was looking for. Once he did, he held the phone out to Ray, but Calvin intercepted it, gave it a once-over, then handed it to Ray.

Ray didn't know a thing about this app, being that he didn't have an account. However, he did know how to read. He saw Sheila's name, beside a small picture of her. Under that, he saw where Jerry texted 'What's up?', followed by a notice informing him that he couldn't respond to the conversation. "So, she blocked you, huh?" Ray finally asked.

"Yeah, she did," answered Jerry.

"That doesn't mean shit!" Calvin persisted. "She blocked him on *that* account, but what about her fake account? Everybody has a fake account. If we scroll down every conversation, I bet we'll find it."

Ray looked at his watch. "I gotta get back to the crib."

Handing the phone back to Calvin, Ray spun on his heels and made for the back door. Now, he was aware of why Calvin wanted him to take this ride: to try and convince him that Sheila was cheating on him with their manager, like he'd been trying to do for some time now. He wanted Ray to experience the same hurt he was experiencing, by knowing that Jerry was laying pipe on his woman. On the surface, he appeared unfazed, but Ray knew better. If he wasn't affected by it, then he wouldn't have abducted Jerry with the intent to toe-tag him.

Getting outside, instead of climbing into the car, Ray walked to the corner of the building, and peered around it, to make sure no one was moving in their direction. The coast was clear, but Ray decided that he would keep watch, until they exited the building.

Just then, he heard two rapid gunshots, which indicated that Jerry was no longer with them. He felt bad for the guy, but there was nothing he could do about it. However, he knew that, after today, things between him and Calvin will not be the same.

Chapter 8

"I got two more grills, Ray," Sheila called out from one of the front registers.

"I'm on it," Ray replied after looking up at the order monitor.

All morning, while trying to keep up with the special orders, Ray kept thinking about Jerry's death. He watched the news on Sunday and saw the reportage on the fire that was set to the closed Dollar General building, but they didn't mention anything about a body being found.

There was another story about the Chevy Caprice that was found in the next county over, charred beyond recognition. When they showed footage of it, Ray was a bit relieved, knowing that whatever prints he left on the vehicle were no more.

Calvin's and Leela's off days had been changed to Mondays and Tuesdays, so Ray wouldn't see Calvin until Wednesday. But, he was more concerned about Toni, Jerry's wife, who didn't show any signs of a grieving widow, as she went about her day as usual.

Perhaps, she was unaware of the tragedy that befell her husband. Ray figured that there was no way she could be that 'normal', if, in fact, she had knowledge of this. However, she hadn't seen, nor heard from him in two days. That was enough to make a worried spouse call the National Guard! Unless she and Calvin were in cahoots, which made a great deal of sense. After all, women are better actors than men.

After fixing the two burgers for Sheila, Ray placed them into a bag, and sat the bag by the soda machine for her to enclose her own fries, or whatnot. Just as he spun on his heels to return to the grill, he caught a glimpse of a Caucasian man standing at the counter, holding up a badge, but did not alter his steps. While clearing the rest of the patties off the grill, Ray heard the man introduce himself as Homicide Detective Brown and inquire about Toni Jackson.

One of the other three cashiers journeyed to the office to collect Toni for the government official, which only took a matter of seconds. The alarmed expression on her face was cogent, but Ray was't buying it.

"Mrs. Toni Jackson?" The detective asked.

"That's me," she answered, her expression still lingering.

"I'm Homicide Detective Brown," he told her, "and this is my partner, Detective Willis. Can we speak in your office?"

"Sure."

Toni logged in the code to the employee entrance, letting the men in. Ray only glanced at them, as the three of them passed him en route to the office. He noticed the worried and inquisitive looks on everyone's faces, but only he knew the true reason Toni was being visited by the two men.

Hell, he knew that, eventually, the authorities would contact her, but he was hoping they'd done it at her home instead of the workplace, because there was a possible chance that every employee would be interrogated for the purpose of the investigation.

However, things continued as usual. Almost thirty minutes had gone by, and the three of them were still in the office with the door closed. At that time, the employees' door came open, and in walked Karen Thompson, the second-shift manager, carrying her usual pocketbook and KFC chicken box. Ray looked at his watch and saw that she was over three hours early.

Being the free-spirited person she's always been, Karen spoke to everyone as she made for the office. This had Ray feeling like they were about to arrest Toni and needed Karen to take over.

About seven minutes later, Toni and the detectives finally emerged from the office, with Toni looking more distraught than before. She had her things, so it was evident that she was gone for the rest of the day, or for however long the authorities planned to keep her.

Ray was running out of meat, so, after flipping over the burgers he already had on, he headed for the office, just as his phone vibrated on his hip. Checking it, he saw there was a text from Joe, telling him to call when he gets a chance.

The office door was standing open, and Karen, who favored brown synthetic weaves that matched her brown complexion, was seated behind the desk, jotting something down in the logbook. Sensing him, she looked up, regarding him through her slightly large glasses that made her look like a naughty schoolteacher from one of the many x-rated videos he'd seen.

"I need more patties," Ray answered her inquisitive look.

Saying nothing, she pulled her sylph-like frame out of her chair and led the way to the cooler. She didn't have much of an ass to look at, but she had a gait that was tantamount to that of a runway model, with the body to match.

"I hope to God that's not Jerry's body!" Karen said as she entered the cooler behind Ray. "Toni did say he's been missing for two days, though."

Making it to the meat shelf, Ray turned to face her. "Two days?" He asked.

"She called and told me this last night," answered Karen. "Now, she's on her way to identify a body that was found burned up inside of an empty building, Saturday. That's crazy!"

"Yeah, it is." Ray turned and grabbed four boxes of meat. When he turned back around, he expected for her to move out of his way, but she didn't.

"Are you and that girl still together?" She asked, drilling those brown eyes into his.

"Of course," he answered, sternly.

"Mmm!" was all the manager offered, before stepping aside.

Ray took that as his cue and got the hell up out of there. He'd spoken to the second-shift manager a few times since he's been working there, but she has never made a pass at him, until now, which was odd, considering what was going on.

As the day went on, Ray only had to make one more meat run, which was different from the last one, because Karen didn't say one word to him. In fact, she unlocked the cooler and let him enter on his own. However, close to shift change, she chose Sheila for the trash detail.

Ray wanted to assist his woman, but he couldn't leave the grill until the second-shift grillman got in. Therefore, he continued cooking and cleaning certain areas of his station. The moment that his relief got in, Ray made for the back door that was propped open.

Grabbing an empty box, Ray exited the building, pulling his cell phone from its case, and dialing Joe's number.

"Is that all you could carry?" Sheila asked, when Ray approached her at the dumpster. "One box?"

"You're lucky I came out here to help your big-head ass!" Ray replied, just as Joe answered his phone. "Tell me something good!"

"Do you remember Alex?" Joe asked.

"I don't know," Ray said. "Should I?"

"He was one of LKS's customers," Joe told him. "The Australian mothefucker. You introduced him to the Queenz, remember?"

"Okay. I remember him," Ray admitted. "What about him, though?"

"He's back in," his friend announced. "Said he's been through some rough times himself, so he can't afford a whole thing right now."

"What can he afford?"

Concluding the call with his friend, Ray helped Sheila with the rest of the trash, then they both went to the office to clock out. By this time, the second-shift assistant manager was present. She and Karen were engaged in conversation when Ray and Sheila entered. Of course, pleasantries were exchanged, but Ray wasn't trying to kick it. Hell, he had to usher Sheila out of the office so that they could get going.

"Why do you think those detectives came and got Toni?" Sheila asked once they climbed into their car, and were waiting for the engine to warm up.

"Karen said something about Jerry being missing for two days," Ray answered.

"Missing!" She let out. "For two days! Do they think she killed him, or something?"

"That's all I know, baby," he told her.

Sheila has been with Ray long enough to know when he's holding out on her, and, right now, she felt that he was doing such. On their drive home, she pondered his response, and the tone of his voice. Yes, something was definitely off, here. Two days? Come to think of it, Ray's demeanor has been a bit shaky these past couple of days. Plus, him accusing her of fooling around with Jerry didn't make matters any better.

As routine, when they made it to Regal Park apartments, Ray dropped Sheila off at the mailboxes, then drove on around to their unit. Sheila didn't have to look directly at the four men to know that they were in their regular spot and watching her as she retrieved the mail. Ready to get the trivial sexual harassment out of the way, she stuffed the mail into her pocketbook and set her feet into motion.

The men were still watching her, attentively. The dark-complexioned man with dreadlocks, who was leaning against the front-end of the Dodge Magnum, stood erect, as if hypnotized. Just as Sheila passed, he grabbed a handful of her ass, which made her stop, immediately, and turn around to face him.

"How did I know you were gonna do that?" She asked in a composed tone. "Because you're a boy, and that's what boys do. Until you grow up you'll never get a woman like me."

With that, Sheila turned and made for Shatera's apartment, hearing the guy's friends clown him for being put in his place. This made her smile while anticipating their next encounter. Sometimes, it takes condescension to make a person respect you. If this doesn't work, she knew that she would have to revert back to her street mentality, and handle things accordingly.

***

Ray was glad to have Alex back as a customer, considering the amount of money he used to spend with LKS. Although he wasn't spending much at the moment, claiming something about falling on hard times, Ray was still willing to deal with him. Besides, he needed as many customers as he could get at the moment.

His appointment was at 7PM, which gave him enough time to shower, eat dinner, and help the children with their homework before leaving out, heading to Atlanta.

Reaching downtown Atlanta, Ray made sure to park as close as he could to the Marriott hotel. With the six ounces in a paperbag stuffed inside of his mid-length leather coat, Ray stepped out of the car, adjusting his skullcap as he moved in the direction of the building, looking around for any signs of potential danger, or a sting operation.

Entering the hotel unscathed, Ray got onto an elevator and rode up to the eighth floor. The room number he was looking for was 812. Finding the door, he rapped on it three times. "Room service!" Ray announced, as advised.

Seconds later, the door came open, and Ray found himself standing face-to-face with a white man in his mid-fifties he figured to be Alex. They've only spoken a few times on the phone when Ray was running his operation under the pseudonym of LKS, and had Joe and Poppo physically interacting with his clients, so he didn't have a clue as to how the man looked.

The older man suspiciously eyed Ray before saying, "You don't *look* like room service."

"I'm here on behalf of LKS," Ray let on, knowing it was him from his accent.

"Is that some kind of service the hotel is offering?" Alex inquired, looking like a younger Hugh Heffner in his complementary robe.

Ray already knew where this was going, which was nowhere. Therefore, retrieving his cellular from its clip, he placed a video call to Joe.

"What's up, bro!" Answered Joe, who appeared to be driving.

"I'm here with Alex," Ray told him. "There seems to be some kind of misunderstanding about room service."

"What kind of misunderstanding?"

"Hold on!" Ray said, handing the phone to Alex.

"Ponytail!" The man beamed at the screen. "How's it going, my friend?"

"I can't call it, Al," Joe said. "What's the problem?"

"It seems that LKS is an equal-opportunity employer," he coded. "Who am I in the presence of?"

"He's a new recruit," Joe answered. "That's my bad, I should've told you this. He's legit, though."

"Thanks, buddy!"

"No problem."

"I apologize for the delay," Alex offered, handing the phone back to Ray. "You can never be too careful."

"I understand," Ray replied.

"Come on in!"

Alex stepped aside. Before Ray could set his feet into motion, he saw two white women in lingerie, sitting atop the bed, snorting cocaine off a small, silver saucer. As he entered, they regarded him like he was a piece of meat or hired entertainment, which made him feel a bit uncomfortable.

***

Sheila had pretty much gotten used to Ray leaving out at different times of the day or night. Hell, it was just like the old days, but she knew that, eventually, she was going to have to get used to spending nights alone when the drug business picks up for him.

After Ray left the apartment, Sheila sent the kids to take their baths, cleaning the kitchen. She thought about the detectives that came to their workplace to collect Toni in reference to Jerry being missing for two days— well, according to Ray.

However, Sheila was determined to find out because there was something quite uncanny about the whole thing and, for some reason, she had a strong feeling that Ray was involved, somehow. First, she has to get the scoop from Brittany, one of her co-workers, which would entail her logging into her Facebook Messenger.

Finishing up in the kitchen, Sheila made sure to check on the little ones before retreating to her own room. Prince Ray was done with his bath and was in his room, coloring in his coloring book. Rachel was still taking her bath. Upon entering her bedroom, she grabbed her phone off the dresser and flopped down on the edge of the bed.

Just as Sheila logged in her passcode, she glanced up at the television and temporarily lost track of what she was about to do, when she saw the news broadcasting that the identity of a body that was found in a burned-down store building, was confirmed. When they showed the picture of Jerry Jackson, Sheila gasped, throwing a hand over her chest.

They went on to explain that he was abducted from the plaza while showing the actual footage of him being assaulted in the parking lot before being forced into the rear of an older-model car. As speculated, the same car was found miles away, after being set afire.

At that moment, there was a knock at the front door which was unusual, being that they didn't get visitors. Thinking it was Shatera, Sheila got off the bed and headed for the door with her phone still in hand. When she peered through the peephole, she saw that it was not Shatera, but the guy who'd grabbed her ass earlier. Instead of asking who it was, she looked back to make sure the children weren't behind her before unlocking and pulling the door open.

"They call me Dread," he said, offering his hand. "What's your name?"

Sheila stepped out and pulled the door close before accepting his hand. "I'm Sheila."

"It's nice to meet you, Sheila," Dread told her. "I want to apologize for my behavior earlier."

"Okay," she replied, wrapping her arms around her for the sake of the cold weather.

"I'd like for us to start over, if that's okay with you."

Sheila smiled, causing him to smile back. Of course, he was smiling, because he felt that he was making progress, but Sheila was smiling because he'd fallen right into her hands.

Chapter 9
Wednesday

"What's your name again, sir?"

Ray, who was tending to the meat on the grill, looked up at Stan, the Caucasian assistant manager from a Checkers restaurant in Clayton County, who was filling in while Toni was out on a hardship leave. "Ray Young," Ray told him.

"Just the first name," he said, writing something down on his clipboard. "How are we looking on meat?"

"I have two more boxes," Ray answered.

"Well, let me know when you need more," Stan told him. "Right now, I'm making my rounds, making sure that everyone has what they need. I mean, that's what I'm here for, right?"

"That's right," Ray replied, not really in the mood to chat, but was glad that the man moved on, leaving him to his thoughts.

Looking up at his monitor, Ray saw that there were two grilled orders from walk-in, and two from drive-thru, where Sheila was working window two. After preparing those sandwiches, he handed a tray of patties over to Calvin, who was working preparations before laying out fresh meat.

"What's up, Sheila!"

The sound of another man saying Sheila's name caused Ray to look toward the drive-thru window to see the red Range Rover that he was tired of seeing, along with its driver and passenger. He'd made it up in his mind that he was not going to tolerate any more disrespect from these clowns. Fuck whatever organization they belonged to!

"How'd you know my name?" Sheila inquired.

"It's not hard for me to get information on someone I'm interested in," Major Gramz answered.

"Here's your food, sir," Sheila said, handing him his order. "I'll be back with your drinks."

When Sheila moved to the soda machine, Ray found himself in a stare-off with the two men. The passenger formed one of his hands in the shape of a gun, aimed it at Ray, and initiated firing it. That did it!

Ray moved toward the window, bumping Sheila in the process. "You got a problem, nigga?" he asked, looking past Major Grams to his protege.

"Whoah! Hold the fuck up!" Major Gramz intervened, "Don't come rolling up on us like you're bullet-proof, or something! I'll have yellow crime scene tape all around this motherfucker!"

"Yeah," the passenger chimed in. "We'll kill everybody, except for that fines-ass bitch of yours. With you out of the way, she might let the whole crew run through her."

"Here's your drinks, sir." Ray heard Sheila say from behind him.

"Can we get our drinks, tough guy?" Major Gramz asked regarding Ray with a taunting grin.

"Back up, baby!"

"Listen to your bitch!" The passenger warned, placing his hand on the chrome handgun in his lap.

Ray was so livid, all he could do was stand there. Maybe, it was pride. Just then, he felt someone tug at the back of his shirt, pulling him away from the window. Ray didn't look back to see who it was until Sheila gave the men their drinks, and they drove off.

"You did better than me," Calvin told him. "I would've dove out the window on them niggas!" With that, Calvin headed back to his station.

For the sake of not letting the drive-thru line get backed up, Sheila went back to filling orders, leaving Ray standing alone, still seething, while the timer on the grill was sounding, indicating that the burgers needed to be flipped over.

"I'm fully aware that some people like their steaks well-done," the surrogate manager offered, approaching, "but we have rules to adhere to, and an annoying-ass timer that makes sure we do just that."

Ray turned to face him. "I need a bathroom break."

"How much of a bathroom break?" He asked, gandering at his watch.

"At least five minutes."

"Okay," he gave in. "I'll man the station until you return."

Without another word, Ray let himself through the employee entrance, and headed for the restroom, hoping it was empty, but it wasn't. There was a guy at one of the urinals, but Ray didn't let that stop him. He marched right into one of the three stalls, locked the door, and selected a phone number from his contacts.

"What's up?" Eric's voice came through the earpiece.

"We need to talk," Ray told him.

"What's it pertaining to?"

"Some middle east shit."

There was a pregnant pause on Eric's end before he said, "It'll have to be later. Give me a minute to text you a location."

"No doubt."

Ray exited the restroom and was about to let himself back through the service door when he spotted Kim in the order line. She wasn't looking at the menu, but looking as though she was looking for someone. Figuring it was him, he rounded the corner.

"Kim?"

"Oh! Hey, Ray!" She said, moving over to him.

"What's wrong?" He asked, seeing the disturbing look on her face that corroborated her bedraggled appearance.

"Are you on break?" Kim inquired, wringing her hands.

"Not at the moment," he told her. "What's going on?"

***

"This is a Coke," the woman in the black Chevy Avalanche acknowledged. "I asked for a Sprite."

"I'm sorry, ma'am!" Sheila offered. "I'm about to get that for you, now."

Sheila has been discombobulated ever since Major Gramz and his disrespectful-ass friend left. She was beyond pissed, so she could imagine how Ray was feeling. It was just crazy how people would disrespect a person they knew nothing about, because she knew, first-hand, that her man had no problem with taking another man's life, which made her think about Jerry. She was just worried that he was going to set out after those guys for the level of disrespect they displayed, today.

After giving the disgruntled customer her correct beverage, Sheila started on the next order, just as Ray entered through the service door. The substitute manager was holding the grill down for him, while he left out to do whatever it was he had to do. Sheila could see their car from the drive-thru window. She didn't see him go to it, so Sheila was a bit relieved to know that Ray didn't plan on pursuing the men immediately.

Ray and the manager shared a few words before the manager made off to the office. While keeping up with the orders, Sheila periodically shot glances over at her man, who visibly looked like he was trying to keep it together, which churned her heart. Considering this, the first chance Sheila got, she crossed over and wrapped her arm around his waist.

"Are you alright, baby?" She asked.

"I'm good," he answered without regarding her.

"I just want you to know that I love you, no matter what."

Leaving him with a kiss on the cheek, Sheila went back to her window. That's when Ray looked over at her. She was his everything. She was a gift to him, as well as a curse, because, the way things were going, she was going to end up being the death of him. Hell, he'd traded his life for hers, once, and would do it a million more times. If a man isn't willing to lay down his life for his woman, as he would his mother, then what good is he?

By the end of the shift, Ray found that he'd calmed down a bit, though he could not stop thinking about the reason why he was in such a state. Moving around seemed to help, which is why he didn't mind when the manager put him on trash detail.

While making his first round to the dumpster, Ray began thinking about the visit he'd gotten from Kim, earlier. She was claiming to have financial problems, and Ray didn't doubt that, but he could sense there was something else she was bothered by. However, he explained to her that we was unable to assist her at that moment, but to give him a few days to figure out something.

"That white boy got you out here in the cold, my nigga?" Calvin said upon approaching, lighting a cigarette.

"It's all good," Ray responded, breaking down boxes before tossing them into the dumpster.

"Major Gramz needs to put a leash on that nigga, No Heart!" Calvin voiced. "He's gotten a little too big for his britches. He thinks that he can go around disrespecting whowever he wants, but I know where one of his aunts live."

Ray perked up at this. "You do?"

"I'm a gang member," he pointed out. "It's required that I do my homework on these niggas. Hell, ever since Saturday, I've concluded that I'm not taking anymore shit from nobody. At the first sign of disrespect, I'm taking a nigga's whole head off! Jerry was the first, but he won't be the last. The nigga ain't even in the grave yet, and I'm already getting my dick sucked by his widow."

Ray shot him an incredulous look.

"She lost her husband— not her hormones, Ray," explained Calvin, pulling on his cigarette. "If you remember the biblical story about Adam and Eve, you'll know that God created women with no compassion, or scruple. Hell, look at the bitch that fucked over that nigga, Sampson. I refuse to let a bitch do me in, which is why, the first chance I get, I'm gonna toe-tag Leela's ass!"

***

It was 8:24PM when Ray pulled to the house that Eric texted him the address to. As far as he could tell, there were no lights on inside the place, and only a silver-looking Hyundai sat in its driveway.

The moment he threw the car into park, a woman appeared in the dark doorway of the house with an active cell phone in her hand. Ray couldn't make out her complexion, but she was wearing jeans and a white shirt that bulged in the mid-section, which could very well mean that she was with child.

With her hand that held the glowing phone, she pointed towards the side of the house where there was a fence with its gate open. Immediately catching on to what she was indicating, Ray killed the engine, donned his skullcap, then got out, tucking his Glock into the waistband of his jeans.

By this time, the woman had retreated back inside. As he reached the fence, he caught a faint whiff of burning marijuana. Rounding the brick house, he saw Eric's dark figure seated in a lawn chair on the small deck.

"I like the setting," Ray commented upon taking a seat in the other lawn chair beside his friend.

"Dark, quiet, and cool," Eric replied, pulling on his blunt. "It kinda reminds you of death. You can't fear something you're accustomed to."

"So, that's Pauline?" Ray asked, jerking his thumb at the house.

"Yeah." Eric was slowly shaking his head. "I fucked around and got her pregnant, again. Anyway, what's this 'Middle East' shit you mentioned on the phone?"

"What'd you know about a nigga by the name of Major Gramz?"

Eric leered at him. "I hope he's one of your allies."

Ray didn't answer.

"Come on, Ray!" He let out. "If you're suicidal, there are plenty of other ways you can go about it."

"I just need guns," Ray told him.

"You'll need more than that, my friend." Finishing his blunt, Eric tossed the butt, then sat in silence for a moment before saying, "I'm not even gonna inquire on the beef between you and this nigga. You're reminding me of Fred, right now, so I know you got your mind made up. I don't have what you're looking for, but I'll place a call to someone who does."

***

"Dread, you can't keep coming to my apartment," Sheila said as she stepped out of the front door, closing it back.

"I saw your boy when he left."

"That doesn't matter," she told him. "The neighbors can see you. And, I'm quite sure you tell your boys everything."

"You're right about the Hills having eyes," Dread admitted, "but you're wrong about me telling my boys everything. I have my personal life, and they have theirs."

"Mm-hmm!"

"How else am I supposed to get to know you?" he went on. "You won't give me your number, and you won't take mine. I'm quite sure you have a Facebook page, but I wouldn't know the first place to look."

"What's yours?" She asked.

"My Facebook info?"

Playa Ray

Chapter 10

The following day, Ray didn't have time to change clothes, which would've made him later for an appointment with a man whose name Eric did not give him, at the gun dealer's behest. All Ray was told to do was meet the man on Simpson Road, at the Tasty Dog restaurant that, as far as Ray knew, wouldn't be open for business at that time of the day.

There were three cars present. Neither one of them had any special effect, so Ray knew that his own car would fill right in as he entered the extremely small lot and parked. He couldn't remember the last time he'd been to the place, but everything still looked the same.

Upon entering, he saw one man who appeared to be doing some maintenance work to the ancient grill. With a pair of pliers in his hand, he turned to face Ray as if waiting for him to say something, although Ray didn't know what to say, being that he was only told to show up.

"We're not open for business, yet," the man told him.

Ray still said nothing. After another moment of silence between the two, the man jerked his head over his right shoulder. Ray already knew there was a small room beyond the door to the left of him, which conveyed three arcade games, a jukebox, and a pool table.

Crossing over to the wooden door, Ray pushed it open and took the one step down into the room, where two men were perched upon the pool table, engaged in conversation. They both looked up as he entered. Quickly scanning their faces, Ray immediately realized that he was highly familiar with one of them.

"What the fuck!" Tommy exclaimed as he slowly eased off the table, looking like he'd seen a ghost. "Ain't no way I'm seeing you right now!"

"I've missed you too, fool!" Ray said, embracing his long-time friend. "How's life been treating you?"

"Pretty bad," Tommy answered. "Considering that I feel like the whole world lied to me about your death. I did hear a couple of rumors that you were still walking amongst us, though."

"Well, you know how those rumors go."

Tommy nodded. "Yeah, I know. So, what about the others? Are they—"

"Deceased," Ray cut in. "Did you buy this place?"

"Hell no!" Tommy let out, making a face. "I still own Club Seven-Twenty. I also still run my gun operation out the back of it, but when Eric hit me up and told me that he had a personal friend who wanted to cop some guerrilla warfare-type of shit, I chose this location, being that I have nothing there that a nigga would even think about going up against Russia with." He indicated the other guy. "That's why I called on my boy, Dirty. He can assist you better than I can."

"That depends on what you're looking for," the light-complexioned man spoke up.

"I'm not familiar with the names of too many assault weapons," Ray admitted, "but I need some shit that'll make a chopper look like a twenty-two rifle."

"I kinda have an idea of what you're looking for," Dirty told him. "Now, it's a matter of quantity. How much are we talking?"

"What am I getting?" Ray wanted to know.

"I don't know what, exactly," the man answered, "but they'll be military-grade weapons. The guy I'm getting them from is a marine who lives in Savannah. I'll place your order with him, and he'll get at me when he comes home on his pass."

"It's all true, Ray," Tommy added. "That boy, Drew, might bring home a damn missile launcher!"

Ray ended up spending a whole hour inside Tasty Dog, mainly catching up on old times with his friend. Upon leaving, he climbed into his car, and, while letting the engine warm up, he placed a call to Joe.

"What's the word?" Joe answered.

"I'm about to buy a new stove," Ray told him. "I'll need a place to put it."

There was a long pause on Joe's end before he said, "Where are you, right now?"

"Atlanta."

"How long would it take you to get to South Cobb Drive?"

Joe's burgundy BMW, with its black, retractable top, was already at the Race Trac gas station when Ray pulled in. Parking beside the BMW and leaving the engine running, Ray got out, and climbed in beside his friend.

"Boy, you smell like a number two, with no onions," Joe bantered, making a face. Despite how he was feeling, Ray couldn't help but laugh. "Plus," Joe went on, "you're starting to look like a light-skinned Samuel L. Jackson!"

"So, you lured me here to hurt my feelings?" Ray smiled. He was grateful to share this laugh with his friend.

"I got much love for you, Ray," Joe said, seriously, once the laughter died down.

Ray regarded him through narrow slits. "You make me feel like I'm about to die."

"Are you?"

Ray was taken aback by the question, which felt like a slap to the face, being that it seemed to come out of nowhere. He knew that Joe was just trying to pull his coattail, as Eric and Tommy had done, but, at that moment, he was actually experiencing chills running through his body.

"I still remember the first time I met you," Joe went on, now looking out of his side window. "You were all about making money and having fun. You had this certain glow that drew people to you, and a sense of humor that made people forget the bullshit they were going through." He turned to Ray. "I was one of those people. I know you've been through a lot, like any other human being, but you act like you lost everything, Ray."

"I have," Ray replied, thinking about his brother, as well as Fred and Black.

"That's a lie!" His friend contended. "I pick up the phone every time you call. Poppo does, too. Plus, you still got your wife and kids. Now, I understand that you're trying to get your paper right so you can take care of them, but you're out here trying to start a war. And you, of all people, know that war is bad for business."

"I'm not starting a war, Joe," Ray explained. "I'm just preparing for one."

Chapter 11
Easter Sunday

"Why haven't you taken the fence down?" Ray asked Robert of the fence he'd built for Ray's dogs years ago, when Ray and Sheila had planned to leave the country.

Being that it's been a long time since Ray has seen his mother and grandmother, he decided that he'd spend Easter with them, taking Sheila and the kids to Alabama with him, arriving Friday night, to the house that his mother shares with her now husband, Robert.

Saturday was spent at his grandmother's house in Mobile, Alabama, and they all had Easter's church service at the church that his mother and Robert attends in Birmingham. Now, Ray and Robert were standing in the front yard while Mary and some of her friends were cheering the children on in their Easter-egg hunt, and others were setting out food dishes on several serving tables.

"I don't know," Robert now answered Ray's question, resting his hands on the fence that stood about five feet high. "I really wanted to keep the dogs, but times got hard. Even your mom had started to like them. She actually cried when animal control took them away."

"She told me," Ray replied, looking out at the number of children who were giggling and squealing while vying to be the one with the most eggs.

"Why are you still in Georgia, Ray?" Robert asked. "It's like you're stuck there. Are you no longer interested in leaving?"

Ray looked at the older man. "I don't know, Rob. It's like, every time I try to leave, something hampers my plans. I was born in Atlanta. Maybe, it's meant for me to die in Atlanta. From the cradle, to the grave."

"Don't start that Tupac shit!" Robert said, grinning. "I'm serious."

"So am I," Ray told him. "I really don't think it's meant for me to leave. If you look at it, I've escaped a lot of shit by the hairs on my chin. Perhaps, there's a shield over me in Georgia. It's possible that the moment I come from under that shield, will be the same moment I meet my fate."

***

Later that night, in one of the guest rooms of his mother's house, Ray lied in bed, staring at the ceiling because he found it hard to sleep. Taking one look over at Sheila who was dead to the world, he slipped out of bed, donned a pair of jeans, slid his feet into his house shoes, then made for the door.

The kids were in another bedroom not too far from theirs. After looking in on them, Ray moved along the quiet and relatively dark house, making for the front door, where he quietly disengaged the locks before easing the noisy door open, and stepping out in the warm and still night, pulling the door back to.

The first thing he did was take a deep breath of the warm air that seemed to smell a whole lot better than that of Georgia, which was quite soothing and welcoming. Ray wasn't out there to figure out why he couldn't sleep— he already knew the various reasons. At that moment, he was trying to figure out how he was going to handle things from here on out.

For the past two and a half months, business gradually picked up, which allowed for Ray to start stacking a good amount of money. Before long, he felt that he'd have enough to cop his own kilos from Big Ru's or whoever he decides to shop with. He, also, hasn't seen, nor heard anything about Major Gramz or his pet, No Heart. Plus, he was still waiting to hear from Dirty's friend, Drew, who hasn't come back from whatever foreign country he was deployed to, to assist some other government-issued party.

Ray's thoughts were interrupted when he spotted a dark SUV to the right of him, slowly approaching with its lights off. The windows were rolled down, so he was able to tell there were three occupants but couldn't make out their features for the darkness.

There was no house directly across the street, which was where the Chevy Tahoe came to a halt. The driver put the gear into park, and the three occupants seemed to just stare at him. Now, Ray was thinking about his family and his gun. He'd left inside, which reminded him of what he told Robert, earlier, about what would happen the moment he left from under the shield he has in Georgia.

"You do know it's not polite to stare and not speak, right?" The driver voiced from his window.

"Ain't no way in hell!" Ray let out, descending the steps of the porch.

Although Ray couldn't make out the man's features, there was no mistaking his voice, which pretty much confirmed who the other two men were. With his heart racing, as Ray closed the gap between him and the truck, their faces began to slowly take shape until they were one hundred percent noticeable. Of course, they were all smiling, happy to see him. Plus, they were all wearing suits and ties.

"Hello, King Ray!" James offered.

"Don't give me that shit!" Ray shot back. "Y'all got a lot of explaining to do!"

"Of course," his brother replied, jerking a thumb over his shoulder. "Get in before you draw unwanted attention!"

Only lingering for a couple of seconds, Ray took a look around before climbing in behind his brother, and beside Black, who was seated in the rear.

"It's good to see you, bro!" Black said, embracing Ray.

"You too, my nigga!" Ray told him, then turned to Fred, who was in the front-passenger seat. "The Mona Lisa picture, huh?"

"I knew you'd figure it out," Fred told him, taking Ray's hand in a firm grip. "It's good to have you back on the throne."

"It's good to be back." Ray squeezed James' shoulder. "I went to your funeral, Jay. How is this so?"

"Yeah, you went to *someone's* funeral," James responded, holding his brother's gaze in the rear-view mirror. "If you thought that dude in the casket looked like me, then that means my money was spent well. Anyway, we felt that it was time to reconnect with you."

"Yeah," Fred added, looking back at Ray. "We've been watching you. You may not be aware of it, but you're traveling down a short highway, with no exit."

"There's a big storm brewing in Atlanta," James went on. "Although you're only in the game to stack some paper, these other niggas have different motives. To them, it's about being the last man standing, which means an all-out war has to take place."

"We can't let you go at this alone, Ray," Black finally conduced to the conversation. "That's why The Kingz are reassembling."

"The streets are way deadlier than they were when we were running them," said Fred. "We'll be getting to the money, but we'll be planting these niggas in the ground, too."

Ray said, "So, we'll be killing for nothing."

"It won't be for nothing, Ray," James pitched in. "Niggas are gonna be gunning for us, so we'll have to beat them to the punch. We're not strangers to this gunplay shit."

"Definitely not," offered Fred. "Just understand that this could be the final reign."

Ray had to cogitate this. There was definitely a storm brewing, and he'd caught a whiff of it not too long ago. On top of that, he was also anticipating his next encounter with Major Gramz and No Heart, which was bound to be quite unpleasant.

Just as Ray thought to open his mouth and tell them about the currently existing beef, the bright headlights of an oncoming vehicle caught his attention. The distinctive shape of the headlights brought on an unwelcoming wave of deja vu, which had him thinking about his gun, again, that was under the pillow his head was resting on just before stepping out of the house.

At that moment, Ray sensed that something wasn't right about this picture. Seeing that his fellow Kingz weren't paying the SUV any attention, he felt compelled to warn them, but when he opened his mouth, nothing came out. It was too late, anyway, because the black H2 Hummer had pulled alongside their truck. It's dark windows immediately began to roll down, revealing four men in ski masks. The driver and the occupant behind him produced AK-47s and wasted no time with squeezing on the triggers, making their barrels spark, as bullets spewed from them.

"Aaah!" Ray cried out.

When his eyes shot open, Ray realized he was sitting on the passenger side of the white Cadillac Escalade he'd leased over a month ago, which was driven by Sheila, as they were on their way back to Georgia upon leaving Alabama. Still frantic from the nightmare, he looked in the back seat for his children. Prince Ray was fast asleep with his head resting on the door, and Rachel was regarding him with a worried look.

"Are you okay, baby?" Sheila inquired.

Just as he was about to regard her, he caught a glimpse of a black H2 Hummer, coming upon the left side of them. Following his gaze, Sheila looked to her left and quickly let her foot up off the gas pedal, as Ray snatched the door to the glove compartment open and took hold of his Glock.

They both watched the glowing taillights of the truck as it moved further and further away, blending in with other vehicles moving along the night traffic. Sheila eased back down on the gas pedal to maintain a proper speed limit.

"They're still alive," Ray finally said.

"What!" Sheila shot a glance at him. "Who?"

Playa Ray

Chapter 12

"Come on in, my friend!" Said Big Ru, who was seated on the living room sofa when Quick Ru let Ray into the house.

Surprised that Quick Ru didn't conduct his unusual weapons search, Ray moved further into the living room and took a seat on the sofa opposite of the one occupied by Big Ru, who was draped in some very expensive pieces of jewelry that complemented the gold-framed eyeglasses on his face.

"You look like you're going to a fashion show," Ray commented, placing the small paper bag he was carrying onto the coffee table.

"Hell, I *am* the fashion show!" The big guy boasted. "I get money, and when I got out, I want niggas to recognize that shit. But, one of our homies is throwing his birthday party at the park, and Quick and I will be on our way once you and I are done."

"Well, don't let me hold you up," Ray told him.

Big Ru asked, "You're copping a ki, right?"

"That was my initial plan," Ray answered. "I still wanna buy the ki, but I need you to front me two of 'em."

Big Ru studied Ray for a moment as if considering his impromptu request. "Yo, Quick!" he finally called out.

Seconds later, Quick emerged from another part of the house with his cell phone glued to his face. "What's up?"

"I need three," he told his right-hand.

"A'ight," replied Quick. "We got twelve on the block, too. I think they're just passing through."

"Keep me posted!" When Quick left, Big Ru looked to Ray. "I got niggas on the block, twenty-four-seven. If an unknown vehicle hits that street, niggas immediately call that shit in. That's why I never worry about the pigs running in on me. My niggas'll turn this bitch into Iraq! I'm like Scarface around this motherfucker!"

Ray nodded his understanding. "That's what's up. So, how well do you know Major Gramz?"

"That nigga is a snake!" Big Ru vented, making a face. "He thinks he's untouchable!"

Says the man who referred to himself as Scarface, Ray thought. "I'm telling you," the big man went on. "He'll shake your hand, then turn around and shoot you in the back! He's not to be trusted!"

Ray left Big Ru's home, thinking about what he'd heard about Major Gramz. He was also thinking about what Calvin had offered in reference to Big Ru. Technically, Calvin and Big Ru are rivals, so it's incontestable that they would say *not-so-nice* things about one another. He didn't know much about the Bloods organizations except that there were many branches of it, and could only assume that most of them didn't get along, which could be ascribed to Big Ru's indignation towards Major Gramz.

"Talk to me!" Ray answered his cell phone as he pushed his Escalade down the expressway.

"There's a marine at my club," Tommy told him. "And I don't think he's looking for me."

***

"Can I have a box of Magnums, too?" Sheila asked the gas station's clerk when she reached the counter with a Fruitopia drink and a pack of Lance cookies.

This week has been quite hectic for Sheila. Especially after leaving Alabama this past Easter. Ever since Ray had that minor episode in the truck, his behavior has become unbearable and a bit scary. Even the children have noticed it and have been walking on eggshells around him.

Since Sunday, he and Sheila only had sex twice, and she could tell that Ray was just going through the motion because his mind was elsewhere. She was still trying to figure out what he meant when he said "They're still alive". Being that he asserted this just after seeing that Hummer truck, Sheila couldn't help but feel like he was referring to some of their past enemies, which surely had her paranoid.

"Which size?" The clerk asked.

"Probably small," Sheila said, almost to herself.

"Small?" the woman shot her an incredulous look.

"Medium."

Sheila didn't need any gas, so she was parked closer to the entrance. Upon climbing behind the wheel, she started the car before greedily downing a large portion of her refreshing drink to get her body temperature down, for the sake of the warm weather.

Extracting the box of condoms from the small paper bag, she stuffed them into her pocketbook, then made off towards the Legion Inn, which was just down the street.

Accustomed to Ray being out all the time at odd hours, Sheila decided to make plans of her own, which is why Shatera was currently babysitting the children and Sheila was now pulling into the lot of the cheap and shabby motel, where she drove around until she spotted the car that she was looking for. She just didn't expect to see its owner standing in front of it, talking on his phone.

Parking across the lot from the Dodge, Sheila killed the engine, popped a Tic-Tac in her mouth, then got out, throwing the strap of her pocketbook over her shoulder. She had to pull the hem down on the white skirt that seemed to have shrunken a few sizes since the last time she'd worn it, before crossing the lot.

While conversating with whoever it was he was on the phone with, Dread seemed to be enjoying the view as she approached, putting on an exaggerated strut. However, she didn't stop when she got to him. Instead, she marched right through the open door of room 27. Only taking a mere glance around the small room, she stopped, and faced the doorway with her hands poised on her hips. Seconds later, Dread entered, closing and locking the door.

"Bragging to your friend?" Sheila asked, indicating the phone he was stuffing into his back pocket.

"What'd I tell your fine ass about that?" He replied, pulling her close and gripping her ass with both hands.

"Uh-uhh!" She expressed, turning her head to dodge the kiss that he was trying to bestow upon her. "No kissing. I don't know where your mouth has been."

"I know where it's about to go," he shot back.

Sheila turned her face back to him. "Words," she offered.

"Words!" He replied defensively.

In response, Sheila tilted her head in defiance, which galvanized him to move her towards the bed, then push her down onto it. With a seductive smile on her face, Sheila scooted to the center, placed her pocketbook beside her, and waited while Dread took off his shirt, revealing his dark, muscular physique that seemed to push the start button on her hormones.

With her head lying on one of the surprisingly soft pillows, Sheila waited until Dread had crawled into the bed and put his face in position before opening her legs, revealing that the skirt and heels were the only things she had on. Obviously, intrigued by this, he hurriedly pushed her skirt up and put his tongue to work, making circular motions on her clitoris, and bringing on a sensation that she, somewhere along the way, had become a stranger to.

It felt so good to her at that moment, Sheila couldn't help but take a handful of his dreadlocks in a tight grip, though she fought the urge to gyrate her mid-section, in an endeavor to assist him.

"Ooh, shit!" She cried out. "Eat that pussy."

***

Back on the westside of Atlanta, again, Ray entered the almost-deserted establishment of Club Seven-Twenty, to see a man sweeping the floor and a woman behind the counter, counting bills.

The man stopped what he was doing to regard him. "Do you need something?" He asked.

"I'm here to see Usher," Ray answered, referring to Tommy by a nickname he no longer goes by.

The man only lingered for a couple of seconds before gesturing for Ray to follow him to the rear, where he rapped on a wooden door, then returned to the front, leaving Ray standing there.

Seconds later, Tommy pulled the door open. "If it ain't Machiavelli!" Tommy jested. "Come on in!"

Ray entered to see Dirty and a dark-complexioned man with a crew cut, whom he figured to be Drew, the marine from Savannah, Georgia. They were standing around a steel table that had a large military duffle bag on top of it.

"What's up, Ray!" Dirty greeted, giving him dap.

"What the move is?" Ray returned.

"I can't call it," he replied, gesturing to the other guy. "This is Drew— the dude I was telling you about."

"What's going on?" Drew offered his hand.

"Nothing but the rent," Ray told him, shaking his hand. "So, you're the man with the plan, huh?"

"I sure hope so."

"Enough of the small talk!" Tommy said, joining them. "He's here. Now, can we see these weapons of mass destruction?"

"Please!" Ray added.

Letting out a tense laugh, Drew untied the top of the bag, then pulled out an assault rifle that Ray knew wasn't legal in the States, being that he'd never seen any outside of military-based movies. He handed the weapon to Ray.

"What's this called?" Ray asked, checking out the unique sight at the head of the barrel.

"It's an M-four," Drew explained as he, one-by-one, pulled three more guns of the same type from the bag. "They're all military-grade with no alterations. Get caught with one of these and you might end up in one of those concentration camps in south Korea, somewhere."

"How much does one of these go for?" Asked Tommy, who was physically analyzing one of the weapons.

"I price mine at five," Drew answered. "That's because of what I have to go through to get 'em. Plus, there's trafficking fees, and other kats on the payroll who are expecting their cuts."

"I hear that," Tommy said. "That's not a bad price, considering you can't get these on the street."

"I'm not sitting on that kind of paper, right now," Ray told Drew. "I want all four of 'em, though."

"Shit, what'cha got, right now?" Drew wanted to know. "I gotta, at least, pay my co-defendants off."

"Okay," Ray said, placing the gun onto the table. "I'm looking at twenty for everything. What if I can compensate you with eight, and allow you to put interest on the rest?"

Drew shifted his gaze to Tommy.

"He's good for it," Tommy replied to the look. "Hell, if he goes off and gets himself killed, again, I'll end up paying it off."

Chapter 13
Wednesday

"Does anybody need anything?" Toni asked, upon exiting her office.

After burying her husband almost three months ago, the now head manager seemed to be in much greater moods as a result of moving on with her life. She's also become a whole lot friendlier, especially with the young assistant manager she had working under her. Ray was kind of glad they sent the young guy from a neighboring Checkers, which took some of Toni's attention off of him, but he was extremely glad that the police department did a half-ass job with the investigation of Jerry's murder, because he didn't trust Calvin being interrogated, given his vacillating mentality.

"Ray, could you empty the trash for me?" Toni asked.

"You're giving me a chance to say no?" Ray inquired, surprised at how she posed the question.

"Hell no!" She said, smiling. "Take the trash out!" With that, she moved on to confabulate with the three women on the registers, one being Sheila.

Ray looked at this watch and saw that he had less than twenty minutes before shift change. Therefore, he began cleaning one side of the grill while waiting for the rest of the meat to cook, and hoping that his order monitor remains clear until the second-shift grillman gets in.

"Here you go, Cal," Ray said, handing the remainder of the cooked patties over to Calvin, who was in preparations.

"I don't want that shit!" Calvin insisted, giving the tray a mere glance. "It's almost time to clock out. Throw that shit away!"

"You better not throw that shit away!" Said Toni, who was passing behind Ray, on her way back to the office. "Calvin, prepare those burgers!"

"I'ma prepare *your* ass!" Calvin shot back.

Ray was not expecting for her to shoot a seductive smile over her shoulder at him, but she did. Well, it's not like they were being disrespectful to their mates, because Jerry was deceased, and Leela, let Calvin tell it, had quit her job after their relationship came to an end two weeks ago. However, Ray was incredulous to his side of the story, considering what Calvin said about sending Leela to join Jerry, the first chance he got. Thinking this, Ray made a mental note to ask Sheila if she'd heard anything from the woman.

When Ray finished with the trash and clocked out, he found his fiancée out in the dining area, chatting with a group of female customers who were pretty much drooling over her three-week-old engagement ring, as Sheila herself was smiling from ear to ear, while showing it off.

Saying nothing, Ray walked past them, making for the exit. He heard Sheila saying her goodbyes, and she managed to catch up to him as he was crossing the lot to the Escalade. Climbing behind the wheel, he started the engine and let all the windows down to relieve the interior of the standing heat, while awaiting the air conditioner to dispose of its hot air.

"The kids want pizza tonight," Sheila informed while searching through her cellular. "Would that suit you?"

"That's cool," Ray answered, backing out of his spot.

"So, you don't have to go out tonight?"

"I do," he said. "If I know that I won't be back for dinner, I'll call and let you know."

By the time he pulled to the exit of the lot, cool air was blowing from the vents, so he let the windows back up before pulling out. Seeing Sheila continued to function with her phone reminded Ray of what he was going to ask her. "Have you heard anything from your friend?" He posed.

Sheila pried her eye from the device to regard him. "What friend?"

"Leela."

"Not lately," she answered, going back to scrolling through her messenger. "She usually posts something on Facebook everyday but I haven't seen anything from her in a while. Why'd you ask?"

"Just curious," Ray offered.

Although Sheila was engrossed in what she was doing, Ray's inquiry into Leela was starting to take shape in her mind. She hadn't given it any thought until then, but it was quite strange how Leela just up and quit her job without warning. Plus, on top of not posting anything on her social media wall since that time, she hadn't come by the restaurant to brag to her friends about a better profession she's started, nor to receive her final paycheck.

Rumor has it that, around the time she called in to inform the manager of her resignation, she and Calvin had called it quits on their relationship, but Sheila was thinking it was something else. Something worse. This made her think of how Jerry came up missing and was subsequently found dead. For some reason, she still had a notion that Ray was, somehow, involved in that.

When Ray pulled into McGees Auto Body Shop, Sheila immediately spotted the Cadillac CTS that still looked the same, although the problem that needed to be tended to was the air conditioner that conked out, Monday evening.

McGee's must've been having a slow day because there weren't many vehicles in the To Be Serviced area. Plus, before Ray could park the SUV, McGee himself, who was a dark-complexioned, balding man in his late forties, came rushing from the small building, dangling the keys in the air. Leaving the engine running, Ray and Sheila got out, and followed the man to the Cadillac, where he took it upon himself to start the car.

"I did your car myself," he told Sheila as he stood back, allowing her enough room to climb behind the wheel. "Country is a good mechanic, but he does a half-ass job, sometimes."

The temperature inside the car had to be close to ninety degrees, which was being added to by the AC unit that was disencumbering stored heat from its duct. Despite the noticeable particles of dust that spewed from the vents, Sheila saw large amounts of it all over the floorboard, and seats.

"What's the matter?" Ray asked, seeing the look on his woman's face.

"It's dirty in here," she answered.

McGee spoke up. "That came from the air duct. The vacuum we have would've just made a bigger mess. Sorry about that!"

"We'll take care of it," Ray promised. "Is it working?"

"I feel air coming from it, now."

"Good! We need to get going!"

Once Sheila paid for the service, they left the repair shop with Ray trailing Sheila to their apartment. Entering the security gate, Sheila stopped at the mailboxes and Ray drove onto the apartment. As always, Dread and his friends were in their same spot, but all they did was watch her as she collected the mail and got back into her car.

Driving around to Shatera's unit, she saw that Shatera and Lavish were sitting on the steps, watching the children play around. Seeing the car, Prince Ray and his sister, Rachel, darted into Shatera's apartment to retrieve their bookbags. Sheila let down the front-passenger window.

"What's up, love birds!" She teased the two.

"I know you didn't!" Shatera shot back, laughing, as Lavish tried his best not to blush. "Don't make me get on you and Crazy Ray!"

"You better leave my baby alone!" Sheila retorted, smiling. "I'll dive through this window on your black ass about my mentally unstable husband!"

"I already know," said Shatera.

"You better know!" Sheila asserted. "What's going on with you, Lavish?"

"Not much," the tall guy responded. "Just taking it one day at a time."

Sheila nodded her understanding. "I know what you mean. Where's Trez?"

"At the studio," he answered. "I'll be on my way, shortly. You need to stop by some time and see us in action."

"Maybe, I will," she replied, just as the kids emerged from the apartment with their bookbags on their backs. "Thanks, Shatera!"

"You're welcome, girl!"

"Are we still having pizza, Momma?" Asked Prince Ray, who climbed into the front-passenger seat as his sister got into the back.

"Of course," she answered, driving on.

"And chicken wings, too?" Rachel wanted to know.

"Whatever y'all want."

"Yes!" They both rejoiced in unison.

Sheila smiled at the fact that she was able to satisfy their little hearts by allowing them to choose what they wanted for dinner. When she pulled around to their unit, she saw Ray exiting the apartment with his knapsack hanging from his shoulder. He'd also traded his Checkers shirt for another one.

Sheila parked, but before she could kill the engine, the kids lunged from the car and ambushed their father with hugs.

"Leaving us already?" Sheila posed as she finally approached.

"Here!" Ray said, handing his set of keys to her. "Give me your keys! I should be able to get the car vacuumed while I'm out."

"Okay." Sheila relinquished her set to him. "Be safe, baby!"

"Always!" He said, kissing her in the mouth. "See y'all in a minute."

Sheila ushered the children inside and locked the door. As bad as she wanted to get back to her social media, she knew that a lukewarm shower was in order, being that her clothes were sticking to her. Therefore, after depositing her things in her bedroom, Sheila gathered her necessities, then made for the bathroom.

***

"Everything's on point," the man, who's known to Ray as Isaac said after removing the last ounce of cocaine from the digital scale, and placing it with the other three on the coffee table. "Hell, I don't know why I even bother to check this shit. LKS has always done good business. When is he gonna get some more weed and pills?"

"I have no idea," answered Ray, who was ready to get out of the uncomfortable, high-backed chair that he was seated in. "I'm just a trafficker. They give me the product and point the finger."

"I hear that," Isaac replied with a chuckle, "Everybody has their own role to play. It's good to be back doing business with him because these niggas be trying to squeeze a million dollars out of a twenty sack!"

"Yeah, you can't be dealing with those type of niggas," Ray said as he stood, stuffing the already counted bills into his bag. "But, I'll let LKS know that you inquired on the pills and weed."

Being that Ray was already in Riverdale, Georgia, upon leaving Isaac's house, he decided to drive out to the house that Sheila bequeathed to Nikki and Ace— the same house that Ebony and Theresa shared, prior to their deaths.

It was Ray's second time ever coming to the place, so there was nothing outwardly different about it. Their family van, along with Ace's champagne-colored Toyota 4-Runner, were parked in its driveway, indicating that they were home. Choosing to dock at the curb, Ray got out, leaving his bag in the car, and made for the front door, where he rang the doorbell.

He was waiting to hear someone's voice to inquire as to who was at the door, but it never came. Instead, he heard the click of a sole lock, before it opened up to Nikki, who was clad in a pair of khaki-colored capri pants that flaunted her every curve, and a green shirt with 'SEXY' on the front. Ray had never looked at Black's woman in that manner, but at that moment, he wouldn't dare contend with the bold statement she was making.

"Hey, Ray!" She greeted with a surprised look on her face.

"I was just in the neighborhood," Ray explained. "Is everything okay?"

"Is that the food?" Ace asked as he came up from behind Nikki. Then, realizing who it was, he said, "What's up, Ray!"

"Not much," he answered, feeling a bit alienated by their facial expressions. Especially Ace's. "I was in Riverdale and decided to drop in on y'all. Is it a bad time?"

"No, it's not a bad time," offered Nikki.

"Just hungry as hell!" Ace added. "This Chinese food is taking forever to get here."

"Yeah, they do be taking forever," Ray agreed. "So, how are the kids?"

"They're great!" Nikki told him, then looked as though she just remembered something. "Ray, do you remember Danielle?"

"Who is Danielle?" He asked, immediately searching his memory bank, only to come up blank.

"She had a daughter by Black," Nikki went on to explain.

"Oh! Yeah, I remember," Ray said, remembering the woman who left for Virginia, taking Black's daughter with her. "I've never met her, though. What about her?"

"She contacted me on Facebook a couple of days ago," Nikki let on. "She claimed that she had no idea that Black was gone until she saw my profile page, and that she was contacting me to tell Black what happened to his daughter."

"What happened to his daughter?" Ray asked, not missing a beat.

"She didn't give me the full details," Nikki went on, "but Kendra was hit by a car and died on the way to the hospital."

"Damn!" Ray sympathized, thinking about the dream he had of his fellow Kingz this past Easter. He still wasn't ready to give up on his theory that they were still alive.

***

"Yeah, that's crazy how she just fell off the face of the earth like that," said Marlene, who Sheila was video chatting with on Messenger. "Whenever I do find a better job and leave Checkers, I'll still stop through from time to time and check on y'all."

"That's my point," Sheila told her. "That heifer would've been pulled up, talking shit."

"You're right about that," her friend agreed. "Maybe, she's going through something. Her and Calvin broke up. Maybe, she's still suffering from that."

"I doubt it."

"Why?"

"Their relationship wasn't a match made in heaven," Sheila replied as her phone vibrated, and the incoming call indicator popped up. "Marlene, that's my baby. I'ma hit you right back."

"Okay."

Sheila switched to the phone app. "Hello?"

"I'm on my way to the self-wash," Ray informed her. "Once I'm done there, I'll be on my way."

"Okay," Sheila replied, noticing he sounded a little different. "I already ordered the pizza. If it gets here before you do, I'll make sure the gremlins don't eat it all."

"Alright," he said, then hung up.

***

Ray's aim was to vacuum Sheila's car, then head on home, but when he pulled into a self-service auto wash and saw that one of the washing stalls was unoccupied, he pulled into it, feeling that he may as well give the Cadillac a full treatment.

When he got out, his nostrils were invaded by various aromas of scented cleaning agents, and his ears were filled with the noise pollution of several sound systems as people went about tending to their vehicles. As customary, Ray took a moment to glance around for any sign of potential danger before dropping coins into the washer.

After rinsing away loosed dirt, Ray switched to the sudsy brush and began lathering the car down. While doing so, his mind reverted back to what Nikki revealed about Black's daughter, who'd left this world, knowing nothing of her father. He wanted to reach out to Danielle but didn't know where to start.

Being that his belief of his brother', and his friends' existence had reached fruition. Ray wondered if Black was aware of his off-spring's demise. Also, why haven't they contacted him yet? What were they waiting for? Surely, they knew where he was. Or, did they plan to just watch over him from a distance? Although it was his personal belief, he knew there was one way to prove if the other Kingz were still walking amongst the living, and that would entail another trip to Birmingham, Alabama.

After rinsing the suds off the car, Ray pulled around to one of the available vacuum stations and pulled all four carpeted mats out before activating the pump, starting on the mats. Finishing with them, he vacuumed the back seats as well as the floor. Then, he moved to the front. Once making sure he got up all the excessive dust and dirt, Ray pulled open the glove compartment to see if it needed to be cleaned, and found himself wishing he'd never ventured that far.

As he stared at the opened box of Magnum condoms, Ray started to perspire, and was unaware that the timed vacuum component had shut off. Now experiencing tachycardia, his mind immediately went back to the day he caught Sylvia performing fellatio on another man, which brought on a whole new wave of anger.

A part of him wanted to blame himself for Sheila's infidelity. Ever since they've been back together, following their incarcerations, things just haven't been the same, and Ray knew it was mainly because of the mentality he'd adopted. As far as he knew, Sheila had been faithful to him, even in his assumed death.

However, the other part of him wasn't trying to hear that bullshit. How could she commit the ultimate betrayal, by letting another man enter her? It didn't matter if Ray wasn't as sexually active as he used to be many years ago— that didn't give her the right to wander off! He just hoped that Sheila knew what she was doing, because, according to the laws of physics, she belonged to him until *he* waves the white flag. And, to his recollection, he didn't own one of those.

Playa Ray

Chapter 14

Knock! Knock! Knock!

The sound of someone knocking on the front door roused Sheila from her sleep. Opening her eyes, she looked to the other side of the bed and saw that it was empty, indicating that Ray still hadn't made it home.

According to the clock on the nightstand, it was 1:52AM. Last night, at a few minutes to seven, she received a call from Ray, informing her that he was on his way to clean her car, then would be on his way home. When nine o' clock came around, and he still hadn't shown up, she called him, only to receive his voicemail. Another call at ten o'clock yielded the same results. Sheila didn't know whether to be mad or worried, though she was conflicted with a mixture of both emotions.

Knock! Knock! Knock!

Sitting up, Sheila swung her legs over the side of the bed and slid her feet into her house shoes. After collecting a housecoat from the closet, she exited the bedroom and encountered Rachel standing in the doorway of her own bedroom, wiping the sleep from her eyes with her tiny fist.

"Who that is, Momma?" she inquired.

"I don't know, baby," Sheila said in passing. "Go back to bed!"

Not waiting to see if her stepdaughter did as she was told, Sheila approached the front door and peered through the peephole, to see a well-dressed white man, holding an umbrella, for the sake of the pouring rain that she didn't know was coming down. Plus, she could make out the badge clipped to his belt.

"Who is it?" She asked anyway.

"Detective Rhodes," he answered. "From the Forest Park Police Department."

Sheila unlocked and pulled the door open, but said nothing.

"Are you Ms. Sheila Griffin?" He inquired.

"I am."

"The significant other of Mr. Ray Young?"

"I'm his fiancée," she told him. "What's wrong?"

"Mr. Young was in a fatal car wreck," Rhodes explained. "He was pronounced dead on the scene. Right now, I need for you to accompany me to the City Morgue for further identification and to claim his belongings."

"Are you sure it's him?" Sheila's voice was barely over a whisper as she placed a hand over her chest that seemed to tighten by the second.

"Unless he was in possession of someone else's driver's license," answered the detective, gandering at his watch. "Are you coming?"

"Let me put some clothes on," she replied, stepping aside. "You can come in out of the rain."

When the officer entered, Sheila closed the door, told him that she'd be back, then made for her bedroom, relieved that the children hadn't come out of their rooms because she was not yet ready to explain anything to them. Before attempting to put on any clothes, Sheila grabbed her phone off the nightstand and dialed Shatera's number, hoping she'd pick up at this time of night.

"Hello?" Shatera finally answered, sounding exhausted.

"I'm sorry for waking you up, Shatera!" Sheila apologized. "But I need you to come over and watch the kids, until I get back from the city morgue."

"The City Morgue!" Shatera became animated. "Girl, why are you—"

"I promise I'll explain later," Sheila cut her off. "Can you watch them for me?"

"I'll be right over," her friend agreed.

By the time Sheila was done dressing, she heard a knock at the front door. Already knowing who it was, she stepped out of the bedroom in her socks. The detective was still standing, patiently near the door.

"That's my babysitter," she told him. "Could you let her in?" Stepping back inside, Sheila sat on the edge of the bed to put on her white Nike Air Max sneakers.

Before she could stand up, Shatera pretty much rushed into the room, looking like she'd seen a ghost with one hand over her chest.

"Girl, tell me it's not Ray!" she spoke, conspiringly, approaching as Sheila got to her feet.

"He was in an accident," she croaked out as tears cascaded down her face.

"Damn, baby!" Shatera moved in to embrace her. "I'm here for you and the kids. Whatever you need, I got you, okay?"

Sheila nodded her head against her friend's shoulder. "He's waiting on me, to take me to the morgue."

"Okay." Shatera released Sheila, then held her umbrella out to her. "Take this with you! It's raining like hell out there!"

Accepting the umbrella, Sheila dropped her phone into her pocketbook before throwing the strap over her shoulder and allowing Shatera to walk her to the front door, where Detective Rhodes still awaited.

"I got the babies," Shatera told her.

Sheila only nodded as she and the detective exited, making for his gray Ford Crown Victoria. It was only a twenty-something minute drive, but Sheila felt like she was on an endless drive to the end of the world, as a million and one thoughts and questions clouded her mind. She was mainly concerned with how she was going to support herself and the children in Ray's absence.

Upon entering the quiet establishment of the city morgue, Detective Rhodes led the way to the front desk that was manned by a large, Caucasian man, who appeared to be in his late thirties.

"Back again so soon?" The security guard addressed Rhodes.

"You make it seem like I was just in here hours ago," he replied. "Where's the M.E.?"

The guard jerked a thumb over his shoulder. "In the back. Room two."

"Thanks, John!"

Just as they were about to enter the steel double-doors, a thunderbolt struck not too far from the place, illuminating the interior and shaking its foundation. It seemed like the closer they got to room two, the more light-headed Sheila became, and the more her legs felt like they were going to give out.

Rhodes didn't bother to knock. He pushed the second pair of double-doors open, and they entered the room, where an older white man in a squeaky-clean laboratory coat was examining the corpse of a black female on one of the gurneys. She was completely naked, and her face looked like she'd been mauled by some kind of animal. It appeared that the medical examiner was washing the blood from her deep facial wounds.

"How may I help you?" He asked, not bothering to look back.

"It's Detective Rhodes again, doc," the detective answered.

"Did you find anyone to identify the male?"

Rhodes glanced back at Sheila. "His fiancée."

"What about the mother and infant?" The examiner inquired, still tending to the corpse.

"Nothing on them, yet."

"What a shame!" The older man dropped his bloody sponge into a biohazard can before moving over to the sink, where the water was running. After finishing his gloves off, he doffed them, tossed them into the same can, then donned another pair. That's when he finally regarded Sheila for a moment with sympathy in his eyes. "I guess we should get started with the viewing," he finally said.

They watched as he covered the dead woman with a freshly new white sheet before moving over to another gurney that contained a corpse in a body bag. First, he appeared like he was about to unzip the bag. Pausing with his hand on the zipper, he looked up at Sheila, who was still standing about seventeen feet across the room.

"I believe you'd have to be closer than that to view the subject," he told her.

Sheila has never been inside a morgue before so, of course, she was going to stand in one spot until advised to do otherwise. Well, after shooting a glance at the detective who was looking back at her, she set her feet into motion, cautiously passing the deceased woman's gurney, as if trying not to disturb her.

"She was a part of the accident," the M.E. explained, then nodded towards a gurney with a smaller figure under a sheet. "Her son had to be no older than two years old."

Sheila said nothing as she approached, and stood on the opposite side of the older man. He gave her another wary look before slowly unzipping the bag. Sheila's right hand was already gripping her chest as her heartbeat increased, and her mouth became parched.

Stopping the zipper midway, he began to peel the top of the bag back, but Sheila was already staring at her fiancée's face that exhibited the same exact injuries as that of the woman. In spite of the mass of blood and particles of glass protruding from his wounds, she knew without a shadow of a doubt that it was her man. The tears began to pour, again.

"I've seen this many times before," the examiner spoke, his voice sounding miles away. "It was a head-on collision. Neither one of them were wearing their seatbelts, which resulted in them being ejected through their windshields. It's sad to say, but this makes you the last Queen standing, Sheila. It's the final reign."

"What!" Sheila let out, now regarding the man who now had a benign smile on his face. "How did you kn—"

Beep-beep! Beep-beep! Beep-beep…

Sheila was awakened by the sound of her alarm clock on the nightstand. Jerking upward in a sitting position, she immediately looked over at Ray's side of the bed to see that it was still empty. Not knowing what to make of this, she silenced the alarm then checked her phone for messages. There weren't any.

"Where are you, baby?" She said, speed-dialing Ray's number. "Please, pick up, baby! Please, pick up!"

Getting the voicemail, Sheila wanted to try again, but thought against it, promising herself that she'd get to the bottom of this, later. Right now, it was time for her to get the children ready for school, and herself ready for work, although she didn't know how she was going to tackle this day mentally, with Ray's absence and that disturbing dream dangling over her conscience.

Of course, Prince Ray and Rachel inquired on whether their father came home last night or not as they got ready for school. As bad as Sheila wanted to lie to them— she didn't. She simply told them that he did not come home. Naive to what that could signify, Prince Ray wanted to know if he could eat the slices of pizza that was left over for his dad, but Rachel's mood seemed to go dark, instantly. Plus, there was a knowing look in her eyes, in which Sheila noticed, when she dropped them off at the bus stop.

When Sheila pulled into the parking lot of Checkers, she was half-expecting to see her car in its usual spot, but it wasn't. Usually, around this time of the morning, the sun would be bathing this side of the planet, in its mildly-warm glow, but the only thing looming in the sky were dark-gray clouds that foretold the tale of a gloomy day.

She took long, deep breaths in an endeavor to mentally ready herself for the every-day madness she has to brook with at her work-place. Feeling like she was, at least, eighty percent competent, Sheila climbed down from the truck, shoved her phone into her pocket, then marched dutifully towards the building.

"I don't know if Ray's coming in or not," Sheila said to the manager, Toni, upon entering the office to clock in.

"He's not," Toni replied from behind her desk, getting Sheila's full attention.

"How do you know that?"

Toni shrugged. "He just called, like, three minutes ago. I thought you guys lived together."

Sheila just scowled at the woman.

"You'll be on window two, today," The manager apprised, pretty much disregarding the look.

Sheila could not believe this! Yes, Ray has been acting strange, but this was new. It was just eating her up inside to know that, while she was sitting outside in the truck, trying to get her mental together for the sake of worrying over his absence, he had the nerve to call in to their manager and inform her that he wasn't coming in, but didn't have the decency to call his own wife-to-be, and explain to her why he chose not to come home, last night.

Oh! She was beyond livid, now! The love she has for Ray is uncompromising, but that didn't mean she was going to continue putting up with his sporadic behavior. Engaged or not, if Ray was foolishly thinking that Sheila wouldn't take the kids and leave him all alone, then he was sadly mistaken. She was a human being, and human beings can only take so much negligence before naturally responding to it.

"Here you go, Sheila," Calvin said, handing her an already wrapped, grilled burger.

"Thanks!"

The first two times were speculative, but when she received the burger from Calvin, this time, Sheila was absolutely certain that he was intentionally touching her hand. Just the thought of it made her want to assail him, but she wanted to save all of her energy for when she gives Ray a piece of her mind, later. Or, whenever the next time she sees him.

Placing the burger into the bag that already contained fries and condiments, Sheila handed the bag and drink out to the awaiting customer, wished him a good day, then continued to prepare the next orders with only a mere glance at Calvin, who was the surrogate grillman for Ray. And, as she thought, he was watching her with a look she'd seen in the eyes of many men.

Sheila didn't see the next vehicle that pulled up to the window for regarding her order monitor. Accustomed to fixing her drinks, first, she set out to the drink machine to fix the next three. Bringing them back to her counter, she still paid no attention to the black convertible Ford Mustang with its top down, as she began preparing the first order.

Finally, with the first order and drink in her hands, she turned to the window and immediately felt that God had chosen this day to test her, because she was surely not in the mood to deal with this clown who was regarding her expectantly through his Steve Urkel-inspired eyeglasses. She bumped the sensor that activated the sliding window.

"Here's your order, sir!" she said, handing the items out to him. "Have a nice day!"

"Damn!" Expressed the man, who she only knows as Major Gramz's sidekick, as he received his order. "Is that how y'all treat customers up in that motherfucker? Whatever I did to you, I'm sorry! Straight up!"

"I have other customers to serve, sir," Sheila told him.

"You don't even have to be doing this." He sat his food and drink down, then pulled a large wad of bills from his armrest compartment. "I believe in paying for what I want. All you gotta do is kick it with me, and you can walk around with shit like this, daily. Trust me, I'm not trying to take you from your man— I just wanna spend some time with you."

"I hear you talking," said Sheila.

"I can back my shit up!" He admitted, with a hint of attitude. "Just write your number down— I'll show you."

"Write yours down!"

He didn't hesitate to jot his name and phone number down on a twenty-dollar bill and hand it to her. After glancing at it to see that his name was 'No Heart', Sheila stuffed the bill into her pocket, told him that she'd make contact, then commenced to prepare her customers' orders, as No Heart rolled on. Just as she turned around, she ran into Calvin, who seemed to be standing behind her with a menacing look on his face.

This had caught her off guard because she'd totally forgotten that anyone standing in the area in which he was standing in could hear whatever verbal exchange taking place at this particular window. Now, she was wondering how he was going to play his cards, because, as far as she could tell, he and Ray has become associates of some sort. So, he was either going to bring it to Ray's attention, or try to blackmail her. Either way, neither option would bring about a favorable outcome for him.

However, Calvin said nothing else to her for the remainder of the day, but she did catch him watching her from time to time. When her relief showed up, Sheila went to the office to clock out, feeling like she was going to have to curse Toni out if she made any kind of remark pertaining to her and Ray's relationship, but that feeling subsided at the sight of the assistant manager, and the two night-shift managers, who were all present. Therefore, she clocked out and got the hell up out of there, meeting Marlene in the dining area.

"Your mom's not here, yet?" Sheila inquired, standing over her friend, who was sitting at one of the tables.

"That damn hooker!" Marlene expressed, smiling. "She's probably somewhere, drunk, with one dick in her ass and two in her mouth."

"Girl, you're crazy!" Sheila let out, giggling.

"She didn't tell you that."

"My dad did," said Marlene. "I'm as black as black can get, and he favors Barack Obama. I assumed they played spin the bottle, afterwards, and he ended up having to claim me."

"Marlene, you're full of shit!" Sheila told her, shaking her head. "I gotta get home to my children."

"And that fine-ass fiancé of yours," Marlene replied with raised eyebrows.

Sheila sighed. "Yeah. That, too."

Marlene threw her hands up in mock surrender. "I won't pry."

"Thank you! I'll see you, tomorrow."

Sheila turned and made for the exit on the side of the building she parks on. The moment she walked through the door, all the anger she was feeling earlier that morning came rushing back to her, unabated, as she laid eyes on Ray who was leaning against the rear of her car with his arms folded over his chest. Besides the sunglasses, he had on different clothing, indicating that he'd been to the apartment.

"I sure hope you plan on explaining to me why you didn't come home last night!" She vented upon approaching.

"Let me get my keys!" Was all he said while holding her set out to her.

"So, you're not gonna say anything?" Sheila pushed, swapping the keys out.

"I'll see you later," Ray told her, moving for the driver's side of the Escalade, deactivating the alarm.

Sheila was at his heels. "How long do you think I'm gonna put up with this shit, Ray?"

Still choosing not to entertain her queries, Ray climbed behind the wheel, started the truck, then handed her pocket book out to her, before closing the door and backing out. As Sheila watched him pull out of the lot, she realized that it was time for her to start putting her foot down.

***

After collecting his truck from Sheila, Ray drove out to RJP Customs in DeKalb County, hoping that Joe was at that particular shop and wouldn't mind the impromptu visit. As he pulled into the lot, he spotted the burgundy BMW convertible that was sitting directly in front of the building. Before he could fully pull into one of the parking slots, he saw Joe exit the building, moving in his direction. When he put the truck into park, Joe slid in beside him.

"What's up, bro!" Joe greeted.

"I can't call it," Ray replied, bumping fists with his friend. "You must've spotted me pulling up?"

"I did," Joe answered, "but I was on my way to grab something from the car. Do you need those, already?"

"No," Ray replied, knowing he was referring to the military-graded guns that he was storing for Ray. "I was just riding and thinking, and ended up at your place of business."

"This sounds serious," Joe acknowledged, regarding his friend with furrowed eyebrows. "Trouble at the crib?"

Damn! Ray thought. *Is it that obvious?* What was he supposed to tell his friend? That he suspects Sheila of cheating because he found a box of condoms in her car with one condom missing? Hell no! That would definitely be a sign of weakness. Shit, Joe probably suspects his wife of cheating, but he's not crying on Ray's shoulder about it.

"The crib is the crib," Ray shot a curve. "I'm just still trying to figure things out. It's like everything is moving in slow motion."

"You already know how the game goes, Ray." Said Joe. You're trying to get rich overnight, and you know that only happens in urban fiction novels."

"Like the ones you read, huh?"

Joe chuckled. "Man, my wife got me hooked on that shit. Right now, I'm reading a book called Bonded by Blood, by some dude named Cash. He's pretty good!"

Ray nodded his understanding.

"I know you're ready to expand," Joe went on, "but the money isn't coming in fast enough. The Kingz had a quick rise to success, but we both know how that came about. LKS just kept the train going. Now, you're an infant, again, and have to learn how to walk on your own, which is gonna take much longer than it would if you had guidance." He fixed Ray with a stern look. "Unless, you plan on knocking off El Chapo."

Ray just looked at him.

"No, Ray!" Joe was shaking his head. "That shit's not necessary! Sometimes, slow money is the best money. You're only doing it to support your family, remember?"

"I need some weed and pills," Ray told him.

"I might be able to arrange that," he replied. "Just give me a few days, and promise me that you won't go knocking off other drug dealers."

Ray didn't respond.

"You can't make your boy that promise?" Joe persisted.

Leaving RJP Customs, Ray decided that he'd head home and put up with Sheila's disloyal ass, although he still blames himself for pushing her in that direction. He was also fully aware that the anger he was currently nursing was only a mere reflection of the fact that he was, indeed, human.

Stopping at a gas station, Ray pulled to an available pump and killed the engine. Just as he exited, a gray, mid-sized Lexus truck pulled up on the opposite side of the pump. Only giving the woman behind the wheel a quick glance, Ray swiped the card to activate the machine, accessed his gas tank, and allowed the gas to pump on its own while he took in the goings-on of the establishment.

"Hey!"

Ray looked back to see the driver of the Lexus, looking over the pump at him, though he could only see her head, which was animatedly coiffed with an excessive amount of blonde weave. If that wasn't enough to flaunt her 'fun' side, the dark-complexioned woman had on a pair of pink sunglasses that were carved into the shape of a flamingo, with wings protruding from the sides.

"Is yours working?" She asked.

Saying nothing, Ray rounded the machine, and couldn't help but be astounded by the woman who was quite attractive in a red and black Chicago Bulls jersey skirt that stretched over her full figure, and a pair of black and red Air Jordan's. Plus, she was like a walking jewelry store with her multiple necklaces, large loop earrings, wrist and ankle bracelets, and rings on every finger, which were all decorated with extremely-long, pink acrylic nails.

"I just got this card," she admitted, revealing an earring in her tongue that matched the one lodged in her nose. "I swiped it. The machine beeped, but nothing else happened."

After studying the machine for a second, Ray pressed start, then removed the nozzle from its cradle as the digitally displayed numbers wound back to zeroes.

"Well, damn!" The 5' 7" woman let out, accepting the nozzle. "I feel like a cavewoman. I guess a fifth-grader would've known to press 'start', huh?

"Not really," Ray replied, getting an eyeful of her cleavage. "I forget, sometimes."

She smiled at the admission. "You're just saying that to make me feel better."

"Did it work?"

"Maybe."

"What's your name?" He asked, right when the nozzle on his side popped, indicating that his tank was full.

"Monica." She answered, then flashed an expensive-looking wedding ring. "I'm not single."

"Neither am I."

"I'd already figured that much."

Ray furrowed his eyebrows. "How?"

"You're a good-looking man," Monica acknowledged, playfully eyeing him. "Plus, you have a sense of humor. There's not a woman, in her right mind, who'd just let your fine ass walk around free. Hell, if I was single, I'd be trying to kidnap you, right now."

"How about we just pretend you're single?" Ray said, which was fueled by the thought of Sheila letting another man penetrate her.

Her smile widened. "So, how long can I hold you hostage?"

At that point, the two of them decided to go in half on a room at one of the nearby motels. Ray didn't know her story, but the moment they entered the room, they were both all over each other, as if they both were going through the same ordeal with cheating mates.

It was like Ray had just thrown caution to the wind, because he was tonguing this strange woman down as if she was Sheila, as he moved her backwards to the bed. When they made it to the bed, they broke off the breathtaking kiss, and began undressing, tossing everything to the floor— including their sunglasses.

Once they were down to their birthday suits and socks, Ray made her sit on the edge of the bed, then stood directly in front of her. Monica didn't hesitate to fill her mouth with his swollen rod, slowly and masterfully going up and down on it while massaging his balls with her right hand, and drilling her brown eyes into his.

"Mmm!" Ray let out, biting down on his bottom lip.

Although she was doing a good job, Ray still chose to assist her by thrusting his hips forward, forcing himself deeper into her throat. Monica gagged, but didn't relent. Intrigued by this, he placed one hand on her shoulder and continued to assault her gullet.

Eventually, Monica couldn't take anymore. She backed up off the dick, retching, as a glop of saliva spewed from her mouth, landing on Ray's foot, though he paid it no mind. While Monica was trying to catch her breath, he lifted her legs, forcing her to lay back on the bed, then buried his face between her thighs, going to work on her clitoris as he inhaled some kind of peach-scented fragrance.

"Ooh, damn!" Monica cried out. "You're rough!"

Ray had never went down on a woman with a clit-ring, but he heard that it amplifies the sensation, so he could imagine what she was going through as he greedily sucked on her love button like a newborn on its mother's nipple. The feeling must've been quite intense because Monica was using her thighs like grip-pliers to keep his head in place, as she moaned in ecstasy, though her grip wasn't tight enough to stop him from dropping his head lower.

"Oh! I love that freaky shit!" Monica exclaimed, as Ray worked his tongue like a snake around the rim of her anus. "Lick that ass, baby!"

Ray knew that he was only doing this because of what he found out about Sheila. Had it not been for that, he wouldn't be inside that motel room, doing forbidden things on a woman he knew nothing about. Hell, he wasn't even enjoying it. Maybe, he and Sheila were finally growing apart, and it was time for them to move on.

"I've never seen a light-skinned man with a dick as black as yours," Monica expressed, smiling, when Ray stood erect, holding his swollen manhood in his hand. "I got some condoms in my purse."

"I'm quite sure you do," he responded, kneeling, and guiding himself inside her.

With her legs over her shoulder, and his feet planted on the carpeted floor, Ray came down with all the force that he could muster, with the impact sounding like someone being punched, as he persistently plunged in and out, making sure that Monica got a full dose of what he was serving.

"Boy, you're about to make me cum!" Monica let out, clawing his shoulders.

"Don't talk about it!" He told her. "Let me feel that shit!"

At first, Ray wasn't enjoying it, but he didn't think that Monica's hot, pink pussy was as tight as it was. He could feel the muscles of her walls contract as she did what she promised, immersing his rod in her sweet juices. That was enough to push Ray to his own peak. He stood up and stroked his throbbing dick until it exploded its load all over her stomach and chest.

"Damn, girl!" he exclaimed while squeezing the remainder of his spill out.

"I got some wipes in my purse," she told him, drilling her eyes into his. "I'm quite sure you're not gonna pass up on *those*."

When Ray returned home, the first thing he noticed was that Sheila's car was missing. Figuring she'd taken the children out for dinner, Ray entered the apartment and decided to go ahead and take his shower before they returned.

While conducting his ablution, which took a little over thirty minutes, Ray listened out for the front door, though his mind was on Monica. When they made plans to go to a motel, Ray was hoping it to be a fling, but things changed during the course of intimacy. Monica made him feel like a man again, which is why he made sure to exchange phone numbers with her before they parted ways. Most people would say two wrongs don't make a right, but he wasn't trying to make shit right— he was doing what the fuck he wanted to do!

Upon stepping out of the shower and drying off, Ray began to wonder why his family hadn't made it home yet. It was almost eight o' clock, which was around the time they put the kids to bed every night. Especially on school nights. Then, when he looked at the toothbrush rack, things started to slowly dawn on him. There were usually four toothbrushes in the rack. Now, his was the only one remaining.

"I know damn well!" He hissed.

With only a pair of boxer shorts on, Ray marched out of the bathroom like a raging bull. First, he peered into Prince Ray's and Rachel's rooms. Nothing appeared out of place. Then, entering his one bedroom, he flung the doors open on the closet and saw that everything seemed the same. He retrieved his phone off the dresser, and dialed Sheila's number, only to get her voicemail. Pausing to take a deep breath, he tried again.

"Yes?" Sheila answered, calmly.

"Where are my kids?" Ray cut to the chase.

"They're in the bed, Ray," she told him. "They do have school tomorrow."

"Don't fucking play with me, Sheila!" He raised his voice. "This shit'll get ugly, real quick!"

"I have to get some rest." Sheila seemed unfazed by the threat. "I'll let the kids know you asked about them."

Click!

Ray didn't know what to do, which is probably why he just stood in that one spot, fuming. There was no denying that he and Sheila were now at war. The only thing that wasn't certain was the outcome. He just hoped she knew what she was doing because she was swimming in shark-infested water.

Chapter 15

Unlike Ray, Sheila didn't stay away from home and not show up for work the next morning. In fact, she showed up for work expecting a physical brawl between herself and Ray. Just because he'd never put his hands on her before, Sheila wasn't a fool to believe that he never would. Especially, considering how he'd been acting lately.

However, Sheila made it to work way before Ray did and was assigned to one of the three front registers, which is where she was when he showed up. Though she furtively watched him from the corners of her eyes, he seemed to pay her no mind as he set the grill up and begun his day.

"Are you okay, girl?" Marlene asked later that day. She was one of the other cashiers.

"I'm just sick and tired of being sick and tired," Sheila answered, casting another glance over at Ray, who still hadn't said one word to her all day.

"Well, I got two words for you," offered Marlene.

Sheila gave her an expectant look.

"Marriage counseling."

"We're not married yet, Marlene."

The dark-complexioned woman shrugged. "Hell, try engagement counseling. If that doesn't work, you can always do what the white people do, and put transmission fluid in his Fruit Loops."

"Girl, no!" Sheila asserted, laughing. "You watch too much Cold Case Files."

Taking another customer's order, Sheila turned to fix it and noticed that Ray wasn't at the grill. After filling a medium-sized cup with ice, she placed it at the soda machine and pressed Fanta Orange. Then, she set out for the burger and fries, which she placed inside a service bag. That's when she notice the leakage at the bottom of the cup, whereas the orange soda was spewing down the machine's drain, being that the cup was default upon receiving.

"Not another one!" She complained.

Putting the food on the counter, Sheila dumped the ice out of the cup, and took it to the trash bin in the back. She underhandedly tossed it at the bin but it bounced off the edge and hit the floor. When she bent to pick it up, she felt someone's hand grip her ass. Of course she thought it was Ray, but when she turned around and saw that it was Calvin, something inside her snapped.

"Nigga, you done last your motherfucking mind!" She voiced, getting into his face. "Don't ever touch me again!"

"Really?" He challenged. "You're giving your number out to random niggas but when I grab you on the ass, you want to act like you ain't no slut."

Slap!

Sheila put all of her might into the slap that forced Calving to stumble a couple of feet sideways, clutching his stinging cheek, with a stunned and enraged look on his face. She'd already vowed that she would no longer tolerate being disrespected nor stepped all over. Plus, she came to work anticipating a physical fight with Ray. She was with whatever at that moment.

"Oh!" You done fucked up!" Calvin recovered, drawing back, with his hand balled into a fist.

Smack!

The fist seemed to come out of nowhere, catching Calvin in the same cheek, knocking him into the plastic trash bin, and causing a loud crashing sound. This time, it was Ray. As Calvin slowly got to his feet, Ray moved protectively in front of his woman, with a crazed look in his eyes that Sheila was familiar with. Plus, Toni, and Daryl, the Assistant Manager, had come out of the office, and others were now watching the disorder.

"You got a nice hand on you, Ray!" Calvin commented, approaching. Then, to Sheila he said, "I'd have a better chance, if I was No Heart, huh?" With that, he moved towards the front of the store.

"Calvin, where are you going?" Toni called after him.

"Fuck that!" He bellowed. Stopping, he pulled his Checkers shirt over his head, and slammed it into the floor, "Fuck this sorry ass job!"

Other employees moved out of the way, as a bare-chested Calvin made for the exit, leaving everyone resembling deer caught in a ray of headlights. De-icing the scene, Toni walked over, and picked up the discarded shirt.

"Um, back to work, everybody!" She commanded. "Unless, the rest of y'all plan on walking out, too. Ray, your meat is burning."

Everyone did as they were told as Toni retreated to her office. Ray shot Sheila a menacing look, before moving towards the grill, where its timer was wailing something awful. Switching it off, he scraped the charred meat off, disposing of it. After cleaning the grill, he put on fresh meat, then pressed the timer.

For the remainder of the day, Ray thought about all the bullshit that he was going through. It felt like God was testing his mental ability to handle certain situations. His relationship with Sheila was on its last leg and far beyond reconciliation, considering the cheating. He didn't want to lose her as his woman, but that's the result of all relationships, right?

Then, there was the new situation with Calvin. There was no doubt in Ray's mind that they'd cross paths again, which would pretty much be unpleasant. He also knew that Calvin's mentioning of No Heart was just to irk him, which is what he'd attempted with Jerry, their late manager.

At the end of the shift, of course, Daryl appointed Ray to trash duty. Upon pulling the first load of trash out the back door, Ray left the cart behind the building, and walked around to his truck. He retrieved his Glock from the glove compartment. He had to untuck his shirt, before concealing it in his waistband. Knowing that Calvin wouldn't hesitate to peel his cap back, Ray decided that he'd rather get caught with it than without it.

He completed the trash detail, unscathed. After clocking out, Ray left the building, hoping to catch Sheila, before she left, but when he got to the parking lot, he saw that her car was already gone. It infuriated him that she would ride off by herself after what happened earlier but she wasn't aware of how dangerous Calvin was. She wasn't there when Jerry was murdered.

Arriving home, and seeing that Sheila wasn't there, made Ray's blood boil over. Before getting out of the truck, he tried her cellular, only to get her voicemail. Finally, after taking a deep breath, he gave up on pursuing her. If she called herself taking a timeout from him, there was nothing he could do but wait.

Entering the apartment, Ray undressed and got into the shower. He was only in it no longer than five minutes when he heard the sound of the front door closing. Without shutting the water off, he immediately got out of the tub, and wrapped the towel around his still wet, and soapy body. Grabbing his gun off the toilet, he pulled the bathroom door open just as Sheila was reaching for the knob, which startled her. She shot a glance at the gun.

"Where are my kids?" Ray asked, trying to maintain his composure.

"I came to talk," she replied.

"Fuck that!" He let out. "If you're not trying to confess your sins, and repent, we don't have shit to talk about. Go and get my kids!"

"Okay," Sheila responded, then headed back towards the front door.

Ray was taken aback at how she gave in so easily. Something was off about her whole demeanor. Did she tell the children to wait in the car? He decided to see for himself. By the time he made it to the door, Sheila was climbing behind the wheel of her car, that was still running. His children were not inside of it. At that moment, all he could do was watch her back out and drive away.

***

"They're asleep," Sheila said of her children, as she re-entered the kitchen, where her grandmother, Dorothy, and Ebony's mother, Elaine, were seated at the table drinking Vodka. Clad in pajama pants and a tank top, she re-took her seat at the table, where her bottled apple juice sat.

"So, what are you and Ray going to do?" Elaine inquired. "You both have been through a lot, together and separately. And you've both been there for each other."

Sheila sighed, fingering her engagement ring. "I know, Momma. I don't wanna just give up on us, but I don't know how long I can put up with Ray's behavior. It seems like I'm the only one that's trying to make it work."

"It always seems that way to us women," Dorothy offered. "Besides bearing children, we were created to endure way more than a man can even imagine enduring. That's why we go through so much. It's not that God is trying to punish us— He's only trying to get us to understand our true worth."

"You're stronger than you think you are, Sheila," Elaine added. "Men are egotistic by nature. Sometimes, you have to swallow your pride, and stick it out until you're at your wits end. Trust me— you'll know when you're at your wits end. Plus, those kids need their dad."

"I'm still waiting for my wedding invite," Dorothy said, taking a sip from her cup.

Sheila smiled.

"Has he even called to check on you and the kids?" Elaine wanted to know.

"I don't know." That's when Sheila realized that she forgot to bring her phone inside. "I left my phone in the car, charging."

"He's probably been blowing you up, worried," said Elaine. "It doesn't take long for a man to realize how much he misses something."

"I know that's right!" Dorothy agreed, holding her cup up, and the women clinked theirs together in a toast.

"I plan on taking the children back home tomorrow," Sheila admitted, standing. "I have to get my phone."

Easing back into the guest room that she shared with the children, who were still asleep in the large bed, Sheila retrieved her keys off the dresser, then left back out. Getting outside, she deactivated her alarm, figuring, after checking for messages from Ray, she'd play around on Facebook Messenger for a bit.

Powering up her phone the first thing she did was check her text app messages. Seeing that there weren't any, she logged into her Facebook account, to see who's posted what. The very first post she saw was from Shatera. It was a picture of her and Lavish. He was leaned against his Lexus, with her cradled in his arms.

Smiling, Sheila texted a comment. Luv @1st sight?

Then, she scrolled down to see one of Marlene's silly posts, whereas she was making a face with her eyes crossed, and her tongue sticking out. It caused her to think about Leela, who'd made a similar post once. After liking, and leaving three hearts on Marlene's post, Sheila continued scrolling, in search of anything from her ex-coworker. Seeing nothing, she went into Leela's profile page, and saw the last post she'd made. It was a picture of her and Calvin, posted almost two month ago.

Seeing nothing that would assist her with Leela's whereabouts, Sheila backed out of Facebook, and logged into her messenger account. There were several messages, though she didn't plan to entertain any of them at this moment. Scrolling down a bit, she was surprised to see a message from Leela that read: *Need 2 talk 2 u.*

Not really knowing how to respond, Sheila texted : *OK.*

Figuring that Leela wasn't online, she logged out, and logged into her bogus account, which had a profile picture of Missy Elliot on it. One friend was online, according to the indicator. Sheila pressed video call and waited for the call to connect. She was looking at Dread, who had his locks pulled back, with a pair of dark sunglasses on his face.

"I didn't know you were in California," Sheila commented.

Dread looked confused. "California?"

"It's dark in Georgia right now."

"Oh!" He said, smiling, removing the sunglasses. "I won these in a dice game, earlier and was trying them on. What's up with you?"

"Not much," Sheila answered, smiling.

"I see you don't check your mailbox anymore."

"I've just been going through some things these past few days."

"That's why you need to let me dick you down, one good time," he offered.

Sheila made a face. "Your dick won't solve my problems."

"It'll solve one of 'em."

"And, which one is that, Dread?"

"Your sexual frustration," he answered. "Then, hopefully, you'll realize that you should be with me, instead of him."

"I thought we agreed to not mention him," she reminded.

"You're right," Dread said, apologetically. "My bad. So, when are we going to get together again?"

"Probably, this weekend.

"Will I get to go all the way, this time?"

"Maybe," Sheila answered, stifling a yawn." Dread, I gotta get some sleep. I'll talk to you some other time."

"Just keep that pussy tight for me!"

"Whatever, boy!"

Sheila logged out, and began thinking about Ray, wondering why he hadn't called to check on her and the kids. Most importantly, she was trying to figure out what had went wrong on that night he chose not to come home. Earlier that day, everything seemed fine. That was before he went out on one of his runs, using her car.

Just then, a thought occurred to her. Sheila opened the glove compartment, and immediately realized what pushed her man over the top. Of course, while vacuuming the car of the debris from the air conditioner duct, he had to also clean the glove compartment, and couldn't miss the box of condoms that she had no business having, being that they didn't use contraceptives.

"Wait a minute!" She muttered, taking hold of the box.

She didn't remember opening the box, but there it was, with its seal breached. Curious, she peered inside, and saw that one was missing. This didn't make sense at all. It was incontestable that Ray had seen the box, but why would he open it? Better yet, why would he take one of the condoms? Did he use it on another woman that night, which is why he didn't come home thinking that he was getting back at her for having them?

Playa Ray

Chapter 16
Saturday

"Daddy, why can't we see the stars in the daytime?" Asked Prince Ray, who was seated in the front passenger seat of Ray's truck.

Ray was glad that Sheila had come to her senses, and brought his children home, because he didn't know how long he could be patient with her, and whatever phase she was going through. Whether he was the reason or not. Though she returned to him, their relationship was still strained, because neither one of them *seemed* to have much to say to one another. No sins had been confessed, yet.

Now, traveling the expressway, Ray was on his way to Alabama to see if he could connect a few dots pertaining to his brother's death. Something was going on, and he had a feeling that his mother, and even Robert played a major role in whatever it was. Well, he was destined to find out because his mother held a vital piece of the puzzle that Ray found himself endeavoring to put together. He didn't ask Sheila if she was up for taking the trip, but he did bring his children, who would've thrown fits if they knew he'd visited their grandmother without them.

"I really don't know scientifically," Ray answered his son's question. "I just know they like hanging out with the moon."

His son giggled.

"They're small planets, Daddy," Rachel offered, from behind them. "You can only see them at night, because they glow in the dark."

"That sounds reasonable," Ray concurred, glancing back at his nine-year-old daughter, who was smiling from ear to ear. "How did the science project go? It was a volcano, right?"

"Yes," she answered. "I think me, and Sherri used too much vinegar and baking soda, because it ran over, and made a mess all over the floor."

"They didn't give y'all measuring cups?"

"They did," said Rachel, "But Sherri was the one who chose not to use them."

"So, Sherri was the mad scientist of the project, huh?" Ray said, making a face that made his kids laugh.

"I want to be a mad scientist," Prince announced.

"You definitely look like one with your hair standing on top of your head like that," Ray replied, reaching over, and ruffling his son's afro that seemed too big for his head.

When Ray pulled onto the gravel of his mother's driveway, he saw Robert inside the fence structure, out front, pouring dog food into two large bowls. Two Rottweiler puppies playfully mauled each other over the rations before Robert could finish pouring.

"Ooh, Daddy!" Rachel exclaimed. "Grandmomma got puppies!"

"Can we play with the puppies, Daddy?" Asked Prince Ray.

"I guess so," Ray answered.

Before he could kill the engine, Rachel and Prince Ray were diving from the truck like miniature paratroopers, which made him smile. By the time he climbed down, Robert was letting himself out of the fence, carrying the large bag of dog food. The children besieged him about playing with the dogs.

"Not while they're eating," Robert told them. "How's it going, Ray?"

"I can't complain," Ray responded, relieving the older man of the bag, then nodding towards the puppies. "Dogsitting?"

Robert grinned. "Not exactly."

"So, my mom actually agreed to having dogs?"

"It was all her idea," he told Ray. "She woke me from my sleep, telling me that she wanted two Rottweiler puppies. She's not scared of 'em. We take turns feeding and bathing them."

"Where is she?" Ray asked, looking towards the house.

"Inside, cutting up vegetables."

Ray indicated the bag he was holding. "Where does this go?"

"Kitchen."

"I'll be back, y'all," Ray said to his kids, who paid him no mind, for being glued to the fence, marveling at the animals.

Upon entering the house, Ray found his mother in the kitchen, standing at the counter, using a large knife to dice carrots, before dumping them into a large bowl containing other particles of vegetables.

"Hey, my son!" She beamed.

"What's up, lady!" He replied, kissing her on the cheek. "I see you've finally became a pet owner. It took you long enough."

"I know." There was a huge smile on her face. "Put that over there!"

After placing the dog food where she told him, Ray approached, and stood on the opposite side of the counter.

"What're you making?" He inquired.

"A chicken and vegetable soup."

"Yuck!" Ray made a face.

"I still don't understand why you hate chicken," Mary said, shaking her head. "So, what brings you all the way to Alabama, all by yourself?"

"I actually brought your grandbabies with me," he told her. "I guess they'll come running in here when they're done playing with the dogs.

"Where's Sheila?"

"Back in Georgia, doing whatever she do."

Mary narrowed her eyes at her son.

"Don't read too much into that, momma!" Ray tried to reason. "I know how you are."

"What's going on with you two?" She asked, placing her knife down on the counter, and thrusting her hands upon he hips.

"We're just trying to stay afloat like any other couple," Ray offered, with a shrug. "But, we're okay for the most part."

"If you say so."

"I say so, momma," Ray said, then remembered his sole purpose for being there. "I want to ask you something."

"What is it?"

"Do you still have the pictures that you took of James' funeral?" He plunged right in, ready to connect dots, and put puzzle pieces in their respectable places.

His mother looked pensive. "You know what?" She asked. "I haven't seen those pictures since we moved here."

"You lost the pictures, Ma'?"

"Let's not forget that you rushed us to move," Mary replied, accusing. "Robert and I left a lot behind, intentionally and unintentionally. The pictures may have been one of my unintentional. I know I looked for them after we settled in. I just haven't seen them."

Ray had to cogitate this. He loved his mother with his whole heart, but something about her story didn't add up at all. These weren't photos of James on some kind of outing— they were of his final moments being seen in physical form. How could she be so careless? Besides, didn't she insert all of her tangible photos inside the large photo album she's had ever since they were children? Hell, she has pictures of Robert in it, so …

"Don't you still have that large photo album?" He finally asked.

"Hey, grandmomma!" Prince Ray and Rachel raced into the kitchen, beaming.

As he watched his kids interact with their grandmother, Ray couldn't help but draw the conclusion that James, along with Fred and Black, had survived the attack on their lives, and his mother, and Robert, were well aware of it. But, why were they so hell-bent on keeping it from him?

***

"That was tight, Trez!" Shatera voiced, when her brother exited the recording booth after laying down his verse to a track produced by Lavish, who she was seated beside at the controls.

"Thanks, sis!" Trez replied, bumping fists with his sibling, then with Lavish. "I'm hungry as hell!"

"What about the ab libs?" Lavish wanted to know.

"After I eat," Trez answered, rubbing his stomach, and looking over at Sheila, who was seated on a black leather couch. "You want to grab something?"

"We can," Sheila answered. "I saw a Taco Bell up the street."

When Sheila awakened that morning, she didn't know how she was going to spend her day. Though she longed for the quality time that she used to share with Ray and the children, as a family, she knew that there wasn't going to be anything of that nature going on. So, when Ray announced to her that he was taking the children to see his mother, and didn't offer her to go with them, Sheila made up in her mind that she was not going to sit in that apartment alone.

Therefore, she placed a call to Shatera, who informed her that she was going out to her brother's studio in Atlanta to sit in while they recorded. Of course, she insisted that Trez would be delighted if Sheila tagged along. Having nothing else going on, Sheila did just that, opting to use her own car as their means of transportation.

"Y'all don't want nothing?" Trez now asked his sister, and Lavish.

"Yeah," Shatera answered. "We like tacos."

Trez held his hand out, as if expecting their pay.

"Shit, I appreciate it, bro!" Shatera said, slapping palms with him.

"You know I got you," Lavish told Trez, seeing the frown on his friend's face.

"Yeah, my baby got you," Trez's sister added. "Stop being so cheap!"

At 2:43pm, the sun still shined brilliantly in the sky as Sheila and Trez exited the two-story building, headed for Trez's black Audi. The moment Sheila climbed into the front-passenger seat, she logged into her messenger to see if there were responses from Leela, but there weren't. Ever since she left the messages a couple of days ago saying she needed to talk, Sheila had been diligently checking for her.

"He checking up on you?" Trez asked, backing out of his spot.

"Huh?" Sheila looked up from her phone. "Oh! No, he's not checking up on me. I was checking my messages."

"I can't believe that I got the legendary Queen Sheila in the car with me," he said with a smile.

"Yeah, what's left of her," Sheila replied, putting her phone into sleep mode. "I feel like a washed-up pop star."

"You may have lost the glint that you had in your eyes," he told her, "But you're still Queen Sheila."

"Aww! How sweet!" She cooed. "So, where's the other half of Southern Comfort?"

"Having women issues," he told her. "It's hard to complete this album when they're not showing up for sessions."

"Do y'all plan on signing to a major label?"

"I want to sign with Rap-A-Lot," answered Trez. "You know I like their whole movement. I tried reaching out to J. Prince, but he's a hard person to get in touch with."

"What about the labels in Atlanta?" Sheila inquired. "I'm quite sure there's at least one that you wouldn't mind signing with."

"Grand Hustle." There was a glow in his eyes, when he asserted this. "T.I. is my favorite rapper. I sent him some of our music. Hopefully, he'll pick us up."

The drive-thru line at Taco Bell was extremely long. While waiting to reach the ordering board, Sheila opened her phone that was still on the messenger page and was surprised to see that she missed a video call from Leela a little over three minutes ago. Just up under the notification, was a text that read, *video call me when u get a chance.*

Seeing the online indicator, she pressed video call, and waited, hoping to finally find out what her ex co-worker wanted to talk to her about. Seconds later, Leela appeared on-screen, looking a mess. Her hair was in disarray, and her eyes were red and puffy, as though she'd been crying.

"Are you by yourself?" Leela asked, in almost a whisper.

"No, I'm not," Sheila answered, reluctant to reveal that she was in the presence of a man, who wasn't her fiancé.

"You gotta hit me back when you're by yourself," she said, before abruptly disconnecting.

Sheila sat, staring at the screen in bewilderment. Her first thought was that Leela was under the influence of some very strong drugs. Then, there was a look in the woman's eyes that Sheila was highly familiar with— fear! But, what was Leela afraid of?

Later, Sheila made it home at 4:38pm, after leaving Shatera at the studio with Lavish. Entering her bedroom, she placed her pocketbook on the dresser. She tried to reach out to Leela but the video call went unanswered. Sheila was beginning to think that Leela was playing some kind of game, though the look on her face was clearly real.

Realizing that Ray never told her if he and the children were planning to spend the night in Alabama, or not, she went out of her messenger, and sent him a text, *Should I prepare dinner?*

Tomorrow, he responded back, quicker than she thought he would.

For some reason, she expected him to acknowledge his love for her, but he didn't. Hell, she couldn't even remember the last time they'd said those words to each other. Was the love still there? Of course, it was. She was tempted to text her love to him but was highly aware of how she'd feel if he didn't respond with his own. Therefore, relinquishing that thought, she logged into her fake account, and pressed video call for Dread. When the call connected, she could tell that he was driving.

"Where you off to?" She asked, taking a seat on the bed.

"To see the Wizard of Oz," Dread answered.

"And, what are you going to ask him for?"

"A new girlfriend," he told her. "My current one ain't acting right."

"I hope you're not referring to me," Sheila said. "You know my situation."

"I'm trying to get you out of that situation."

"No," Sheila contended. "You're trying to get between my legs. Once you get this pussy, you'll be on to the next one."

"Is that what you think of me?"

"I think of all men that way."

Dread shot her a look.

"Except for him," she answered the look. "He didn't pursue me in the beginning— I did all the pursuing. Of course, he stiff armed me, but I kept pursuing him, because I knew he was different. I knew he was what I was looking for. I knew he wasn't the type to hit it and quit it."

Dread put on an exaggerated yawn. "That's a beautiful love story! I think it would make a great novel."

At the moment, Sheila wished that she could reach through the phone, and choke the life out of him, but she dared to let her visage reveal her true feelings. She pretended to laugh it off.

"Boy, you're crazy! She let out. "Anyway, what kind of plans do you have for tonight?"

"Why?"

"Because, my husband and kids are in Alabama, and won't be home until tomorrow.

"Does that mean I can swing by?"

"Hell no!" Sheila answered. "I told you about that."

"Well, can we get a room?" He sounded hopeful.

"Maybe."

"You're just going to keep stringing me along, huh?"

"Not really," Sheila said, really meaning it. "The only way I'll let you go all the way is if you play out one of my fantasies with me."

"I'm not putting on no fucking diaper!" Dread let out. "You can hang that bullshit up!"

'Who said anything about a diaper?" She asked, regarding him suspiciously. "That sounds like one of *your* fantasies. Do we need to play that one out, first?"

"Girl, stop playing!" He voiced. Then, after a moment's pause, he asked, "So, what's this fantasy of yours?"

132

Chapter 17
Monday

Again, Ray had decided to drive to work alone, being that he was to meet up with Joe, afterwards, which was why he was now in route to RJP Customs shop on Browns Mill Road, in Atlanta. When he pulled onto the shop's property, Joe, who was already standing outside, climbed in beside him.

"He's going to meet us at the park not too far from here," Joe informed. "I'm not supposed to be present, being that it's personal, but he asked me to tag along."

"Why would he do that?" Ray asked, already knowing the answer.

Joe shrugged. "Ain't no telling. Maybe he's concerned about not getting paid. You know how white people get sometimes."

"Yeah," Ray said, thoughtfully, keeping his eyes on the road.

"I got in touch with the dude that I was telling you about," Joe went on. "He's willing to cut you a deal on the weed and pills."

"I gotta run some more paper up," Ray said, glad to hear that his friend made a little progress. "Hell, I'm still paying on that stove."

Joe sat quiet for a moment, before finally saying, "What if I tell you that I saved up a nice piece of change?"

Ray glanced at him but said nothing.

"Don't give me that shit about not looking for a handout!" Joe told him. "I already know that. That's why I'ma loan you the money. Just pay me back what I give you, deal?"

Ray only nodded.

"That's his car, right there," Joe informed, when Ray turned into the community park.

Ray spotted the green Toyota sitting alone, though there were only a handful of other vehicles present. Once he parked two spots away from it, Joe pushed the passenger door open.

"I'll let y'all chat," he told Ray before getting out.

Upon noticing Joe, the occupant of the Toyota, emerged, clad in a gray suit, red tie, and carrying a large manila envelope, and a small camcorder. Approaching, he and Joe spoke, before Joe crossed the lot, and the private investigator, whose name Ray didn't remember, got into the passenger seat.

"How's it going?" The white man asked, extending his hand.

"Your payment," Ray said, handing him the white envelope that was under his armrest. "What'cha got for me?"

"Video, first," he answered, placing both envelopes in his lap, then activating the camcorder, and unfolding its screen, before handing it to Ray. "I edited it between locations, "he added.

Looking at the screen that had Saturday's date, and 11:24 am on it, Ray saw Sheila getting into her car. She drove around to Shatera's apartment. Once Shatera joined her, the image switched to Sheila's Cadillac pulling into the lot of some small office building, that was at 12:02pm.

After the women entered, the image switched to show Sheila and some man exiting the building at 2:43pm and climb into a black Audi sedan. Ray didn't know the guy but he was sure he'd seen his face in the general vicinity of their apartments. The two of them ended up riding out to the nearest Taco Bell restaurant, then returning to the building.

Shortly after three o' clock, Sheila exited the building, alone, and drove back to the apartment. Considering the time she got in, Ray figured it was the time she texted him about dinner. Ray thought that was the end of Sheila's escapade, until he saw her exit their apartment at 7:08pm, wearing a black patent leather skirt that he didn't know she owned, with Prince Ray's book bag slung over her back. He assumed she was off to spend the night elsewhere.

It was confirmed, when she pulled into the Legion Inn Motel. The investigator seemed to lose her, as he searched for a spot to park. Then, the image showed Sheila entering a room where the door was standing open, with the bookbag on her back. There was a man standing just outside the room, smoking what appeared to be a blunt, and yapping away on his cellular. Before the investigator zoomed in on him, Ray had already identified the dreadlocks wearing guy as one of their neighbors. Flicking the remnant of his blunt, he concluded his call, then entered the room, closing the door behind him.

Ray was furious as he watched his woman carry on without a care in the world. As though she didn't belong to him anymore. Did she? Hell, she seemed to be having her way when they're not together. And it's not like she was seeing one, but she was stepping out on him with two men.

At 9:47pm, the video showed Sheila exiting the motel, pulling the door close. Though she still had on the book bag, she was now wearing a pair of blue jeans, and a black shirt. What threw him about the scenario, was that she had on a pair of sunglasses, and a ball cap, though it was dark out. Again, the investigator followed her home. That's when the video ended. Ray looked to the investigator.

"I concluded my investigation at midnight," he handed Ray the manila envelope. "These are just stills that corroborate the video. They're yours. I'll delete the footage, now, unless you want to view it, again.

"You can delete it," Ray said, pulling a stack of computer generated photographs from the envelope, that were as the man advertised, showing Sheila with the two men from the video.

"I hate having to bring people this kind of result," he said, apologetically.

"It's what you get paid to do, right?" Ray said, stuffing the photos back into the envelope, and extending his hand. "I appreciate your services."

"You're quite welcome!" The man shook Ray's hand, then exited.

Seeing that Joe had his back turned, doing something on his phone, Ray blew the horn, getting his attention. Concluding whatever he was doing, Joe waved at the investigator while crossing back over. Ray stuffed the manila envelope inside the glove compartment, just as Joe was getting in.

"Everything good?" Joe inquired.

"Yeah," Ray answered, pulling out of his spot.

"Are you sure?"

"You don't trust my word?" Ray challenged, leering at him.

Joe threw his hands up. "Hey! I was just asking, bro." Then, after a long pause, he asked, "Are you going to accept the loan from me, or not?"

"Of course," Ray said, figuring that he wouldn't let Sheila's infidelity prevent him from getting his paper right.

"Great!" Said Joe. "I'll call and set up an appointment for you to meet up with dude."

After dropping Joe back off at his shop, Ray drove away, thinking about Sheila, and wondering what he was going to do about the situation, now that it was confirmed. Should he bring it to her attention that he knew what she was up to? Or, should he carry on like everything was normal, to see how things would play out? Just then, his cellphone vibrated in the cupholder.

"What's up?" He answered it.

"Are you busy?" Monica's voice came through the earpiece.

"I should be asking *you* that," Ray said, happy to hear from her.

"I'm definitely not busy."

"Good!" He replied. "I'm in Atlanta. Get a room and call me back with the location!"

"Aye, aye, Captain!" She giggled.

Not really having a destination in mind, Ray found himself driving through Bland Town, his old neighborhood, where all the old houses had been torn down. They were currently being replaced with new ones that were still under construction. Cruising through Knight Park, he saw that it also had received a slight facelift. There were people milling about, but none were familiar to him.

As he left Knight Park, coming upon the Fulton County Jail, the call finally came in from Monica, informing him that she'd managed to get a room at a motel on South Cobb Drive, which took a little over thirty minutes for Ray to reach.

Finding a spot beside her Lexus truck, Ray got out and made for room 13. Before he could reach the door, it came open to a smiling Monica, who was wearing a burgundy skirt, and bare-footed. With no words exchanged upon entering and closing the door, Ray pushed her up against the door and shoved his tongue into her mouth. She reciprocated by moaning in ecstasy. Finally breaking the kiss, Ray roughly spun her around.

"Put them hands up there!" He commanded.

"Am I being frisked?" She asked, doing as she was told.

"You're being fucked," Ray replied, hitching up her skirt, revealing her bare assets.

After pulling his shirt off and tossing it, Ray dropped his pants and boxers to his ankles, and didn't hesitate to ram his throbbing dick inside of her warm, and wet love box. He was blinded and driven, by images of what the private investigator revealed to him today.

***

Getting out of the shower, Sheila exited the bathroom with a towel wrapped around her. Before heading for the bedroom, she peered into the kitchen to see that the children were still busy with their homework. Closing her door, she approached the dresser, where her array of cosmetics sat.

While applying deodorant to her underarms, her eyes were drawn to her cellular that was also atop the dresser. She'd already decided that she wouldn't try to contact Leela until tomorrow but something was telling her to try it at that very moment. Giving in to what she was feeling, Sheila grabbed her phone and opted for the messenger video call again. To her surprise, Leela's image came upon the screen instantly, though she still looked haggard and afraid.

"I'm alone, Leela," Sheila beat her to the punch, "What's going on?"

"Can you come to me?" Asked Leela.

"Do what!" Sheila let out. "Girl, no! I have my kids with me, and Ray's not home yet."

"I wouldn't ask you if it wasn't important, Sheila."

Sheila let out a sigh. "Let me see if my babysitter would watch the kids for a few. Where am I driving to anyway?"

"I'm staying at a friend's place out in East Point."

Once getting the address, Sheila phoned Shatera, who obliged to sit with the children until either Sheila or Ray returned. Sheila was dressed and ready to go by the time Shatera showed up with her son. Sheila gave her thirty dollars to order pizza, then was out the door.

The sun had set but it wasn't dark out when Sheila reached her destination in East Point, Georgia, parking at the curb of a two-story house that had a white Infinity midsize SUV in its driveway. Not knowing if she should honk the horn, or get out, she put her car into park, and waited.

Almost a minute later, Leela emerged from the home, wearing white tennis shoes, jeans shorts, and a gray sweater. As if it was cold out, she had her arms folded over her chest. Plus, she was cautiously looking around as she approached.

"I'm glad you still got this same car," Leela expressed upon climbing in beside Sheila. "If it was any other car, I wouldn't have come out."

"What's going on with you, Leela?" Sheila inquired, regarding her with a concerned look, being that she'd never seen the woman in such a state.

"I know that I look different," Leela explained. "I'm just going through a lot right now. I'm scared out of my mind and I don't know how much longer I have to live."

Sheila was confused. "What are you talking about?"

"Calvin's going to kill me."

"What!" Sheila exclaimed. "Why would you even—"

"He told me that he was gonna kill me," Leela cut her off. "Just like he killed Jerry."

"Why would he kill Jerry?"

Leela just gave her a knowing look.

"Girl, you were fucking Jerry?" Sheila was in disbelief. "You weren't?"

"Hell no!" Sheila made a face. "Why would I fuck Jerry?"

"Well, Calvin found out that I was fucking Jerry," Leela admitted, ringing her hands in her lap while gazing out of her side window. "He told me that he'd killed Jerry before I even saw it on the news. We broke up a couple of weeks before that. When he came to my mom's house, threatening me, I moved out here with a friend

138

he doesn't know. I don't know how long I can hide from him, though. I wouldn't be surprised if he already knows where I am."

"So, where do I fit into all of this?" Sheila finally asked.

Leela looked Sheila in the eyes. "There's something I need done," she said, "And you're the only one I trust to do it."

Playa Ray

Chapter 18

"Ray?"

At the sound of his name being called, Ray opened his eyes to Monica, who was sitting up on the bed, with her back against the headboard, and her cell phone in her hand. Initially, he didn't plan to spend the night with Monica, but after they sexed for a whole hour, Ray still felt that he wasn't ready to face Sheila. So, he deferred to his emotions, and remained. However, Monica did leave, returning with an overnight bag.

"It's almost seven," Monica now told him. "You can shower, and probably make it to work on time. I have an extra toothbrush, washcloth, and towel in my bag. I also hand washed your boxers. They're hanging up in the bathroom. They should be dry by now."

Saying nothing, Ray pulled his naked body out of bed, retrieved the necessities from Monica's bag on the floor. He made for the bathroom, where his boxer shorts were indeed hanging on the shower curtain railing.

Thirty minutes later, Ray emerged from the bathroom, feeling refreshed, though his boxers were a little damp. Monica was still sitting in the same spot, engrossed in her phone.

"You're watching a movie?" He asked, pulling on his pants.

"The news," she answered, without looking up. "They're talking about a body being found inside a motel room, bound and gagged. It was discovered by a maintenance worker, who got a whiff of the odor while cleaning a vent in a room beside it."

"So, the person had to have been dead for some days."

"Pretty much."

"Which motel was this?" Ray wanted to know, as a feeling came over him.

"The Legion Inn, in Forest Park," she answered.

He moved over to her. "Let me see that!"

She handed him the phone but not the cordless earphone in her ear, so Ray had to view it without sound. The first thing that stood out to him was the heading that read: Man Found Slain in Forest Park Motel Room'.

It was almost like he was looking at the screen of the private investigator's camcorder, again, because the same room he now saw several government officials going in and out of, was the same one he saw Sheila exiting. That's when it dawned on him that when Sheila exited the room and closed the door behind her, she had some kind of cloth in her hand. It was as if not to leave her prints on it, in which Ray was sure that the investigator, however professionally trained he were, had seen.

"That's sad," Ray offered, handing the phone back. "I got to get going. Are you staying?"

"Just for another hour," she said, "Then, I'll be on my way to work."

"That's what's up," he said. "You know my number."

Putting back on his Checkers shirt, Ray made his exit, headed for his truck and thinking about how one innocent decision he made could get his woman the rest of her life behind bars. After starting the engine, he phoned Joe.

"What's up?" His friend answered in a groggy voice.

"We need to meet up, asap," said Ray.

"I haven't even gotten out of bed, yet," his friend complained.

"It's beyond important, Joe."

After a moment's pause, Joe finally said, "Meet me at the shop in Conyers.

While in route to Conyers, Georgia, Ray racked his brain, trying to put everything in proper perspective. There was no doubt in his mind that Sheila had murdered the man from their apartments, but why? And what was the story with her and the other man she was seen with at that building out in Atlanta? Could he be the one that was gradually taking Sheila away from him? The one who Sheila bought the condoms for? He remembered Calvin mentioning No Heart. Could she have something going on with him, also?"

It was 8:39 am, and daybreak was in full swing when Ray made it to RJP Customs. It was deserted and he parked near the office. After seeing the news, he knew that he wasn't going in to work but he felt that he could at least call in.

"Checkers!" Daryl, the Assistant Manager, answered.

"It's Young," Ray announced.

"Please tell me that this is not a sick call, Ray!"

"It's not."

"Great!" The Assistant Manager let out. "So, you're on your way?"

"I'm not on my way, Daryl," Ray answered, as Joe's car pulled into the lot. "I don't feel well at the moment."

"That sounds like a sick call to me."

"Just sympathize with me, right now. Tell Toni I'll make the day up."

"I guess we're obligated to show a little sympathy," said Daryl. "I'll run this by Toni. Just be ready to make this day up."

"I will," Ray replied when Joe got in beside him. "And thanks!"

"Where's the fire?" Joe asked when Ray got off the phone.

"I need to find that investigator!" Ray told him, then explained what the investigator revealed to him, lining it up with what he seen on the news.

"Damn!" Joe said, reflectively. "So, he could easily send the cops her way."

"He's got to go!" Ray pointed out.

Joe was nodding. "I overstand that. I don't know where he lives but I know where his office is located."

***

"Here you go, sir!" Sheila said, handing the older man his food and drink out the drive-thru window. "Have a nice day!"

Sheila's mind was so boggled. It was a wonder how she was able to function as properly as she did with worrying about Leela's situation, and Ray's dementia like behavior. He'd spent another night God-knows-where without even calling to let her know that he was okay.

It was evident that there was someone else in his life. He was brazenly throwing it in her face as if trying to force her to leave him because he didn't have it in him to break it off with her. Sheila felt that if that was the case, then Ray was in for a rude awakening because when she does leave, she's taking the children with her with no intentions of him seeing the three of them again.

"Ouch!" Marlene cried out, pulling Sheila from her abstract musing, and drawing her attention to the grill where Marlene was substituting for Ray.

"What's wrong, girl?" Sheila inquired. "I just burnt myself, again," Marlene answered like a small child. "You need to kick Ray's ass for me. That was the third time I damaged my beautiful, black skin."

"You act like you ain't never used a stove before."

"Girl, I'm from Africa," Marlene claimed. "We used fire barrels and long ass tree branches."

Despite how Sheila was feeling, she couldn't help but laugh at her friend's witty comment.

"Don't let me find out you knocked Ray's ass off," Marlene went on. "I saw the news."

"Girl, what're you talking about?" Sheila asked, while preparing the next order on her monitor.

"They found a man dead at a motel, not too far from y'all," explained Marlene. "I think somebody smelt his stank ass and called the police. You're the first person I thought about when I seen that shit. I was like, "Sheila done fucked Ray up!"

This had caught Sheila by surprise. Surely, Marlene wasn't making this up. Although, she had a bizarre imagination. Sheila intentionally told Dread to rent the room from Saturday to Tuesday, knowing that his body would be discovered Wednesday morning at wake-up call. However, according to what she was hearing, she miscalculated the deterioration of a flesh wound corpse because she definitely slit his throat after seducing him into allowing her to bind him with silk scarves.

She could still see the greedy look he had in his eyes when she ordered him to get naked and began stroking his already rock-hard dick. Though she felt guilty for doing it, she licked the tip of it, and told him that she'd finish sucking him off, once he was her *prisoner*.

Honestly, she expected Dread to find out, but she also knew that he wanted her so bad, that he would have jumped off the tallest building in the world if it meant that he would land between her legs. So it went, he obediently lied down on the bed while she started with his wrists, binding his hands in front of him. After restraining his ankles, she stuffed the third scarf into his mouth. *"So, that no one would hear you scream,"* she'd told him.

Not there to waste time, after Dread was incapacitated, Sheila retrieved a box cutter from her son's bookbag that she came with. Dread saw the weapon, and his eyes instantly became clouded with fear but he only froze for a short moment before trying to break free. Sheila quickly straddled him, releasing the razor from its shell.

"This is for all the times you disrespected me as a woman, and as a Queen," she informed him, before swiping the extremely sharp razor across his throat.

Sheila had never done this before, but she knew that she would get blood on her. She just didn't expect to have to tolerate that annoying, horn-like noise that escaped his trachea as the life slowly drained from him. After Dread had given up the ghost, Sheila was able to shower, sanitize the bathroom, change clothes, and even wipe her DNA form his worthless penis.

"You can lead the horse to the water, but you can't make it drink," No Heart quotes when Sheila leaned out the drive-thru window, handing him his order. "I'm done chasing you, though. I ain't never got to beg a bitch for no pussy. I got hoes lined up, in all kinds of states, begging for me to fuck 'em."

"I've been busy, No Heart," Sheila offered. "I still have your number but if you can't give me time to get myself together, then I'd be more than happy to rip that little twenty-dollar bill up."

"Damn, baby!" He seemed to soften a bit. "You don't have to get gangsta on me like that! I just thought you were playing games."

"I don't have time for those," she told him. "But, I do have other customers to serve."

"True that," he acknowledged. "If you need some paper, let me know!"

"I'll see if you're a man of your words," Sheila replied, then moved away from the window to tend to her next customers.

While doing so, she thought about how No Heart was another dupe, who could easily be lured in by what most women refer to as the *Power of the P*. As she thought about it, there aren't many men who could resist just the thought of that sweet sensation that a woman's love canal can produce, which makes it easy for women to tame, seduce, and murder their no-good asses.

    ***

The private investigator, whose name was Peter Lymm, had an office inside a plaza on Defoors Avenue, which was off of Howell Mill Road. It was 9:52 am when Ray pulled his truck into some apartments that sat on the other side of the road from the plaza, which he couldn't see for the apartment buildings.

Joe was able to provide Ray with a .38 caliber for the mission. Being that Ray still wore his Checkers shirt, Joe also gave hm black t-shirt, a black ball cap, and a green bandana that he now had tied around his neck.

Now, as Ray glanced around the residence, he only saw a few people milling about and heading to their vehicles as if on their way to their occupations. Once the coast was clear, he got out, tucking the revolver into the waistline of his pants while taking another furtive glance around. Then, he moved towards the entrance of the apartments.

Making it to the road, he saw that there weren't many vehicles in the lot across the street, being that those particular businesses in the plaza didn't open their doors until ten o'clock. But he did see the investigator's green Toyota sitting in front of a small shop that advertised his name and profession on its storefront glass.

Ray looked both ways before crossing the busy street and entering the lot, making sure to keep his head lowered at an angle, for the sake of any camera that may be able to identify him. As he neared the establishment, he noticed a middle aged white woman exiting her car and seemed to be headed in the same direction. Not once did she look back to see if anybody was behind her.

Momentarily, she reached the investigator's office. When she pulled the entrance door open, Ray, who was a couple of feet behind her, pulled the bandana up over the bottom part of his face, and drew his weapon. By this time, the woman must've felt his presence because she began to turn around, just as he caught the door that was closing behind her.

Before the woman could get a look at him, Ray shot her in the hip. She let out a scream as her body collapsed onto the floor of the large room that consisted of two desks, an array of file cabinets, and other miscellaneous items. Of course, Peter Lymm was seated behind his desk regarding the scene with a great deal of apprehension in his eyes.

Only taking a few steps towards him, Ray raised the gun, and squeezed off on the trigger, five times, pinning fatal shots to Lymm's upper chest, knocking him out of his chair. Already figuring that the investigator was expired, he turned, and stepped over the whimpering secretary, tucking his gun, while approaching the entrance.

After a quick look around, Ray pulled the bandana down, then casually exited the place. If anyone heard the shots, there were no indications of it because he didn't see anybody coming out of other establishments as if they had. But, he did see a police car enter the lot and move in his general direction.

***

Upon leaving Atlanta, Ray drove home, thinking about his family. For some reason, he felt that he wasn't going to be around long enough to see his children grow into adults and have children of their own. It was a sad thought but a true assessment. Plus, he didn't know which way his relationship was going with Sheila, who's become some kind of monster, considering what she'd done at that motel. Of course, he had no intention of letting on that he knew anything about that.

After showering, and donning fresh clothing, he chose to lounge on the living room sofa where he first placed a call to Joe, to let him know that everything was everything, and that he would dispose of the weapon later. Joe informed him that he had the money ready for him and that the weed and pill supplier wanted to meet with him on Saturday.

Getting off the phone with his friend, Ray called to check on Monica, who was at her salon, but wanted to know when they could get together. Ray liked the woman but he knew that if he had any plans of making things right with Sheila, then he'd have to drop his side piece. But, first, he'd have to find out the chemistry between his fiancé and the guy she was with in Atlanta.

"Hey, Daddy!"

Ray didn't know that he'd fallen asleep until his kids came barreling through the front door, cheerfully. He had to sit up to intercept the hugs they bestowed upon him while Sheila locked the door back and proceeded on to the bedroom without saying a word.

"Daddy, our school is going on a field trip," Prince Ray announced.

"To another planet?" Ray asked, making a face.

"No, Daddy," Prince Ray laughed. "We're going to the zoo."

"Are you going, too?" Ray asked his daughter.

"Yes," She answered. "But not on the same day as his class. Every grade has their own day."

"And, how much is this going to cost me?"

"Seven dollars," his son answered.

"Momma got the papers y'all got to sign," Rachel added.

"I'll check 'em out," he promised, getting to his feet. "Go ahead and start on y'all homework."

While they set off to do as they were told, Ray journeyed off to the bedroom where Sheila was gathering her things for her shower. He sat on the edge of the bed as she chose a panty and bra set from the dresser.

"Are you alright, baby?" He asked.

"I'm fine, Ray," she replied with an expected attitude but didn't look in his direction.

"After you shower," Ray went on, "Can we all go out for dinner? As a family."

"That's fine," she said, heading for the bathroom with her things.

Though he didn't get much out of her, Ray figured that it was a start. His mind was made. He was not going to let another man take Sheila from him while he's still breathing. Their engagement was a promise to get married and he planned to make good on that promise until death brought them to an end.

Playa Ray

Chapter 19

Ray couldn't believe he'd let Big Ru coax him into accompanying him and some of his affiliates to a club in Decatur that was owned by another one of their brothers. Being that most suppliers are prone to do this in an endeavor to get more acquainted with a customer, Ray obliged, riding with the four members in Big Ru's Denali. He left his own truck at the supplier's house.

Extravagant to his heart, Big Ru paid everyone's way in, copped one of the two VIP sections and must've ordered six bottles of Grey Goose. Of course, his showing off drew the attention of a handful of women, who he ended up giving his permission to join them. The women entered the small section like professional call girls, smiling broadly, and choosing a lap to sit in. The one that sat in Ray's lap only said, "Hi!" before helping herself to some alcohol.

While both groups drank, smoked weed, and conversated, Ray bobbed his head to the music and observed the atmosphere. Moments later, he spotted a large group of men entering the club, which was headed by none other than Major Gramz and his sidekick, No Heart. Noticing Big Ru's flashy ass, the arriving party threw up acknowledging gang signs as they filed into the other VIP section that was right across from theirs.

Ray's focus was on Major Gramz and his pet, but he couldn't help but notice that one of the other men seemed to be staring him down and it only took a split second for him to recognize his newest enemy. But, what the hell was Calvin doing in the presence of his rivals? Did he cross over?

"Look at your boy!" Big Ru said to Ray, who he was seated beside. "He's the true definition of a dick rider. A real groupie."

"Yeah, I see that," Ray replied.

As if competing with Big Ru, Major Gramz had several bottles brought to their area. Ray noticed Major Gramz speaking to the manager before pointing in their direction. That's when the manager crossed the floor of dancing customers, with a bottle of Ace of Spades, and approached Ray.

"Major Gramz sends this as a peace offering," he told Ray. Not waiting for a response, the man placed the bottle on the table and went about his way. Ray looked across the room to see Major Gramz holding a bottle up as if making a toast, in which he only nodded his response to.

"Don't trust that shit, Ray!" Big Ru warned. "He'll shake your hand and shoot you in the back with that same smile on his face."

"Can we start on this?" The woman sitting in Ray's lap asked him, indicating the newly arrived bottle.

"It's yours," he told her.

Then, not wanting to spend his night staring at the guys across from them, Ray went back to watching the crowd. That's when he looked towards the entrance and saw Monica and two other women enter. The burgundy weave that looked like it was stacked on top of her head by a blind stylist was not hard to miss.

As the three of them moved through the crowd, Ray was hoping like hell that Monica didn't see him. Just as they were passing, she turned and looked directly at him as though she knew that he was there. At the moment, he was half expecting for her to throw a fit and attack the woman in his lap, but she smiled, waved, and continued on. For some reason, Ray didn't think it coincidental that out of all the clubs in Atlanta and Decatur, that she would end up at that particular one. There was a feeling at the pit of his stomach, telling him that something wasn't right.

***

The following day, Ray was awakened by the sound of a door being opened and closed. He opened his eyes, just as Monica placed a McDonald's bag onto the bed, and two cups of orange juice on the nightstand. He didn't think the two of them would link up last night after Monica passed the booth until she texted him almost ten minutes later asking him about the *floozy* sitting in his lap.

Eventually, their texting became sexting before Monica chose Facetime. She activated her phone's light, and shoved it under her sundress, giving him a view of her clean shaven pussy. When she offered to suck him off in the restroom, Ray almost jumped to it.

Instead, being that she'd turned him on, he insisted that they got a room.

"Two sausage and two steak sandwiches," she told him, taking a seat on the bed and pulling the food from the bag. "I hope you like apple jelly because that's all I grabbed."

"That's fine," Ray replied, helping himself to a sausage and biscuit sandwich. "You move like a damn cat! I didn't even hear you leave out."

Monica giggled. "Hell, you were snoring so loud that I barely heard myself leave out. I guess my *cat* has that kind of effect on men."

"Yeah, toot your own horn," he said, smiling. "Can I have my beverage?"

She handed him one of the cups of orange juice.

"We have to slow down on this," Ray got straight to the point after washing his bite down.

Monica took a sip of her own juice. "Slow down on what, baby?" She asked.

"Us."

"Don't tell me that you're catching feelings for me."

Ray shot her a look.

"It happens," she told him. "If you don't want to see me any-more, stop beating around the bush, and just say it! I'll understand."

"I'm about to get married," Ray let on.

"You were about to get married when you met me." Monica pointed out. "What makes things any different now?"

"I have to concentrate on her a little more."

"So, I've become a distraction, huh?" There was a sinister smile on her face.

"Yes, you have," Ray admitted. "All I ask for is a little space so that I can make things right with my woman. Could you grant me that?"

"Does that mean you'll block my number?"

"I won't block your number, Monica," he told her. "We can still chat."

"Promise?"

Ray's first appointment was at three o'clock with the weed and pill man and he managed to make it to the guy's house in Summer Hill, at 2:49PM. Joe had already put Ray on point about the dude. His name was Jeffe and he was a part of the Inglewood Family Gang, which meant that he was one of Major Gramz's foot soldiers. However, this didn't matter to Ray because it wasn't like the beef between he and Major Gramz, was legit.

"What's up, homie!" A man greeted, upon opening the door for Ray.

"You must be Jeffe?" Ray inquired.

"The one and only," the man replied, offering his hand.

"Joe spoke highly of you."

"Yeah, I'm quite sure," Ray said, shaking the guy's hand.

"Come on in!"

Ray entered and was immediately impressed by the layout of Jeffe's living room. The white, leather couch, twin-seat, and re-cliner, with metallic gold trimmings, harmonized elegantly with the white curtains that were parted and held in place by gold ribbons. Then, there was the transparent coffee table that's glass was held up by the branches of a golden structure of a tree. The only thing this setup was missing was an immaculately white carpet, but the spit shined hardwood floors seemed to do the trick.

"You don't have to take your shoes off," Jefe said, clearly see-ing the questionable look on Ray's face." It's clean, because I keep it clean."

Jefe took a seat in the chair and Ray chose the twin seat as ordered. The man had six pounds of weed, and two Zip-lock bags containing ecstasy pills, sitting on the table, along with a scale. Plus, there was some kind of tool kit on the table, closest to Jeffe that Ray has never seen before and what appeared to be a gold Rolex watch with its back off.

"You can't smell 'em, huh?" Jeffe asked, indicating the weed, as he picked up the watch.

Ray took a sniff at the atmosphere. "No, I can't."

"I used to be a trafficker," he went on to explain. "The dude I was moving for had an international clientele. I was pushing shit through planes, trains, and automobiles. The reasons why he had so much clientele, and made so much money is because he knew how to build secret compartments, and he was a whiz at wrapping that work up. Once he taught me that shit, I brought it back to the hood. I can't risk my customers getting pulled over and them folks smelling that shit."

"What about the dogs?" Ray asked.

"Especially the dogs," Jefe emphasized on *'especially'*.

"That's why when I set my prices for the work, I make sure to include the price for the wrapping."

"Hell, it's worth it," Ray offered, nodding at the watch. "You fix timepieces?"

"I went to school for it," he answered. "I got a booth inside the West End Mall."

"What's wrong with that Rolex?"

"Just needs to be re-calibrated," Jefe told him. "You want to weigh the weed up, and count the pills?"

***

"Momma, can I eat my ice cream, now?"

Before hearing her son's voice, Sheila's mind was on Ray, and their impending wedding day, which was to take place within another month. In fact, he was the one that insisted upon it. However, just when Sheila thought that things were about to get back on track between the two of them, he goes off and pulls another Houdini act by not coming home last night.

Sheila was nobody's fool. He wasn't staying out at night, just to be doing it. He was sticking his dick in another bitch and the missing condom was certified evidence of that. If he thought that their marriage was going to be like this, then he was sadly mistaken.

"Finish your food, baby!" Sheila now answered Prince Ray. "That ice cream is not going anywhere. It's not going to melt."

"It's called a *Blizzard,"* rectified Rachel, who was seated beside her brother.

Sheila regarded her with furrowed eyebrows. "Blizzard, Snow storm, Tornado. It's not going anywhere, mad scientist."

Rachel giggled.

Picking her phone up off the table, Sheila scrolled through her messenger to see if there was anything from Leela, being that they both agreed to check in with each other daily. Sheila sent her a thumbs up yesterday and Leela has yet to respond to it. Backing out of her messenger account, she accessed her contacts list and found herself staring at a phone number that had NH above it.

"I'll be right back, y'all," she told her children as she got to her feet. "Don't go nowhere!"

Exiting the Dairy Queen restaurant, with her phone in hand and pocketbook dangling off her shoulder, Sheila crossed over to the public service phone, making sure to sanitize it with one of her wipes before putting the receiver up to her ear and dialing the number from her contacts.

"Who the fuck is this!" No Heart answered his phone.

"Take a wild guess," Sheila replied.

"Man, you still ain't paid your phone bill?"

"I'll pay it when I get my check next week," she told him, even though Checkers paid out yesterday.

"Next week!" Exclaimed No Heart. "That nigga can spend money on hoes at the club but can't give his main woman money to pay her cell phone bill?"

"Excuse me!"

"I saw your man at one of my bro's clubs last night." He went on. "He was popping all kinds of bottles with bitches like he'd just hit the lotto."

Sheila automatically knew that this nigga was lying, because Ray doesn't drink alcohol. Although, lately, she's been wondering if he's been sampling his own product.

"Are you sure that it was him?" Sheila pressed.

"I know what that nigga looks like." No Heart caught attitude. "Hell, I got a picture of him with a bitch sitting in his lap on my phone. I would send it to you but I don't think you'll be able to see it through the payphone."

Sheila didn't reply. The thought of Ray's mistress being revealed was gnawing at her conscience because she pretty much had an idea as to who it might be.

"Look," No Heart resumed. "I got five hundred dollars for you, but you'll have to come and get it."

"I got my kids with me, right now."

"Well, whenever you decide that you need the money, you know my number," he said, then rung off.

Hanging the receiver up, Sheila crossed back over to the restaurant, thinking about this picture that No Heart claims to have. Perhaps, it was true that Ray had attended a club with his side piece, at her behest. From the way No Heart described it, it sounded like a special occasion. Her birthday, maybe?

***

Upon leaving Summer Hill, Ray phoned Joe, who'd already told him that he'd help break down the pounds and separate the pills. They met up at Joe's home in Douglas County, where they chopped everything up. Knowing he had an appointment with Big Ru at eight o' clock, Ray decided to stay at Joe's, until the time arrived.

Being that Jeffe didn't share his secret wrapping recipe, the broken down weed that was now inside two, black trash bags in the rear compartment had the inside of the truck smelling like a medical herbal dispensary, which had Ray riding with the window cracked.

It was 7:40pm when he pulled up in front of Big Ru's house, parking behind a dark-green Jaguar convertible. For the sake of the police riding by, and getting a whiff of the drug, Ray made sure to roll the windows up before stepping down and approaching the house where Quick Ru let him in.

As he lifted his shirt for Quick Ru's visual inspection, Ray noticed two guys in the living room with Big Ru. They were all standing as if the two men were about to leave. One of the men was light-complexioned with natural reddish-orange hair, and the other was brown-complexioned and looked like he'd been bench pressing school buses.

"Come on in, Ray!" Big Ru prompted. "Let me introduce you to some real O.G.s." He indicated the light-complexioned man, first. "This is Pistol Pete, the highest-ranking Bishop in Georgia. And, that's Ice Man. The name speaks for itself."

"What's up!" Ray shook the men's hands.

"They were telling me about sparring gym that they just opened up." Big Ru went on.

"It's for children and adults," Pistol Pete took over. "We also have self-defense classes for women and children. The name of the place is 'Above It All', and we're located in Buckhead."

"I'ma checkout that clothing line," Big Ru promised. What's the name of it, again?"

"Official Gentlemen," answered Pistol Pete. "I just got the website up and running today.

"I hope you got something I can fit in," Big Ru said, then looked to Ice Man. "I ain't trying to be busting out of my shirt like Popeye over here."

This tickled Ice Man. "Ain't that somethin'!" He said. "Big man's got jokes!"

Once the two men made off, Big Ru offered Ray to have a seat and sent Quick Ru to gather Ray's order.

"You must've left the club last night and went straight to the trap?" The big guy asked.

"Why'd you say that?"

"Because, you still have on the same outfit."

Ray looked down at himself. "Oh! It's a long story."

"Had you one of those late night flings, huh?"

"Pretty much."

"That's two and a half," Quick Ru said, upon entering the living room with a large paper bag, in which he placed on the table.

"I need two for Say No More," Big Ru told him. "He should be on the way."

"Bet!"

"I see you're slowly trying to climb your way back to the top," Big Ru acknowledged when Quick Ru left.

"Yeah." Ray placed a band of bills on the table. "It's a slow process."

"A *very* slow process when you're doing it alone," he told Ray. "You need a team. And you definitely need some more Kingzmen, because these niggas ain't bullshitting out here. Everybody wants to lay claim to the streets and niggas are doing whatever it takes to make that happen. Hell, I just lost a customer a couple of days ago to that street beef shit."

Ray thought about Big Ru's words on his drive home. Of course, he needed a team but who could he trust outside of Poppo and Joe? Niggas were playing the cutthroat game so he was not about to set himself up like that by recruiting somebody he knew nothing about. A person can't buy loyalty.

Just as he was about to exit off on the Forest Park exit, Ray looked into his rear-view mirror and spotted an SUV about thirty yards behind him. Although it was night time, he could tell that it was occupied by three men by the vehicle behind them.

After that dream he had in Alabama, he's been noticing different vehicles with three occupants, trailing him, periodically. At that very moment, as he took the off ramp, Ray decided that this was the last straw. If the Kingz were to reassemble, then it was going to be tonight.

The SUV, which he noticed was a Ford Explorer, had closed the gap between them by fifteen yards. Once they made it onto the main road. Not taking a chance on them evading him tonight, Ray drove for close to a minute before slamming down on the brake, and throwing the gear into park.

With total disregard for the other motorists traveling the four-lane road, Ray lunged from his truck, moving toward the Ford like a man with a purpose. That's when he was able to see their faces, and neither one of them matched those of Fred, Black, nor James.

Ray slowed his momentum, just as the three men began to exit the Explorer. Calvin, who climbed from the front-passenger seat, aimed a black handgun at Ray between the hinge of his door, which galvanized Ray to instinctively feint to his right.

Boom!

Chapter 20

"I don't have to lie to you, shawty," No Heart said, handing his phone over to Sheila, who was seated on the passenger side of his Ford Mustang.

Immediately upon looking at the digital photo of the interior of a club, Sheila used her two fingers to enlarge it, being that it was taken at long range. She couldn't make out the features of the apparent target or the female sitting in his lap, because the picture had become grainy. She clearly remembered the colors that Ray had on when he left the apartment yesterday, which were shared by the man in the picture. However, her main focus was on the woman with her hair cropped like someone that she and Ray were highly familiar with.

"He's a real bitch ass nigga!" No Heart ranted on. "What if something happened to you or your kids, and you couldn't call this nigga because your phone is off?"

"Yeah, I know," she said, maintaining her composure, although she wanted to push his head through the glass of the driver's door. She handed the phone back to him. "You don't know the girl?"

"She didn't look familiar to me," he told her, putting his phone up, then handing her a wad of bills. "Pay your phone bill and do something nice for them kids!"

"Thank you!"

Sheila placed the money inside her pocketbook, then looked out her side window at the house that they were parked in front of. As rap music played from the stereo, her mind was on the upcoming wedding that she was not sure of.

"Don't let that shit get to you!" No Heart said, placing a hand on her thigh.

She looked at him. The lust in his eyes was striking.

"I wanna take you inside," he told her. "But my people are up. How long do I have you for anyway?"

"Not long," she said, regarding her watch. "My babysitter has to get up in the morning."

He reclined his seat and began undoing his shorts. "How about five minutes with that sexy ass mouth of yours?"

When Sheila licked the tip of Dread's dick, she felt a tinge of guilt. Now, as she sized up No Heart's fully erect manhood, it seemed like her emotions were out of order. Besides, he gave her five hundred dollars. It was the least she could do.

Adjusting in her seat, she reached over, took hold of his rod, and started stroking it. No Heart moaned. Figuring she would gone and get it over with, Sheila got her mouth as moist as she could, then leaned over.

Tap! Tap! Tap!

"What the fuck!" No Heart exclaimed as he struggled to pull his shorts up over his erection. He was clearly pissed that someone had chosen the wrong time to be tapping on his window.

"Come on, nigga!" Said the intruder whose face Sheila couldn't see. "Major Gramz just called a whoop."

"Damn!" No Heart looked to Sheila. "We'll do this some other time."

"Okay."

Sheila's car was parked behind No Heart's. As she got out, she saw another car behind hers but she didn't bother with trying to see who was occupying it. She climbed behind the wheel and started the engine. She thought that she would go ahead and pull off but the car behind her sped by with No Heart trailing behind.

Ruminating this, Sheila pulled her cell phone from under her seat with the intent to call and let Shatera know that she was on the way but there was a text from Ray that said, *I'm at Grady Hospital. Accident.*

***

Sheila still ended up calling Shatera but not to tell her that she was on the way home but on her way to the hospital. Empathetic to the situation, Shatera promised to keep the kids until she got there, even if it was the following day.

After getting Ray's location from the receptionist, Sheila got onto an elevator, still struggling with her emotions. She was there because she loved and cared deeply for Ray. Although, she really wanted to kick his ass for what she just discovered. It's not like she didn't expect it. Hell, it's been on her mind for a very long time now.

The door to Ray's recovery room was standing wide open. When Sheila entered, she instantly became enraged to see Precious standing over him like a grieving widow and holding one of his hands. Upon noticing her, Precious let his hand go, pretending to check her watch.

"Hey, girl!" Precious greeted in a hushed tone.

"What's up?" Sheila responded, approaching the opposite side of the bed.

"I thought you were already here."

"No, I'm just now getting here," Sheila told her. "How long have you been here?"

Precious looked at her watch again. "For a little over ten minutes," she said. "He still hasn't awakened. The nurse said that he was hit by a car, but it wasn't going fast enough to break anything. His right thigh is swollen and they stitched the gash up on his forehead."

"How'd you know that he was here?" Sheila questioned, eyeing the woman, who reflected a brown-skinned version of T-Boz of TLC, with her professionally cropped, sandy-brown hair.

"He sent me a text."

"He did?"

"Yeah." With her phone already in her hand, Precious showed the text to her, which was the same one she received verbatim.

That's when Sheila finally looked down at her man, whose head was bandaged. His eyes were closed but there were no other visual injuries. He was covered up with a white bedspread. At that moment, all she could do was watch his chest rise and fall as he slept. For some reason, she started to feel like she didn't belong there.

"Hey, y'all!"

They both looked to see Kim approaching with her ten-year-old son, James, trailing behind.

"Hey, Kim!" They both spoke in unison as Kim stopped at the foot of the bed, regarding Ray like she was at a wake.

"Hey, Auntie Sheila!"

"Hey, James!"

"What happened to Uncle Ray?" He inquired.

"He was hit by a car," answered Sheila. "As far as I know, it wasn't that bad."

"Was it a hit-and-run?" Kim wanted to know.

Sheila looked to Precious, who apparently knew more than she did.

"Not as far as these people know," Precious answered, acknowledging Sheila's look. "How'd you know about it?"

"Ray sent me a text," she answered. "I didn't know if he wanted me to come here or if he was just letting me know."

"Girl, I'm in the same boat," Precious told her. "I didn't know what to do either."

"Today's your birthday, right?"

"It was yesterday."

"I hate that I missed it!" Kim let out. "Happy belated birthday."

"Thanks!" Precious replied. "I didn't do anything special. Just hung out with a couple of friends."

Yeah, I just bet you did, bitch! Sheila thought, as she eyed the woman that had Ray's heart way before she came into the picture. Men are dogs by nature and are prone to indulge in their own vomit but if these two thought that this shit was going to continue after she becomes *'Mrs. Sheila Young'*, then they didn't know with whom they were dealing with.

***

"Mr. Young?"

Ray's eyes immediately shot open, at the mentioning of his name. The first person he noticed was Sheila, who was seated in the chair beside his bed looking like she was just awakened. With his head throbbing and a burning sensation in his right thigh, Ray turned his head in the opposite direction, to see a Caucasian man in tan slacks, a purple Izod shirt, and a badge clipped to his belt. Plus, he was carrying a small notepad, and pen.

"I didn't mean to wake you," he said, apologetically. "But I need to get this report filed. My shift ended three hours ago. I'm Detective Holins, by the way. How are you feeling?"

"I feel like I'd been hit by a train," Ray answered, truthfully.

The detective nodded. "That's understandable. However, I've already spoken with the driver of the vehicle that you were struck by. Now, all I need is your account of the incident. Care to tell me what happened?"

"Somebody bumped the back of my truck," Ray gave the story he'd come up with. "I pulled over and got out to assess the damage. That's when I was struck."

After jotting something down, he regarded Ray with a look of uncertainty. "What kind of truck were you driving?"

"Cadillac Escalade," Ray told him. "White in color."

"Do you remember what kind of vehicle that struck your truck?"

"Some kind of black sedan," Ray lied.

Holins chewed on the top of his ink pen for a moment before asserting. "Neither of these vehicles were present at the scene. The only vehicle present was the one belonging to the driver that plowed into you. She claimed that you came out of nowhere as if crossing the street but you seemed to jump in front of her."

Ray's mind went back to the scene. He vividly remembered looking down the barrel of Calvin's gun before dashing out of the way to keep from being shot. He wasn't sure if Calvin had fired the weapon for the sound of the car ramming into him. Everything went blank after that, which was probably the result of the head injury but what the hell did he mean that the Escalade wasn't at the scene?"

If Ray's truck wasn't at the scene, this meant that Calvin had taken it. Not only did he have the truck but he was in possession of the two and half kilos, the weed, and the pills, which had Ray wondering if Calvin had been following him all day anticipating the chance to rob and kill him. Whatever the case was, injured or not, Ray intended to comb the streets of Georgia, find this nigga, and carve the skin off of his soul!

Playa Ray

Chapter 21

"Breakfast, Ray!"

Opening his eyes, Ray saw Sheila standing over him with a plate of food in her hand. Still in pain, he managed to pull himself into a sitting position, planting his back against the headboard. The prescribed pain medication commingled with the fact that they made it home from the hospital after 5am, had him struggling with a level of exhaustion that he'd never known. He was hoping to shake the fatigue because he had some calls to make, starting with the reporting of his missing truck.

"I know you're still hurting," Sheila said, handing the plate to him, "But I need you to watch the children while Shatera does my hair."

"I can do that," Ray replied, noticing that she was already dressed with one of his ball caps pulled down on her undid hair. "I may need your phone."

"For what?" She asked, a little more defensive than he expected.

"I need to report my truck stolen and make a few other calls."

"Where's *your* phone?" She was trying to remember if they'd left it at the hospital by mistake.

"It was in my truck, Sheila."

This wasn't making sense to her. "So, how'd you send that text?"

"What text?" Ray asked, genuinely confused.

Sheila pulled her cell phone from her pocket and showed him the text that she received, last night, informing her that he was in the hospital. Ray studied the text for a few seconds. It was definitely sent from his phone, but how? Did Calvin send it, in an endeavor to lure Sheila to where he could harm her?

"Kim and Precious got the same text," Sheila went on.

Ray looked up at her. "Did they show up at the hospital?"

"Precious got there before I did," she offered, accusingly. "They tried to stay until you woke up."

"I don't know how y'all got those texts," Ray said, pondering. "But, I didn't send 'em."

This had them both addled. Ray didn't tell Sheila what really transpired last night so she was a bit more confused than he was. After making sure to log out of her social media accounts, she relinquished her device to him.

"I'll change your bandage when I get back," she said, before leaving the bedroom.

Ray looked down at his plate that consisted of grits, eggs, and pancakes. He was hungry but for some reason, he could not bring himself to eat. Just then, Sheila re-entered the room with a concerned look on her face.

"Your truck is outside," she announced, jerking a thumb over her shoulder.

"How is it outside?" Ray inquired, hoping for a little more clarity.

"It's parked beside my car."

Then, as if it was nothing, she turned and left back out. Ray heard her say something to the children before leaving out of the front door. At that moment, he knew that he wasn't going to be able to eat. Placing his plate on the nightstand, he grunted while enduring the excruciating pain of getting his legs over the side of the bed.

Only clad in a pair of boxer shorts, and a T-shirt, Ray looked down at his right thigh that was swollen and bruised with a purple hue. Figuring it would be more painful to try putting on a pair of pants, he grabbed his crutches that were leaning against the wall beside the bed and used them to pull himself up. Then, he made for the front door.

"Hey, daddy!" His children greeted in unison from the kitchen table where they were eating their breakfast.

"Hey, my children!" He replied, offering a plausible smile.

"What happened to you, daddy?" Rachel wanted to know.

Finally making it to the door, Ray stopped, and looked back at them. "I had a small accident," he answered. "I'll be okay."

"Daddy, can we have some more pancakes and bacon?" Prince Ray asked, which seemed to be his only concern.

"Y'all can split my plate," Ray told his son. "It's in my room."

There was genuine smile on Ray's face, as he watched his children race towards his bedroom. With his mind back on his mission, he got the front door open and just stood there staring at his truck as if it belonged to someone else.

The detective claimed that it wasn't at the scene of the accident, and it definitely wasn't parked there when he and Sheila made it home that morning. Somebody had to have parked it there between then and now. A game was being played and Ray knew that Calvin was mentally and dangerously capable of doing such.

Pulling the apartment door closed, Ray took his time studying every vehicle that he could see before approaching the driver's side of the Escalade. Peering inside, he saw his keys dangling from the ignition, and his cell phone sitting in the compartment beneath the control panel. He also saw that his alarm was no longer activated as the switch was flipped down.

After another look around, Ray propped one crutch against the truck, then pulled the driver's door open. His nostrils were greeted by the scent of the weed, but it was faint. Grabbing his phone, he powered it on, and went to his Textnow app. There were messages from Joe, Kim, and Precious. He also saw the texts that were sent out to them last night. The same exact text that Sheila had shown him.

His mind seemed to shift into overdrive. He could understand why Calvin would send the text to Sheila, but why to Precious, and Kim? Or, why send them at all? It was like he was making sure that they made it down to the hospital to check on him. And why return the truck?

This definitely had *'James'* written all over it.

Snatching the keys from the ignition, Ray used the one crutch to get to the rear of the truck, where he wasted no time opening the fifth door. That's when a new wave of confusion surfaced. James would have sent the texts, and returned the truck, but he wouldn't have taken the drugs. However, the drugs were indeed missing.

***

Ray didn't like visiting people's homes unannounced but something had to give. This visit was to ensure that after he does

whatever he has to do to Calvin, there won't' be a lynch mob awaiting him, considering Calvin's affiliation.

Docking his Escalade behind a white Toyota Land-Cruiser on
chrome wheels that was parked in front of Perk G's house, Ray used
the one crutch he'd brought along to climb down from the truck.
Getting to the house, he stopped and frowned at the steps that led
up to the porch. Then, at that time, as if a Godsend, Perk's wife,
Yasmine pulled the front door open.

"Boy, who's girlfriend did you try to steal?" She bantered,
while descending the steps, to assist him.

Ray couldn't help but smile. "Mr. Biggs, I guess."

They both laughed as she helped him up the steps. Ray couldn't
help but notice that she smelled of freshly-smoked weed, and some
kind of sweet fragrance. He didn't expect for Perk to be alone but
when he entered the living room, Ray didn't expect to encounter
one of his old associates.

"That boy, Ray!" Young Cap expressed from the sofa that he
was seated on, opposite of the one Perk was occupying. "You look
like an injured Vietnam vet."

"I see you're still the comedian," Ray replied, as Yasmine
helped him down on the sofa beside his old friend. "Thanks!" He
told her.

"You're welcome!" She grabbed a rolled blunt off the table.
"I'll be in the room."

"Girl, you better bring that blunt back!" Perk gave voice.

"Hell no!" She shot over her shoulder but kept going.

"I hope your ass choke!" He insisted on having the last word,
then turned to Ray. "What happened to you?"

"I came to talk to you about Calvin," Ray told him.

"We were just talking about him," Young Cap cut in.

When they were much younger, BJ introduced Ray to Young
Cap, who was also a resident of the East Lake projects. Together,
the three of them started pulling off pedestrian robberies. After a
couple of home invasions, Cap became obsessed with the act, while
Ray and BJ transitioned to stealing cars. The last time he'd heard of
the big guy, who was dark-complexioned with a long scar across his

left cheek, was when he made the news for a home invasion. He tied some man's grandmother up and tortured her until the man gave up his stash.

Perk asked, "What'cha got?"

Taking a deep breath, Ray started with what Calvin did to Jerry and went into how they got into it at work over him being disrespectful toward Sheila. Then, he explained last night's incident, making sure to mention the texts, the returned truck, and the missing drugs.

"We already knew about the restaurant manager," Perk said, once Ray was done. "But, that other shit doesn't sound like Calvin. I can understand him taking the drugs but why would he bring your truck back and park it in front of your apartment?"

"Calvin would've set that bitch on fire!" Offered Young Cap. "And, I don't get why he would send those texts out to your people if he didn't plan on ambushing them?"

"Yeah, I'm still lost on that myself," admitted Ray, who was starting to feel like a complete idiot.

"Well, on top of going renegade," Cap went on, "Calvin is on the run from the law for violation of parole."

"We also got word that he was putting in work with the opposition," Perk added.

This made Ray think about seeing Calvin at the club with Major Gramz and his entourage but he dared to say anything about it.

"I made a call to the boys in Chicago," Cap went on. "Once they hear back from Larry, they'll contact me, then we'll know how to go about dealing with Calvin."

"I know you want his ass, Ray," Perk asserted, "But we can't' move on him without going through the chain of command."

"Yeah," Cap looked his friend in the eyes. " 'We can't move on him."

It didn't take long for Ray to catch on to that. They were basically giving him the green light to handle this nigga however he pleased and were prepared to turn a blind eye to it.

***

After getting her hair fixed, Sheila rushed home, thinking about her phone, and hoping that Ray didn't go through her contacts list because she didn't erase the phone number with No Heart's initials above it. A wave of relief came over her when he told her that his phone was inside of his truck and didn't need hers.

Ray was still close-mouthed about his incident, so Sheila was still in the dark about it, though she wanted to question him while changing his bandage. It didn't take a scientist to tell her that he'd gotten himself caught up in something extremely bad. Had it not been for the detective, she wouldn't have bought the car incident. Her initial thought was that he was beaten in the process of being car jacked.

This morning, when she saw Ray's truck parked out front, it frightened her because she'd seen these kinds of things happen in Mafia movies. She really thought that the ignition was rigged with explosives. Whatever the situation was, Sheila just wished that he didn't keep her in the dark about it because if she and the kids were in any danger, she'd want to know so she'd know how to move.

When Ray insisted that he had to make an important run, Sheila didn't try to reason with him. Instead, she decided to take the kids picnicking at the park, where they were now, lounging on a blanket in the grass, enjoying tuna sandwiches and chips.

When she checked her messenger earlier, there was still nothing from Leela. Now, she grabbed her phone off the blanket and logged back into her account. For some reason, she found herself sighing inwardly when she saw it. Clicking on Leela's name, she read, *Leela told me to contact you if something ever happened to her*, twice before clicking on the link below it which was a YouTube news clip.

Sheila's heart seemed to drop to her stomach when the video started playing and a photo of Leela was the first thing she saw, accompanied by an active crime scene and a heading that read, *Woman Found Slain.* The volume of her phone wasn't all the way up so she knew that the children couldn't make out what the reporter was saying. She had to put it close to her ear, to catch the reportage, which was short and concise. There were no leads on any suspects and she was shot dead the day before.

When the clip ended, the wheels in Sheila's brain began to turn. She was sure that the message was sent by the woman that Leela was staying with. She was also sure by what Leela revealed to her, that Calvin was responsible for the demise. For some reason, Sheila felt that this was all related to Ray's incident.

***

Ray left Perk's house mentally putting his plan in place. Perk and Young Cap had already put him on point that Calvin was highly influential and could assemble a nice sized army at will. Plus, he was associated with Major Gramz, who was over every Inglewood Family member in Georgia.

As bad as Ray was willing to go at this alone, he knew that he couldn't. He had the guns, but not the men to wield them. Hell, he didn't know the first place to look for his arch enemy but he was sure that Leela could point him in the right direction. He was sure that Sheila was still in contact with her. At that moment, his cell phone vibrated in the cupholder.

"Yeah?" Ray answered it.

"I got your message," Joe told him. "Is everything good?"

"Not yet," replied Ray. "I'ma need that stove back in a minute."

"What's a minute?"

"In about a couple of days."

"That's what's up," said Joe. "I'll unwrap it. Just let me know when."

"No doubt."

Concluding the call, Ray turned into his apartments at approximately 5:51PM. He parked beside Sheila's car but before he could put the truck into park, she was emerging from the apartment with her phone in her hand and a disturbing look on her face. Seeing that she was moving towards the passenger side, Ray left the engine running.

"I need to show you something," she said, upon sliding in beside him, and holding her phone out. "Press play!"

Accepting the device, Ray pressed his thumb on the video that was a still of Leela, who resembled an American hostage in a foreign country by the distraught look on her face.

"Hi!" Leela started timidly. "I'm Leela Counts and I'm making this video in the event that something happens to me. As of now, I'm constantly getting threats from my ex-boyfriend, Calvin Franklin telling me that he killed Jerry Jackson, our former manager at Checkers. I'm currently hiding out at a friend's house. To my knowledge, he doesn't know where I am. Anyway, to whoever's watching this if I end up murdered, I want you to know that Calvin Franklin did it. Please investigate him!"

"Erase that shit!" Ray told her, handing the phone back. "What do you plan on doing with it?"

"I made a promise to Leela," she answered, sternly. "Calvin murdered that girl. He also murdered Jerry."

"Can you prove it?" Ray challenged.

Sheila didn't respond.

"He did kill Jerry, though," Ray said, looking out his side window.

Her eyes widened. "Ray, did you have something to do with that?"

"No, I did not."

"Well, how do you—"

"I was there, Sheila." He cut her off, now facing her. "I didn't know the shit was about to go down but I had nothing to do with it."

For some reason, Sheila's believed him but something was still off about his demeanor. Clearly, he was upset about something and didn't seem too anxious to share it.

"What really happened to you, last night?" She finally asked.

"I was hit by a car," he said, matter-of-factly.

"I want the whole rundown, Ray!"

"People in hell want ice water!"

Sheila scowled at him.

Exhaling sharply, Ray directed his attention out of the window again. After a pregnant pause, he said, "I saw a truck following me and thought it was James, Fred, and Black."

"You what!" Sheila couldn't believe that he was still chasing the notion that the other Kingz were still alive.

"When I got off the expressway," he went on, "I stopped and got out to see if it was really them but it wasn't. It was Calvin and two more niggas."

"Calvin!" She exclaimed.

"The nigga tried to shoot me," Ray told her. "That's how I ended up jumping in front of that car."

"So, who brought your truck back to the apartment?"

"I still don't know yet," he answered, thinking about the drugs. "But, I'm on the hunt for this nigga. You can go ahead and erase that video."

With that, Ray killed the engine, signifying that this meeting was over. Taking that as her cue, Sheila climbed down and circled the truck, to assist her man. As she helped him down, she caught a whiff of some sweet-smelling fragrance wafting off of him.

This reminded her of what Ebony went through with Charles, who she subsequently discovered was cheating on her with Pam but Sheila didn't have to investigate. She already knew who Ray's mistress was. It was just a matter of time before she put the kibosh on their little *sideshow*.

Playa Ray

Chapter 22
The Following Day

Leela's video like Ray told her to. It was hard because she made a promise to Leela that she'd get the video in the hands of the proper authorities if something ever happened to her. On the other hand, she didn't want to get the police involved and Ray ends up getting caught in the mix while trying to retaliate on Calvin. Especially, if he ends up being watched by the law.

Sheila still struggled with this decision on her drive to work and while she worked the grill in the place of Ray, who was out on medical leave. And Marlene wasn't making the situation any better by periodically approaching and expressing her sentiment on Leela's death. Other employees expressed their own feelings but Marlene was carrying on like she'd lost her best friend when they were anything other than.

"Girl, I just thought about something," Marlena approached for the hundredth time, still using her hushed tone.

"What now, Marlene?" Sheila asked, rolling her eyes.

"I think Calvin killed her." She let on.

Sheila finally faced her. "Why would you say that?"

"I just have a hunch," her friend answered. "His ass is already crazy. Then, he was beating on her."

"Marlene, you can't be speculating!" Sheila was really hoping that Marlene left her alone because she had a great deal of other things to think about.

"You can't be that naive, Sheila," Marlene pressed. "The nigga was beating the dog shit out of Leela! We used to talk."

"You got customers." Sheila was glad to announce, seeing more customers approach the counter.

"I'll be back," Marlene promised, rushing off.

Sheila shook her head as she resumed with tending to the meat on the grill and entertaining her thoughts of Ray, and how he was going behind her back to dally with his ex. If that wasn't a slap in the face, the bitch had the gall to pretend like everything's fine between the two of them.

"Sheila?"

Sheila looked to see Toni and the assistant manager, Daryl approaching.

"Go ahead and take your break," Toni told her. "Daryl is gonna take over until you get back."

"Okay."

After clocking herself out, Sheila fixed herself a large Coke, then went out to her car. She'd already planned to call No Heart on her break to keep the play going. Especially since he gave her money to *'supposedly'* pay her phone bill. For the sake of the heat, she started the car before using her phone.

"What's up?" No Heart answered, sounding angry.

"It's Sheila," she announced. "Did I call you at a bad time?"

"Naw, baby," he replied. "I'm just tired of having to penalize niggas for doing shit that they have no business doing. Is this your number?"

"It is," she told him. "Thanks for the money!"

"It's all good," said No Heart. "Are you on break?"

"I only have a few minutes left," Sheila lied.

"That's cool. When's the next time you'll be free?"

"I don't know. This weekend, maybe."

"I can dig that," No Heart told her. "Just let me know before Friday."

"Alright."

Disconnecting with No Heart, Sheila devised a plan on how she was going to deal with him. At that same instance, she thought of how she was going to also deal with Precious, which is why she killed the engine, got out, and made for the public telephone on the property. After inserting coins, she dialed the phone number that she was all too familiar with.

"Hello?" The recipient picked up.

"Hey, Precious!"

***

"I got orders coming in," Ray was saying to Joe on the phone, "But I don't have any product."

Before leaving for work, Sheila awakened Ray to change the bandage on his head. He'd been up since, trying to formulate a way to compensate himself for the loss he'd just taken. After forcing himself to consume a bowl of cereal, he made calls to some of his customers, telling them that his product was running late. Now, he was sitting up on his bed talking to Joe on this phone.

"Yeah, that's a major setback," Joe admitted. "I think I can pull a couple of strings and get you a couple of things to help you get halfway back on your feet. I know you don't like handouts but—"

"It seems like my only option right now." Ray cut him off. "It'll put me further in debt but I'll pay it off."

"I ain't tripping on the money, bro." Joe let on. "I'm just trying to make sure you're good."

"I appreciate that!"

"You know it's all love," said Joe. "I'll let you know when I make that move. Just let me know when you'll need that stove."

"Will do."

Just as Ray hung up, he heard the sound of the front door opening. His first thought was that Sheila was on her break and had come home to check on him, but as he sat staring at the threshold of the bedroom, all he heard was the brief rustling of plastic. He heard the sound of the front door closing. After another moment, she still hadn't entered the bedroom and the apartment was once again silent.

Now alarmed, Ray pulled his Glock from under his pillow. After waiting for another beat, he grabbed one of his crutches to help himself off the bed. The pain was a lot more bearable now, being that the swelling in his thigh was going down.

As cautiously and quietly as he could, Ray exited the bedroom, making for the living room, where his nose was instantly assaulted by the smell of marijuana. That's when he spotted the black trash bag on the kitchen table, which sent a chill up his spine. There wasn't an ounce of doubt in his mind that it was the same bag stolen from his truck.

He rushed over to the door and tried to pull it open but it was locked. Whoever entered, had taken the time to lock it back with their own key. Getting the door open, Ray limped through the threshold with gun behind his back as he looked for anything out of place.

Seeing nothing, he closed and locked the door back and then crossed over to the kitchen. He could tell that the bag had been untied, and re-tied, because it wasn't his work. Untying it, Ray saw that there was another plastic grocery bag other than the one that contained the two kilos.

Pulling it out, Ray placed it on the table, and tore the bag open to find a leather bound folder with a Velcro latch.

Curious, he peeled the latch back and flipped the cover open to a stack of typed documents and photographs but what got his undivided attention was the typed heading that read: *'Investigating Subject: Kingz'.*

The following page contained a list of names, accompanied by titles and aliases, starting with James Young, Ray Young, Frederick Mills, and Keith Daniels. The next name was Steven Chambers, with his title as 'Worker/CI'.

For some reason, the letters 'CI' stood out to him, although he had no clue as to what they meant. As Ray sifted through computer-generated photos of he and the other Kingz, the only person he could think of was FBI agent Brian Bishop, who was *'very'* deceased.

This sent another chill down his spine. It's incontestable that someone was playing some kind of game with him. Now, he was sure that it was someone from one of the various law agencies, which definitely meant that he was still being watched, and was probably about to be arrested again.

Considering this, Ray, not realizing he'd taken a seat, continued sifting through the file to see if there were anything recent on him. He came upon information on the Queenz that went into a file titled 'LKS', listing Joe, Poppo, BJ, and Rick as other players. This went all the way up to the date of Ray's arrest.

The next section was titled 'Queen Sheila'. Here, he came across the letters 'CI' again, but they were beside Ace's government name. Then, there were sworn affidavits written by people whose names he was surprised to see. Just as he started to read the one written by Bobby Johnston, he heard the ringtone of his cell phone in the bedroom.

Leaving everything, including his gun on the table, Ray hobbled back into the bedroom. The phone had stopped but he reached it just as it started back up. Seeing Monica's number, he declined the call. Before he made it back to the kitchen, a text came through, from Monica, that read, *You should have received my gift by now, I guess you'll thank me whenever you're done dodging me.* Seeing this, Ray immediately called her back.

"I'm here," she answered.

"What gift are you talking about?" He asked, cautiously.

"I left it on your kitchen table," she told him.

"How'd you get a key to my apartment? Ray inquired, now thinking about the safety of Sheila and the kids.

"I had a copy made while you were asleep."

"You're the one that brought my truck back," he said. "That means you were following me that day."

"You'll have to think farther back than that, Ray," Monica advised. "Better yet, let me help you. I've been following you for almost a year now."

"So, the day we met wasn't a coincidence," he finally put it together.

"No, baby."

"And, I'm guessing your name is not Monica."

"It's Monique Bishop," she responded. "I'm Brian Bishop's widow."

Right then, the warning bells went off in his head. "So, what? Am I about to be arrested?"

"I don't know," she answered. "Are you?"

Ray didn't know how to respond to this."

"Oh!" Monique let out. "I'm really a hair stylist, not an FBI agent."

"Why would you give me this?"

"I figured you would like to know how it all unfolded," she offered. "I've been over it several times, and I'm quite impressed with my husband's work. His dedication."

"I saw a couple of pictures of me with hearts drawn around them," Ray told her. "What's that all about?"

Monique giggled. "I was perplexed by that myself. I think my husband had some kind of obsession with you."

"Obsession? Really?"

"I mean, it's understandable," she let on. "While I was going through the file, I found myself curious about your sexual performance. I guess it kinda rubbed off on me."

"I'm not understanding your intentions right now." Ray was ready to get this over with. "You returned my truck. You returned my merchandise. Then, you hit me with this file. What are you expecting from me?"

"A *'thank you'* would be in order," she said. "I mean, I wouldn't mind continuing our fuck session, but you've pretty much nipped that in the bud. It's cool, though. Just be a good husband to Sheila."

"I'll try," Ray told her. "Thank you!"

"You're welcome, Ray," said Monique. "I really enjoyed you."

"I guess I'll take that as a compliment."

"You should," she replied with a giggle. "Well, I guess this is goodbye. Oh, yeah, you should dispose of that file when you're finished with it. Especially, if you plan on taking any adverse action."

"Yeah, I guess," Ray said, still processing her words. "Before you go, I want to ask you something."

"What is it?"

"What does 'CI' mean? He asked, thinking about Steve and Ace.

Monique was quiet for a moment before saying, "Confidential Informant."

Right then, Ray's mind started spinning out of control. He wasn't the smartest person in the world but from what he gathered from the file, Steve assisted the FBI agent in the Kingz's investigation, and Ace helped him with taking Sheila down.

Now, he was seeing a mental image of Steve and how he found Steve's body at The Palace. Perhaps, James had gotten a whiff of what Steve was up to and snatched him up with the intent to execute him before the Crown, which never took place, due to the demise of the other Kingz. For some reason, Ray didn't think that Black, nor Fred, knew of this. Well, there was nothing he could do about Steve but Ace would definitely have to answer for his involvement in Sheila's arrest.

***

After picking the kids up from Shatera's, Sheila drove around to their apartment, expecting not to see Ray's truck, being that he'd sent her a text letting her know that he was out and wouldn't be home for dinner.

This was a relief for Sheila because she wasn't in the mood to cook. Therefore, after showering, and getting dressed, she treated the kids to Long John Silver's, where they dined in, taking their time while enjoying each other's company.

It was 7:22PM when they made it back home. Ray was still out. Being that Rachel and Prince Ray had completed their home-work before they all left out for dinner, Sheila let them watch TV until eight o' clock, then sent them to bed.

As nine o' clock drew nigh, Sheila donned a black T-shirt to go with her black jeans she already had on, then picked out one of Ray's ball caps to complete her ensemble. After stuffing her cell phone between the mattresses on her side of the bed, she opened one of her dresser drawers, pulled a nickel-plated .38 revolver from beneath her folded pants and dropped it into her pocketbook atop the dresser.

Hoping to avoid encountering Ray, she looked in on the kids to see that they were asleep. She exited the apartment, making sure to lock the door back. The night sky had pretty much just set in and there were only a handful of people milling about the neighborhood, who probably gave her a mere glance as she drove toward the en-trance of the apartments.

This was one of those nights that Sheila hoped that Ray planned to stay out all night because if he makes it home before she gets back and find the children there alone, not only would he be angry, but he would be able to put two and two together and link her to tonight's venture.

It took more than twenty minutes to reach the small, nondescript gas station, though she drove right past it. The car she expected to see was already there, parked on the side of the store with the only other vehicle being the one belonging to the only employee.

Further down the dark and almost deserted road, Sheila found the dirt road opening to the adjacent wooded area and turned onto it. She was thankful that the trail wasn't muddy. Figuring her car was well out of sight of any passing motorists, she killed the engine, grabbed her pocketbook, and got out.

Using her penlight, Sheila trekked through the woods in the same direction she'd come from. These weren't that many trees, so it was pretty much a straight shot, which brought her to the rear of the gas station.

This is where she stopped and slipped a black glove over her right hand. Rounding the store, she saw Precious, sitting in her car engrossed in her cell phone. Sheila could tell this, because there were no lights on this side, which made it easy for her to approach the car, unnoticed, pulling the pistol from her bag.

"Sheila!" Precious exclaimed when she looked up and found herself staring down the barrel of the revolver.

"He's *'my'* man, bitch!" Sheila let out, before injecting three slugs into the face of Ray's ex-girlfriend.

Chapter 23

"Are you sure you don't need me to go with you?" Sheila asked Ray while changing his bandage.

Unbeknownst to Ray, Sheila had a hard time sleeping last night for struggling with images of Precious in her last moment of existence. This was something that Sheila would have never dreamed of doing to Precious but she was going against the 'girl code', by sleeping with Ray behind her back. Therefore, Sheila was indisposed to feeling sympathy for the traitor.

"They're just taking the staples out, Sheila," Ray now answered her question.

"Okay," she deferred, figuring he intended to link up with Precious before or after his appointment. "I guess we'll see you later."

Sheila kissed him on the jaw, then crossed over to the dresser where she grabbed her keys, phone, and pocketbook and exited the bedroom, closing the door behind her.

Ray, who was sitting up, on the edge of the bed, listened as Sheila and the kids exited the apartment. He got up, and moved over to the closet to find something to wear to his appointment, which was at ten o'clock.

While he dressed, Ray thought about the kiss Sheila planted on his jaw. It felt awkward because she hadn't done it in some time. He didn't know what to make of it. Maybe, she was trying to rekindle the fire in their relationship, being that they were set to tie the knot in another three weeks.

Finally exiting the apartment and climbing into his truck, the stench of the weed brough Ray's mind back to the FBI file that was also in the rear compartment. He'd taken his time to read the affidavits written by Bobby, Trina, Kim, Steve, and some of their customers and employees. He still didn't know what to do about this but he'd already decided that he wouldn't tell Sheila about it.

"Mr. Young?"

Ray, who'd been sitting in the waiting area, on the sixth floor of Grady Memorial Hospital for over forty minutes, looked up from the movie playing on his phone, to see a Caucasian female with dark hair, and black-framed eye-glasses, holding a clipboard. He'd never seen her before but she was regarding him with a look of recognition.

"This way, please!" She said, indicating the service door she'd emerged from.

Stopping the movie, Ray got up and allowed the nurse to escort him through the door and to an awaiting examination room, where she insisted he sit upon the examination table. She was still giving him that look.

"Do we know each other?" Ray finally inquired.

"It sure feels like it," she answered. "My name's Kim. You don't know me, but you know my boyfriend."

"Who's your boyfriend?"

"His name is Queail," she told him. "He said that you guys met in juvenile, and he has a lot of pictures of you, him, and some other guy."

Ray knew that she was telling the truth, and the *'other guy'* she referred to was Tommy. The three of them met each other in the same place and became best friends. Although their paths ended up diverging, causing them to lose contact with one another. The last thing he heard on Queail, was that he was in prison for drug and assault charges.

"Yeah, I know him," Ray admitted. "Is he out?"

"He's out," Kim answered. "Right now, he's not working, so he could use a little help."

Ray handed his phone to her. "Put his number in there!"

She did, then handed the phone back. "He's gonna be glad to hear from you," she told Ray. "I'm glad that we finally met. Anyway, I have to gather other patients. Dr. Pratt will be with you, shortly."

"Thanks!"

***

Again, Sheila was assigned to grill duty. She was kind of glad that Marlene was off today because she really needed the time to think. She knew that Ray was going to insist upon them attending Precious' funeral, and would need some time to mourn her death, which was okay, because once he got over losing the bitch, she was going to begin working on the process of repairing their relationship.

"Excuse me? Is your manager in?"

Hearing this, Sheila looked towards the front counter to see a white male in casual attire. Even without the gun and badge clipped to his waist belt, she was able to tell that he was a government official. One of the cashiers went to gather Toni from the office. When the manager reached the counter, she and the officer exchanged a few words before Toni turned toward Sheila.

"Sheila?" Toni spoke. "This detective wants to have a word with you."

Sheila's heart dropped to her stomach. Her gut feeling was telling her that this was about Precious, which had her wondering if she'd covered all her tracks. There were no cameras at the gas station. She didn't take her phone with her, and she was highly confident that she'd buried the gun in a good spot. The only way she could be linked to the murder of Precious is if Precious had informed someone of the meeting, beforehand.

After Toni found someone to relieve her, Sheila joined the detective in the dining area, where they were now seated across from each other, being watched by everybody inside the restaurant.

"Thanks for joining me, Ms. Griffin!" He said, flipping through this small notepad. "I'm Detective Knox from the homicide division, and I'm investigating the murder of Leela Counts. You two were friends, right?"

"I guess you could say that," Sheila answered, not thinking about Leela's video that she still has on her phone.

"Well," he went on. "I was told by a mutual friend of Counts that I should speak to you, regarding her murder. What can you tell me about it?"

***

Ray didn't eat anything prior to leaving the apartment, so upon leaving the hospital, he stopped by a Burger King restaurant, where he was now waiting in the drive-thru line. At that time, his cell phone vibrated on top of the armrest.

"Yeah?" He answered it.

"Hey, Ray!" Nikki's voice came through the device. "How're you doing?"

"I'm good, Nikki," he replied. "I just got my staples taken out and the swelling in my thigh has went down. What's going on with you?"

"Not much," she said. "I'm calling around to see who all's gonna pitch in on her funeral."

"Whose funeral." Ray piqued up.

Nikki was quiet on the other end before asking, "So, you really don't know?"

"Know what, Nikki?"

"Precious was murdered last night."

This came to Ray like a slap to the face. Nikki wasn't the type to participate in any kind of prank, so this was definitely true but who on earth would murder someone like Precious? She was pretty much an angel.

"How was she murdered, Nikki?" Ray asked.

"I don't know the details," she admitted. "But it was on the news. She was found in her car on the side of some unknown gas station in Forest Park."

Ray was familiar with this 'unknown' gas station that Nikki spoke of but he couldn't fathom why she was at such a place at such a time.

"Did they say that it was a robbery?" Ray inquired, trying to connect a few dots of his own.

"If I can recall," answered Nikki. "They said it wasn't a robbery and that nothing seemed to be taken from her."

Ray let out a sigh. "Yeah, I'll pitch in on the funeral. Just hit me up later."

"Okay."

Now, with a loss of appetite, Ray steered his truck from the drive-thru line and drove away with no destination in mind. It was hard for him not to be touched by Precious' death, even though they hadn't been together in almost eight years. As the tears welled up in his eyes, all he could think about was finding out who did it. Another call came through on his phone.

"What's up?" He answered it.

"I got some information that you might be interested in," Big Ru let on.

"I'm listening," Ray told him.

"You're still looking for Calvin, right?"

It took no time for Ray to reach Big Ru's house. This time, Quick Ru didn't bother to search him. He just led Ray to the kitchen, where Big Ru was seated at the table, running bills through a money counter.

"Have a seat, my friend!" Big Ru offered, wrapping a rubber band around a stack of bills before placing another stack into the machine.

Ray took a seat across from him. "So, what's the four-one-one on this nigga?"

Big Ru smiled. "That's what I like about you," he said. "All business, no bullshit. Anyway, I got word that Calvin has been hanging out in Mechanicsville. He's fucking some chick over there but he mainly hangs out with Mankey, who also stay's there."

"This is Puff's shooter, right?" Ray remembered the young man.

"Yeah," answered Big Ru. "He's a hothead. Plus, Mechanicsville is pretty much 'Bloods city'. So, if you go over there looking for Calvin, you may not get the results you're looking for. Especially, if you go alone."

"I'll take my chances."

***

Sheila was surprised to see Ray's truck when she pulled around to their apartment with their kids in tow. Entering the apartment, she found Ray in the bedroom, looking through the closet, as if for something to wear. He only glanced back at her, then went back to sifting through the hanging attire. He wasn't propped up on his crutches, nor did he have the bandage around his head. In fact, there was a small band-aid on his forehead where the staples were.

Sheila didn't know if the children would enter the room to greet their daddy or not but she closed, and locked the door, to make sure that they didn't. Then, she sat her keys and pocketbook atop the dresser, before crossing over to the bed, and perching on the edge of it.

"How did the appointment go?" She inquired.

"They took the staples out," Ray answered with his back still to her. "Gave me some more antibiotics."

"Did they say anything about your leg?"

"Just to keep pressure on it," he told her. "I'll go back to work, Monday."

Sheila knew what she had to say, but she was hesitating. After taking a deep breath, she said, "A detective came to see today."

Ray finally stopped what he was doing and turned to face her but said nothing.

"He was asking me about Leela," she resumed. "I think the girl that Leela was staying with sent him to me."

"Why would she do that?" Ray wanted to know.

Sheila lingered.

Ray furrowed his eyebrows at her. "Did you erase that video?"

"Right after he left."

"So, what did you tell him?"

"I told him what I didn't know anything about Leela's murder," Sheila answered. "He asked if I knew about any men she was dating, and I said no. He left."

While digesting this, Ray limped over to the dresser, and leaned against it. After a brief pause, he said, "Precious was killed last night."

"What!" Sheila feigned surprise, placing a hand over her chest. "Are you sure?"

"Nikki called me about it," he told her. "When I got home, I pulled it up on the internet. It's true."

"Oh, I'm sorry, baby!"

Playing her part, Sheila got off the bed and wrapped her arms around him, burying her face in his neck. Him embracing her back came as a surprise to her. In fact, his touch alone, was turning her on but she knew it would be selfish of her to give in to her hormones at such a time.

Just then, Sheila felt a wetness on her cheek, and looked up to see the tears cascading down Ray's face, which churned her heart. Although, she was the cause of it.

"It's okay, baby," she whispered, wiping his tears with her thumb. "I'm here for you."

Sheila knew that she was going out on a limb but she felt that this was the best time to make her first of many moves. Still looking into his eyes, she leaned in and began kissing him, not knowing if he would reciprocate but he did. When their tongues touched, Sheila knew that it was genuine, which brought tears to her own eyes.

Taking advantage of this moment, Sheila began undoing his pants. She didn't expect for Ray to have an erection but his rod was standing at attention and seemed to have gotten bigger. Breaking the kiss, she didn't waste time dropping to her knees and taking a great portion of her man into her mouth.

Despite his current emotional state, Sheila's mouth was performing a miracle because with every stroke, Ray could feel the weight of the world lifting up off him. It felt so good. He closed his eyes and gripped the edge of the dresser with both hands.

Knock! Knock! Knock!

"Momma!" Prince Ray's voice came through the door. "I left my crayons at Shatera's house."

Stopping mid stroke, Sheila looked up at her man.

"You know he's going to have a fit about those crayons," he told her.

Playa Ray

Chapter 24
Saturday

Precious' funeral service didn't last as long as Ray thought it would but there were a great number of attendants, mostly people he was familiar with. It was Sheila's idea to not let the children attend, so they were at her grandmother's place for the weekend.

At the burial site, while the pastor was conducting the final eulogy, Ray, through the dark lenses of his sunglasses, kept cutting his eyes at Ace, who was accompanied by Nikki, and their children. Kim and her son, James, were also in attendance. She seemed to be intent on avoiding him but Ray couldn't understand why. He'd read the affidavit that she'd written, claiming that she had nothing against her ex-boyfriend, James Young, and knew nothing about what he participated in on his spare time. So, why was she acting strange?

Before Precious' casket was lowered into the earth, people paid their last respects by placing flowers on top of it. Sheila placed hers, but Ray lingered. He didn't move until Ace and Nikki stepped forward. Without a word, he placed his flower, and embraced Nikki, then slid Ace a note, while shaking hands with him.

With that, Ray threw his arm around Sheila's waist and they made off towards Sheila's car, where Ray climbed into the passenger seat, and loosened his tie.

"Are you hungry?" Sheila asked, starting the engine.

"Not really," he told her. "You can grab something if you want."

Sheila drove on, not saying if she was going to grab herself something to eat or not. In fact, the drive was as quiet as it was on their way to the service, which was okay with Ray, because he had a lot on his mind.

"Ray, can I ask you something?" Sheila finally spoke as they traveled along the expressway.

"I'm listening," he said.

"Were you still seeing Precious?" She asked. "Sexually, I mean."

Ray looked at her. "Why would you ask me something like that?"

"I'm not stupid, Ray," Sheila voiced, but maintained her composure. "You weren't staying out all those nights just to be by yourself. Are we lying to each other now?"

"I should be asking you the same question," Ray shot back. "Or, did I not find a box of condoms in your glove compartment? An opened box of condoms, with one missing."

"Yeah, I had the box," she admitted, "But I never opened it. Stop playing mind games with me, Ray! If I no longer satisfy you, I can understand that. I considered Precious a friend. All I wanna know is if she was going behind my back."

"No, she wasn't, Sheila," Ray answered. "On the same day that I found those condoms, I met someone. I only fucked her because I was mad about finding out that you were fucking off behind my back. But, if it makes you happy, I'm no longer seeing her or any other bitch."

"Ray, I've never fucked another man behind your back," Sheila told him. "I can't believe that you'll even think of some crazy shit like that."

Ray shook his head. "I see you just refuse to tell the truth, huh?"

"What the fuck do you mean, Ray!" Sheila spat, not liking what he was implying. "I am telling the fucking truth! I ain't never—"

"What about Shatera's brother?" He inquired, recently ascertaining who the guy was that Sheila was seen within Atlanta. "The nigga that you were in Atlanta with?"

"We went to listen to her brother record music, Ray," Sheila admitted, wondering how he knew about that. "Nothing happened."

"Yeah, whatever!" Ray asserted, directing his attention out his side window. "You had a box of used condoms in your car, which means that you were doing something with somebody. I admitted my wrong. I stepped out on you, a few times, but that's over. And, neither one of those times were with Precious."

With one hand still on the wheel, Sheila put a fist up to her mouth, as if to parry bile. Ray caught this from the corners of his eyes and couldn't help but wonder if Sheila had murdered Precious out of jealousy. She was definitely capable of it, considering what she'd done to Dread at that motel. However, he was only hoping that she didn't do that selfish-ass shit.

When they made it home, Sheila made for the bathroom. While Ray retired to their bedroom. Of course, she didn't have to use the toilet, which was why she let the lid down, and sat on it. Sheila didn't know how an anxiety attack started but she felt like she was on the verge of one.

Sheila's chest felt like it was getting tight, as tears flooded from her eyes. She couldn't believe that she let her jealous emotions cause her to take Precious' life. This hurt because she really considered Precious a friend. She didn't deserve to die like that but there was no way to bring her back. Sheila knew that she could never break down and confess this to Ray. She would definitely have to take this one to her grave.

***

Ray and Sheila didn't have much of a conversation upon returning home from the funeral service. After changing out of his dress clothes, Ray decided to go ahead and leave the apartment, without informing Sheila of when he'll return.

Now hungry, Ray stopped by a Captain D's restaurant, where he dined in to waste a little time. Afterwards, he drove out to Atlanta. If Ace took heed to the note he'd given him, then they would be meeting in another two hours.

As promised, Joe was waiting for Ray on an unpopulated back street with a stolen, white Chevy Astro van. His car was parked behind it with him seated in the front-passenger seat, and someone at the wheel. Joe got out when Ray parked behind his car, and they met up at the driver's door of the van.

"It hasn't been reported stolen, yet," Joe told him. "The gun is on the seat, and the gas can is in the back."

"Thanks!" Ray said, bumping fists with him.

"It's all good, bro," his friend responded. "Just make it back! And you need to go and see Poppo. He'll be doing morning service tomorrow but he'll be holding bible study at night, which won't be a large crowd."

"I'll remember that," Ray said, pulling the driver's door open. There was a chrome .38 pistol on the seat. Ray tucked it in his pants pocket before climbing behind the wheel of the van that was already running and making a U-turn.

It took about forty-two minutes to reach Kroger City on Cleveland Avenue. To Ray's surprise, Ace's SUV was already in the lot parked closer to the road. Pulling alongside it, Ray motioned for Ace to join him but left the engine running, and was thankful that it was dark out.

"Did you tell Nikki where you were going?" Ray questioned when Ace got in beside him.

"Hell, no!" He answered. "Today's my mom's birthday. I told Nikki that I was going to see her. So, what's this money scheme that you want to talk to me about? I damn sure need it!"

"I understand," Ray offered. "But, there's no money scheme, Ace. Just a bunch of disappointment."

"What are you talking about, Ray?" There was apprehension in Ace's eyes.

"I'm talking about you helping the Feds to take Sheila down," Ray dove right in.

"What!" Ace feigned surprise. "Ray, I would never—"

"Don't do that!" Ray cut him off. "I hear enough lies at home."

"Why would you think—"

"I'm not *thinking* shit!" Ray voiced, ready to get this over with. "I saw the FBI's file for myself, nigga! We trusted you. The most fucked up part about it is that Sheila doesn't even know you fucked over her."

Just then, as Ray reached into his pocket for the revolver, Ace reached for his door handle, but it wasn't there, being that Ray told Joe to displace it. It only took a couple of seconds for Ace to realize that his fate was sealed. He slowly turned to face Ray, who had the pistol held low, aimed at his chest.

"You know what?" Ray asked. "I don't even want to know why."

As though sensing his final moment, Ace attempted to reach for the gun. Ray threw his right arm up, redirecting Ace's aim before squeezing the trigger six times, ending his natural existence.

Sticking to his original plan, Ray pulled out of the lot with Ace's cadaver lying between the front seats. Making it back to the spot, where his truck was still parked, he drove the van further into the woods and got out, opening all of the doors.

Just as Joe promised, the gas can was sat the rear of the van. After dousing the whole interior with the flammable agent, Ray pushed the electric lighter in. When it popped back out, he tossed it onto the rear seat, and waited until it ignited before walking off, headed to his truck.

***

"I wish that I could take you to the Cancun or something," No Heart said through the phone. "I think we both deserve a getaway."

"Amen to that!" Sheila replied.

She'd just gotten out of the shower and was still wrapped in a towel while going through her cosmetics atop the dresser, where her phone sat, on speaker. When Ray left the apartment, without a word to her, Sheila took a long, warm shower, until being interrupted by her cell phone. She and No Heart had been talking ever since.

"If it wasn't for this gang shit," No Heart went on, "I'd probably be living in another country."

"And, which country would that be?"

"It don't even matter," he said. "I'd close my eyes and just pick a place on the map. Go somewhere where nobody knows me."

"That would be nice," Sheila said, going into her underwear drawer for a pair of panties and bra.

Upon closing that drawer, she noticed a piece of cloth sticking out of Ray's pants drawer, which was probably a result of him rushing out to get the hell away from her. She opened the drawer, intending to correct the position of the disrupted pair of pants, but her intuition was telling her to explore the small area.

After straightening the top pair of pants, Sheila began looking under each pair, one at a time, until she came across something that she did not expect to come across. She picked the cellular phone up, looking it over. She couldn't imagine someone buying a second phone that was completely identical to their first one.

This was definitely Ray's initial phone, but why would he hide it there, and leave out without it? Well, of course, Sheila knew the reason for using such a tact, because she'd done it, but she didn't particularly know what he was up to. Perhaps, he was still trying to hunt down Calvin.

Chapter 25
Sunday

"I'm on my way to pick up the kids," Sheila announced upon entering the living room, where Ray was sitting on the sofa talking on his phone. "Do you need anything while I'm out?"

Ray hadn't said one word to Sheila, since their disagreement yesterday and he wasn't responding to her now. All he did was shoot her a scolding look before resuming his conversation. However, Sheila pretended to not let it bother her and exited the apartment.

Climbing into her car, she started the engine, and sat there, trying to keep her tears from escaping her ducts. Of course, she was affected by this minor setback. She thought Precious death would bring them closer together, but it seemed like she was taking one step forward and two steps back. And, it didn't help at all to find out that she'd liquidated Precious for no reason.

"Come the fuck on!" Sheila bellowed, holding a hand up to one of her vents that was blowing out hot air. "Not again!"

Pissed about this, Sheila shut the AC unit off, then let all the windows down before backing out of her spot. By the time she made it to the front gate, her cell phone vibrated in her lap. She wasn't in the mood to talk but after checking the caller ID and seeing that it was Trez, she answered it

"Hello?"

"Are you busy?" He asked.

Sheila exhaled. "No, Trez. I'm on my way to pick my children up. How's everything going on your end?"

"Everything's good," he answered. "We just finished the album. Fabo and Tripp James did a couple of features on it."

"They're both from Bowen Homes, right?"

"Yeah," Trez replied. "Tripp James got a nice buzz going on right now."

"I've heard some of his music."

There was a pause before Trez asked. "What are you doing after you pick up your kids?"

"Heading back home," she told him. "I have to go to work in the morning."

"That's what's up. When will you have some free time."

***

Ray was on the phone with his childhood friend, Queail when Sheila left out to pick the children up from her grandmother's house. It wasn't a secret that things were not the same between them. Ray felt like he was on an emotional rollercoaster. At first, it was him. Now, it's Sheila with her tit-for-tat methods. Even when he admitted to cheating on her, Sheila still refused to come clean. And he was still under the notion that she murdered Precious.

Shortly after Sheila left, Ray got dressed and made his own exit, driving out to Atlanta, where his first destination was the BP gas station on Ashby Street. Before he could pull into the establishment, he spotted Queail, who was 5' 7, and 196 pounds, standing at the entrance, smoking a cigarette. Seeing Ray, he grounded the cigarette out then made for the truck.

"Boy, you got this bitch smelling like a whole weed factory!" Queail commented, as he got in.

"Here!" Ray handed him the paper bag containing the product he promised.

"Are you sure I don't owe you?" Queail inquired.

"Just get on your feet!" Ray told him.

"I'm gonna definitely do that," he promised. "So, what's up with this suicide mission you're about to go on?"

"I didn't say it was a *'suicide'* mission."

Queail smiled at him. "I know you, Ray. You'll burn down a house with you in it just to get a nigga that crossed you . Hell, if a nigga crossed you and you're after him, I want in!"

At that time, Ray's cell phone vibrated in the cupholder.

"Yeah?" He answered it.

"Ray!" Nikki's voice came through, breathlessly, "Ace left out yesterday, and didn't come home last night. And, he's not answering his phone."

"Did he say where he was going?" Ray made sure to ask, just in case Ace lied to him.

"He was going to see his mom for her birthday," Nikki confirmed, "I called her and she said that he never made it. I tried to file a missing person's report but the police department told me that I have to wait forty-eight hours. Ray, I'm worried!"

"Yeah, I know," he replied, wondering if Nikki knew that her husband was a rat. "Right now, I'm in the middle of something. When I'm done, I'll check around and see what I can find out."

"Okay. Thanks, Ray!"

"You're welcome!" Concluding the call, Ray looked over at his friend, "So, you want in?"

"Nigga, you know I'ma ride with you!" Queail stated. "Just give me the full layout!"

"Alright. I'll pick you up on Saturday. You'll get the full scoop, then."

"That's a bet!" After bumping fists with Ray, Queail reached for the door handle, then paused as if remembering something. "Oh!" he let out. "I be seeing your boy, BJ."

Ray piqued up at this. "Where?"

"He be coming through Beckwith Street to fuck with some chick that stays out there."

***

Poppo's church, 'Lift Every Voice', was located in Roswell, Georgia. As Ray pulled into the massive lot, he marveled at the size of the building. This was well beyond his expectations. He was greatly proud of his friend.

Ray managed to find a place to park closer to the building, being that there were no more than twelve vehicles present. Getting out, he buttoned up his gray blazer and adjusted his burgundy tie as he made for the entrance of the church that seemed quiet on the inside.

Upon entering, he doffed his sunglasses and looked up and down the curving hallway that he was standing in before entering a door before him. It led to the heart of the two-story building that was decked out with rows of burgundy-cushioned chairs and matching carpet extending all the way up to the low stage. Poppo was standing behind the podium, reading words from his bible to a small crowd of worshipers.

Not wanting to disturb anyone, Ray sat on the very back row. Poppo wasn't using the microphone, which was why Ray couldn't hear anything from outside. However, he could hear his friend now, though his mind was on BJ.

The last time that Ray had seen or heard anything from BJ was the night he took BJ to the Greyhound station, and BJ had mysteriously disappeared, which was the same date that showed up on the affidavit he'd written. He was claiming that he would testify against Ray in court of law if called upon to do so. Queail had given Ray the address so he was definitely going to pay the traitor a courtesy visit.

At 7:12pm, the bible study group began to slowly make their exits as Poppo hugged and shook hands with them, bidding them good night. Most of them spoke or just nodded at Ray upon passing.

"Blessed is the King who comes in the name of the Lord!" Poppo quoted, as he approached with a broad smile on his face.

"I need all the blessings that I can get," Ray said, standing, and embracing his friend. "How are you, brother?"

"I can't complain," Poppo told him. "Just serving my purpose."

"Yeah, I hear that." Ray took a seat, allowing for Poppo to sit beside him. "You did well with the place! Do you ever have a full house?"

"Just about," answered Poppo. "How's the family?"

"Everybody's good. How yours?"

"Blessed." Poppo lingered before asking, "So, what brings you by?"

"Just thought I'd stop by and check on you," Ray offered. "Let you know that I'm still alive and kicking."

"I hear that from Joe."

Ray narrowed his eyes at Poppo. "What else do you hear from Joe?"

"The usual," Poppo replied, "He doesn't talk to me about what you got going on in the streets if that's what you're asking. I'd rather hear that from the horse's mouth. So, what's going on in the streets?" Anything I need to be concerned with?"

Playa Ray

Chapter 26
Wednesday

Still empathetic to Ray's incident, Toni refused to put him on trash detail but chose Sheila to do it. Being that Marlene's relief had gotten there early, Sheila lobbied Marlene's assistance. They saw Ray drive off, while pushing their second load of trash to the dumpster.

"Why don't y'all ride together anymore?" Marlene questioned what she clearly thought was asinine. "Gas ain't as cheap as it was in the nineties."

"I have to pick up the kids from the babysitter," Sheila explained, "And Ray has other errands to run. It all works out."

Marlene was shaking her head. "Y'all are the strangest couple I've ever met! I thought Tommy Lee and Pamela Anderson were fucked up."

"You've never even met them, Marlene," Sheila pointed out, smiling.

"Thank God for that!" She let out, making Sheila laugh.

It doesn't matter what kind of stupor Sheila may find herself in, Marlene always seemed to pull her out of it. Upon leaving work, Sheila drove out to McGee's Auto Body Shop, to see if she could get someone to look at her air conditioner unit, because she could not stand another day, driving around in that sweatbox. She made sure to place a call to Shatera and informed her that she'd be a little late.

Being that McGee's had a sign that advertised their closing time at 5:30pm, Sheila knew that she was pushing it by pulling up at 5:07. Parking, she got out and entered the building looking specifically for the shop's owner, who she found by one of the oil pits, observing one of his workers.

"Mr. McGee?"

The older man turned and seemed to admire her for a moment before asking, "How may I help you?"

"I don't know if you remember me," she started, "But you fixed the air conditioner in my car not too long ago."

"I remember," McGee admitted, glancing at his watch. "We're close to quitting time. Did the unit go back out?"

"I think something came unhinged," Sheila offered. "Can you spare a few minutes to look at it?"

The man let out a sharp breath. "Alright." Looking down at his worker, he said, "I'll be back, Larry."

Sheila led the way. Knowing that he was watching her, she put a little more bounce in her gait, to wet his appetite some more. Making it to her car, she deactivated the alarm, climbed behind the wheel, and started the car as McGee got in on the other side, tampering with the functions of the AC unit.

"Okay," he said after a while. "I know exactly what it is. I'll be right back."

As he retreated back to the building, Sheila stood outside the car, hoping that she wouldn't have to sustain the sweltering heat for too long. About six minutes later, he returned, carrying some kind of tool bag, and sat back in the front-passenger seat.

"I know exactly what it is," he reiterated, almost to himself. "This shouldn't take long."

Just as promised, the mechanic completed the job in less than fifteen minutes. He took another minute or so to experiment with the controls before tossing his tools back inside his bag and getting out of the car.

"There you go!" He announced. "It had something to do with how I wired it. Being that it was my fuck up, I can't charge you."

"That's good to know," Sheila replied. Then, a thought occurred to her. Can I ask you something?"

"I'm pressed for time," he said, looking at his watch again. "What is it?"

"On my last visit," she began, "You serviced my car. Did anybody else have access to it?"

He gave her a quizzical look. "Not that I know of. Why?"

"Someone stole a condom from my glove compartment," she dove right in. "You wouldn't do anything like that, right?"

McGee cast his eyes to the ground, then back up at her. "I can't even lie to you," he said. "I did get one of 'em."

"Why the fuck would you do some dumb ass shit like that!"
Sheila bristled, feeling her blood boil over.

"Whoa, lady!" He exclaimed, pulling a wad of bills from his
pants pocket. "I'll pay you for the damn thing!"

"It ain't about the fucking money!" She told him. "You started
a fucking war that should have never been started!"

***

Ray had been parked on Beckwith Street for almost forty
minutes, watching the house that was three houses away from where
he was stationed, but saw no signs of life. There wasn't any kind of
vehicle parked in front of it.

While sitting, Ray thought about his impending wedding date,
which was eleven days away. Having second thoughts, he was
tempted to call the whole thing off or just be an asshole and not
show up. He knew that would embarrass the hell out of Sheila. Honestly, at the rate their relationship was going, he didn't think that
'jumping the broom' would make things any better.

For some reason, the thought of their wedding made him think
about Nikki and Ace. He couldn't believe that he forgot to call and
make a show of consoling her, in the absence of Ace. Realizing this,
he grabbed his phone and dialed her number.

When Nikki answered, he heard her sniffle before saying,
"Hello?"

"Are you good?" Ray tried to sound concerned. "Have you
heard anything on Ace?"

"They found his body, Ray," she said, her voice cracking.
"Somebody set him on fire. I can't believe somebody actually did
that to my baby."

"Where'd you get this from, Nikki?"

"I filed the missing person's person report," she told him. "A
detective called me this morning and told me that they found his
remains yesterday and were able to identify him by his teeth."

"Look," Ray said, upon seeing a car pull up in front of the
house that he was watching, "I'm in the middle of something. Once
I'm done, I'll be right over, okay?"

"Okay."

Disconnecting, Ray looked at the house where a blue Nissan Sentra had parked. At that time, a female was emerging from the driver's side and a male from the passenger side. Of course, the man was none other than BJ.

Starting the truck, Ray put it into gear and pulled up to the house just as they were about to ascend the steps that led up to the porch. On instinct, they stopped and looked back. If Ray was reading it right, BJ looked like he was ready to try out for the Olympics Track and Field. That's, of course, if he was reading it right.

"Step into my office!" Ray said, as cool as he could, so not to alarm BJ or his female companion.

BJ said something to his woman, then waited for her to start climbing the steps before crossing over to the truck. Upon getting in, his eyes landed on the .38 revolver in Ray's lap before trying to penetrate the dark lenses of Ray's sunglasses.

"How'd you find me?" BJ asked as the truck moved forward.

"It's good to see you too, BJ," Ray replied.

"Come on, Ray!" BJ voiced. "You know I'm happy to see you. I'm just surprised at how you found me, that's all."

"What happened that night?" Ray dove right in. "At the Greyhound station?"

"Oh!" BJ looked out his side window. "That FBI agent snatched me out of line. The same one that did your case."

"Really?" Ray didn't try to hide his incredulous tone.

BJ looked at him. "He had a gun on me, Ray. He said that if I didn't go with him, he was gonna lock you up that night. He knew that you were there, that night."

"Grab that out of the glove compartment!"

Opening the glove compartment, BJ pulled out a folded piece of paper, and opened it.

"That was the same night you wrote that, right?" Ray pointed out. "It has the same date on it."

Visibly swallowing, BJ looked at Ray. "I only wrote this, so he'd leave me alone. He was threatening to charge me for what happened on the expressway that night. Like I was shooting at my damn self, and intentionally killed everybody in the fucking camper." He paused for a moment before going on. "We've known each other for too long, Ray. My loyalty is something you'll never have to question and you know that."

Ray narrowed his eyes at him. "Do I?"

Playa Ray

Chapter 27

It was finally Saturday, and Ray was anxious to find Calvin, and put him out of his misery. Leaving the apartment around 4:28p.m., he met Joe at the shop on Browns Mill Road to pick up the assault weapons he'd bought from Drew. Then, he drove out to Ashby Street to collect Queail before heading for the Tasty Dog restaurant on Simpson Road. They were now pulling up in front of.

"Do you have your phone on you?" Ray asked his friend, as he shut off the engine.

"Yeah," Queail answered.

"Leave it in here!"

When they exited, Ray retrieved the duffle bag containing the rifles from the backseat, then Queail followed him into the restaurant. They went straight to the back room, where they encountered Tommy, Drew, and some other man, who was a little older than the three of them. Not knowing who the man was or if he should even speak in front of him, Ray laid the bag down on the pool table, then looked at Tommy.

"Who is this?" Ray asked, jerking a thumb in the man's direction.

"Sean P.," Tommy answered. "He owns the restaurant."

"I respect that, but you know—"

"He's our alibi, Ray," Tommy cut his friend off. "You know just in case we need one."

Ray eyed Sean P. "Can we trust you?"

"I hope that's a rhetorical question," the man shot back.

"Let's go ahead and get started, Ray!" Tommy intervened. "We gotta have this shit mapped out to a T."

Realizing that Tommy was right, Ray looked to Drew. "Drew, I appreciated you for tagging along," he said.

Drew shrugged. "Hell, I was bored. Besides, this is the type of shit they trained me for."

"Did you bring the vests?" Ray inquired.

"Yeah," he answered, gesturing to a black trash bag that was also on top of the pool table. "Kevlar, Military-grade."

"Great!" Ray finally dumped the guns out of the bag. "But before we try those on, I'll need you to break down the functions of these weapons."

***

"I'll have to see if I can get away from the apartment tonight," Sheila said through her cellular as she drove.

"Ray was home when I left and I can't say if he'll leave out later."

Again, the children were staying with Dorothy and Elaine for the weekend. Sheila had spent the day with Nikki, who was still grieving the loss of Ace, whose remains have still not been released by the Homicide Division, which was holding up the funeral process.

She and Ray were still alienated but tried not to show this in front of the children. Although, Sheila knew better than to think that they were raising fools. Their wedding date was set for next Sunday and Sheila's heart was truly not in it. She couldn't imagine walking down the aisle and saying 'I do' when she was feeling otherwise. And there was no doubt in her mind that Ray was nursing the exact same notion.

"That sucks!" No Heart now replied. "It seems like I'm just having a hard time with getting my hands on your fine ass. I can't win for losing, huh?"

Sheila giggled. "It's not that bad. We both just have a lot going on in our lives. If it's meant to happen, it'll happen."

"It's definitely meant to happen," he assured.

"You might be right," Sheila said when she reached her apartment and saw that Ray's truck was not there.

***

After Drew showed everyone how to operate the M-4 rifles, Ray laid out his plan with a contingency and an escape route. Then, to waste a little more time, Sean P. had his cook to make everyone dinner. At 7:40PM, Ray, Tommy, Drew, and Queail exited the restaurant wearing the Kevlar vests under their dark clothing and Ray carrying the duffle bag of rifles.

Tommy climbed behind the wheel of a blue Volkswagen Passat and the others got into a black Chevy Yukon with Queail at the wheel. As their small convoy rolled out, with Tommy leading the way, Ray, who was in the front-passenger side of the truck, began thinking about Sheila. They had their issues like any other couple but that was no reason to throw in the towel on their relationship. Especially with their wedding date looming. At that moment, Ray decided that once this thing was over with Calvin, he was going to put his all into trying to make things right between them.

They followed Tommy to a closed body shop, not too far from the Mechanicsville housing projects. Being that the Volkswagen was for reconnaissance, and evacuation, Ray, Queail, and Drew exited the truck and joined Tommy, who started the car back down Glenn Street.

As planned, when Tommy reached the apartments, he entered them through an unnamed road that passed through them like a divider. It was dark but the community's night lamps made it easy to make out the facial features of any wandering residents. They were certainly able to make out the ones of the large group of men that were huddled in front of one building to the right of them. Calvin's face was the first face recognized by Ray.

"He's here," Ray announced from the rear of the car. "Like I said, expect for these niggas to shoot back. Especially Mankey. He's the tall, light-skinned nigga with the Atlanta Falcons shirt on. Drew, I'ma need you to make him your primary target."

"Got'cha!" Drew replied

Having driven the length of the community, Tommy made a right on Fulton Street, got to the stoplight, made another right on McDaniels riding past the front of the apartments. The next stoplight brought them back to Glenn Street. Tommy made the right turn and headed back towards the body shop, where they all climbed into the Yukon.

"It's 'go' time, fellas!" Ray said, handing everyone a rifle. "There's no reason to hesitate. Hop out, spray the scene, and get the fuck up out of there! And, also, watch out for anybody that might come to their rescue. We all got to make it out of here, alive."

At his final statement, it dawned on Ray that he was actually responsible for the lives of the three men that were accompanying him on this mission. He knew for a fact that they were all capable of handling themselves but if something happened to either of them, he would be deeply affected.

As part of the plan, Tommy drove past the unnamed road that ran through the apartments and made a left on McDaniels. The thing was to re-enter the apartments through the way they exited them. When they entered Mechanicsville from the other side, everybody donned their ski masks and switched on the infrared beams of their weapons.

The group of men were still in the same spot. As the truck neared, Ray saw that the men weren't paying them any attention. Then, at that instance, while the others were talking, smoking and laughing, Mankey turned and looked directly at the oncoming vehicle. Ray felt like the young gang member was looking right at him.

Tommy slammed down on the brakes but before he could put the gear into park, Ray and the others lunged from the truck. Rounding the front of the truck, Ray's eyes were on Calvin, who was still unaware of the imminent attack but he couldn't help but see Mankey pull a pistol from his pants, and dive to the ground. That got the attention of the others, who eventually went for their own weapons.

Mankey's gun went off repeatedly but before the others could get their guns out, Ray had the M-4 raised, looking through the sight, with the beam aimed at Calvin's upper body, just how Drew instructed. He squeezed on the trigger, sending a barrage of slugs at his acquired target. Calvin's body jerked with every impact before he and his gun crashed to the ground.

The other goons were suffering the same fate, as they endeavored to defend themselves as Ray's team did what they were instructed to do. Mankey managed to get off the ground, still firing at them while trying to round the building but he was hit several times and was forced to the ground. His cartridge went dry.

Hearing someone cry out in pain caused Ray to look to his men to see Tommy doubled over as a result of being wounded. Seeing that Calvin, and the other men were out of commission, Ray lowered his gun and rushed over to assist his friend.

"Where're you hit at?" Ray asked, physically assessing Tommy.

"In my thigh," Tommy grunted. "I got hit in the chest, too."

"Help me get him in the truck, Queail!" Ray barked. "Drew, you'll have to drive!"

Just as they got Tommy settled in the rear seat, more shots rang out from other directions. Like the trained Marine that he was, Drew immediately returned fire with Ray and Queail following suit. Running out of ammunition, they hurriedly climbed into the truck as more residents opened fire on them.

Throwing the gear into drive, Drew stomped down on the gas pedal as two of the rear windows crashed in on them and bullet peppered the vehicle like a hailstorm.

***

Usually, Sheila would be worried about what time Ray would be returning home but since they've been partially invisible to each other lately, she really couldn't care less. She moved along the expressway, amongst the evening traffic on her way to Atlanta, Georgia.

For some reason, she started to get a bad vibe about tonight. She didn't know how she allowed herself to become the 'Angel of Death', avenging herself of anyone who disrespected her as a woman, and Queen, but she promised herself that it would stop tonight. This was not something that she wanted to make a career out of because eventually, she knew that it would catch up with her.

As promised, No Heart was sitting in his car that was parked in front of the same house. Parking behind his car, Sheila killed the engine, grabbed her pocketbook, then exited. Knowing that No Heart was watching her through his rear-view mirror, she made a seductive show of pulling at the hem of her black leather skirt before passing between the two cars and climbing in beside No Heart. She was making sure that her skirt rose high enough for him to get a glimpse of the red panties she had on.

"I don't smoke," she said, declining the blunt he held out to her.

"Do you drink?" He asked.

"No alcohol."

"Well, damn!" No Heart took a pull on his blunt. "I can't see how you do it. When you're under the influence, it makes the sex better. Hell, I was high when I got my first piece of pussy and I was only ten. I felt like I was on another damn planet!"

Sheila forced a giggle as she looked out at the house. "I thought we were going inside."

"We are," he told her. "My mom's about to head to her boy-friend's house and do whatever it is that old people do when they're home alone." He looked past Sheila. "It's about damn time!"

Sheila followed his gaze and saw a woman leaving the house, heading for a white Mercedes-Benz truck that sat in the driveway. She looked to be in her mid-forties and she was wearing a tight blue skirt, some kind of kitten-heeled sandals, and what was clearly a blonde wig. Sheila didn't at all find it strange that as she walked to her car, she was intently staring in their direction as if trying to fig-ure out if Sheila was a familiar face. It was quite dark out. Sheila diverted her gaze to avoid recognition.

"Don't have that fast ass girl in my house, Quan!" She voiced upon reaching her vehicle.

"I love you too, momma!" No Heart shot back.

They both watched her get into her Mercedes, back out of the driveway, and drive in the opposite direction.

"She's not coming back until tomorrow night," No Heart in-formed Sheila.

"Well, you know I can't spend the night," she reminded.

"I know that." He took another pull on his blunt. "We can head on in when I finish with this."

"Do you have condoms?"

No Heart looked at her. "I was hoping 'you' brought some."

"I think I may have."

Digging inside her pocketbook, that was in her lap, Sheila made like she was rummaging around in it before gripping her .380 in her right hand. Feeling like it was now or never, she lifted the weapon from the bag and immediately fired a succession of four shots into No Heart's chest.

The look in his eyes was none other than the look of death as he slowly expelled the remaining air from his lungs and expired with his head rested on the steering wheel. Placing the gun back into her pocketbook, Sheila pulled out a handkerchief, in which she used to pull the door handle with. Ready to get as far away from the scene as she could, she pushed the door open and found herself looking down the barrel of a gun a split-second before sparks flashed from it, and everything went black.

Playa Ray

Chapter 28
One Week Later

"Y'all can go on home," Ray told Dorothy and Elaine, who were standing to the right of him, doing their best to console Prince Ray, and Rachel while struggling with their own grief. "I'll check on y'all, later."

While the women ushered the children away, Ray looked back down at Sheila's casket that the groundskeepers were shoveling dirt onto. He still couldn't wrap his mind around the murder scene that was illustrated to him by a homicide detective. He could understand the part about her murdering No Heart, but he was lost on the part where she was murdered, just after committing the act.

Ray hadn't been back to work since. He'd been beating up the streets, trying to find out who killed his woman, while the children shacked up with Elaine and Dorothy. Considering No Hearts affiliation, he already figured it was one of his affiliates. Of course, Major Gramz was Ray's number one suspect. He was just waiting to hear back from the streets before moving in on anyone.

"You good, bro?"

Ray looked up to see Poppo approaching. "Yeah, I'm good," he answered. "Thanks for doing the service for me!"

"You know it's all love," said Poppo. After a short pause, he said, "Look, I know that I made a promise to God but Sheila was family, so when you find out who did this, I want in!"

"I know you do, P.," Ray replied, patting his friend on the shoulder before turning and walking away.

Making it to his truck, Ray climbed behind the wheel, and just sat there, thinking about nothing. He hasn't been spending any time at the apartment since Sheila's death. He wasn't going anywhere near that place any time soon. Just then, his cellphone vibrated inside his blazer's interior pocket. He wasn't in the mood to chat but after seeing the information on the screen, he immediately answered.

"I hope you got some news for me!"

"Calm down, King Ray!" Big Ru said, chuckling. "You know I got some news for you."

"I'm listening."

"Major Gramz called it," the big guy informed. "He had one of his other men on No Heart. I didn't find out who he was, but—"

"Where can I find Major Gramz?" Ray cut him off, only concerned with the person who greenlighted his woman's demise.

***

Still not interested in going home, when Ray got off the phone with Big Ru, he drove out to Simpson Road to get a couple of handguns from Tommy, who was doing better after being wounded in the shootout. It was thanks to Queail's girlfriend, Kim, who doctored on him in their living room.

Leaving there, still clad in his black dress suit, Ray drove out to Decatur to meet with Big Ru but at some other house he'd given Ray the address to. Reaching the home, which seemed very much abandoned, he parked in front of it, behind a black, '97 Chevy Impala.

For some reason, the whole setup looked suspicious to him, but Ray wasn't worried because if Big Ru had something up his sleeves, Ray was prepared to go down with his guns blazing.

Killing the engine, Ray stepped down and tucked both nine millimeter handguns in the waistband of his pants. After looking up and down the street for anything out of place, he moved towards the house. Before he could reach the door, it came open to Quick Ru, who had one hand behind his back, concealing a gun.

"I'm strapped," Ray let him know, upon approaching.

"I hope so," Big Ru's shooter replied, stepping aside for Ray to enter.

The house was definitely unlived in, though it had all the signs of a campsite for junkies. As Ray stepped over all kinds of discarded trash, he studied the faces of the three men that Big Ru was standing in the center of the living room with but didn't recognize either of them.

"He should be here, shortly," Big Ru informed Ray as Quick Ru closed the door back.

"Are you sure he'll come here?"

Big Ru smiled. "Of course. Especially after what I told him."

"Which was?" Ray inquired, now sensing that something wasn't right.

"Well," the big man began, "He recognized your girlfriend as No Heart's killer and immediately put a price on your head. A big ass price."

"So, you're using me as bait," Ray surmised.

"It was all I could come up with," he purported, with a shrug. "Major Gramz and I are not the best of friends but there's no legitimate beef between us."

"So, what's the plan?" Ray posed, eyeing the three men flanking Big Ru.

"Shit, you want the nigga dead, right?"

"What's in it for you?" Ray answered his question with another one.

"Yeah, what's up?" Quick Ru answered his phone, getting everyone's attention. "Aight." He looked to Big Ru. "He's on the way. Three cars."

Ray directed his attention back to Big Ru, who'd, somehow, brandished a gun during the course of Quick Ru's phone conversation. He had it held at his side. As if not perceiving the threat, Ray reached for one of his own guns.

"I wouldn't advise that!" Big Ru warned, raising his weapon and prompting his concomitants to draw theirs.

Ray lowered his hand back to his side as one of the men lifted both of the nine millimeters off of him.

"You don't even look surprised," Big Ru resumed. "In fact, you're cool as a motherfucker, right now."

Ray didn't reply.

"Well, I guess you already know what's about to go down," he went on. "But, don't worry, I'm gonna handle Major Gramz for you. That way, you'll get to settle your score with him in the afterlife." Big Ru paused, clearly expecting for him to say something. After getting no response, he said, "You know what? I'm not even gonna leave it on that note. Major Gramz didn't kill your girl. I did."

Ray lunged at him, but the big man must've anticipated it, because he took a quick step back, avoiding the blow and firing a shot, which was followed by the discharging of the guns of his men. The many slugs to the upper body caused his legs to give out, dropping him to his knees before landing on his back.

At that time, Ray's vision was blurry as he looked up at the men that were now looming over him. He'd never been shot before, so it felt like a candle was left burning inside of him. Although, he dared to give these fuckers the pleasure of knowing that the pain was unbearable.

"I never wanted it to end like this, Ray," Big Ru insisted. "Not with you. I was gonna end up taking over the streets eventually, but your plate would've remained untouched. In fact,"

Boom!

The sound of the front door being kicked in cut off the big man's words. Ray shifted his gaze, despite the distortion of his retinas, he was sure that he saw Major Gramz rush through the threshold with some kind of submachine gun in his hand, followed by other men.

That's when the shots rang out from both sides. There were shouts of pain, and bodies hitting the floor. The commotion was very loud but as Ray's eyesight slowly gave way to darkness, the noise slowly faded. That's when he realized that it was his time. After escaping the snares of death on numerous occasions, King Ray had indeed come to his final reign.

The End

Lock Down Publications and Ca$h Presents assisted publishing packages.

BASIC PACKAGE $499
Editing
Cover Design
Formatting

UPGRADED PACKAGE $800
Typing
Editing
Cover Design
Formatting

ADVANCE PACKAGE $1,200
Typing
Editing
Cover Design
Formatting
Copyright registration
Proofreading
Upload book to Amazon

LDP SUPREME PACKAGE $1,500
Typing
Editing
Cover Design
Formatting
Copyright registration
Proofreading
Set up Amazon account
Upload book to Amazon

Playa Ray

Advertise on LDP Amazon and Facebook page

***Other services available upon request. Additional charges may apply
Lock Down Publications
P.O. Box 944
Stockbridge, GA 30281-9998
Phone # 470 303-9761

Submission Guideline

Submit the first three chapters of your completed manuscript to ldpsubmissions@gmail.com, subject line: Your book's title. The manuscript must be in a .doc file and sent as an attachment. Document should be in Times New Roman, double spaced and in size 12 font. Also, provide your synopsis and full contact information. If sending multiple submissions, they must each be in a separate email.

Have a story but no way to send it electronically? You can still submit to LDP/Ca$h Presents. Send in the first three chapters, written or typed, of your completed manuscript to:

LDP: Submissions Dept
Po Box 944
Stockbridge, Ga 30281

DO NOT send original manuscript. Must be a duplicate.

Provide your synopsis and a cover letter containing your full contact information.

Thanks for considering LDP and Ca$h Presents.

<u>NEW RELEASES</u>

GRIMEY WAYS 3 by RAY VINCI

HEAVEN GOT A GHETTO by RENTA

SOSA GANG 2 by ROMELL TUKES

KINGZ OF THE GAME 7 by PLAYA RAY

STRAIGHT BEAST MODE III

De'Kari

KINGPIN KILLAZ IV

STREET KINGS III

PAID IN BLOOD III

CARTEL KILLAZ IV

DOPE GODS III

Hood Rich

SINS OF A HUSTLA II

ASAD

YAYO V

Bred In The Game 2

S. Allen

THE STREETS WILL TALK II

By Yolanda Moore

SON OF A DOPE FIEND III

HEAVEN GOT A GHETTO III

SKI MASK MONEY II

By Renta

LOYALTY AIN'T PROMISED III

By Keith Williams

I'M NOTHING WITHOUT HIS LOVE II

SINS OF A THUG II

TO THE THUG I LOVED BEFORE II

IN A HUSTLER I TRUST II

By Monet Dragun

QUIET MONEY IV

EXTENDED CLIP III

THUG LIFE IV

By **Trai'Quan**

THE STREETS MADE ME IV
By **Larry D. Wright**
IF YOU CROSS ME ONCE III
ANGEL V
By **Anthony Fields**
THE STREETS WILL NEVER CLOSE IV
By K'ajji
HARD AND RUTHLESS III
KILLA KOUNTY IV
By Khufu
MONEY GAME III
By Smoove Dolla
JACK BOYS VS DOPE BOYS IV
A GANGSTA'S QUR'AN V
COKE GIRLZ II
COKE BOYS II
LIFE OF A SAVAGE V
CHI'RAQ GANGSTAS V
SOSA GANG III
BRONX SAVAGES II
BODYMORE KINGPINS II
By Romell Tukes
MURDA WAS THE CASE III
Elijah R. Freeman
AN UNFORESEEN LOVE IV
BABY, I'M WINTERTIME COLD III
By **Meesha**

QUEEN OF THE ZOO III
By **Black Migo**

CONFESSIONS OF A JACKBOY III

By Nicholas Lock

KING KILLA II

By Vincent "Vitto" Holloway

BETRAYAL OF A THUG III

By Fre$h

THE MURDER QUEENS III

By Michael Gallon

THE BIRTH OF A GANGSTER III

By Delmont Player

TREAL LOVE II

By Le'Monica Jackson

FOR THE LOVE OF BLOOD III

By Jamel Mitchell

RAN OFF ON DA PLUG II

By Paper Boi Rari

HOOD CONSIGLIERE III

By Keese

PRETTY GIRLS DO NASTY THINGS II

By Nicole Goosby

PROTÉGÉ OF A LEGEND III

LOVE IN THE TRENCHES II

By Corey Robinson

IT'S JUST ME AND YOU II

By Ah'Million

BORN IN THE GRAVE III

By Self Made Tay

FOREVER GANGSTA III

By Adrian Dulan

GORILLAZ IN THE TRENCHES II

By SayNoMore

THE COCAINE PRINCESS VIII

By King Rio

CRIME BOSS II

Playa Ray

LOYALTY IS EVERYTHING III

Molotti

HERE TODAY GONE TOMORROW II

By Fly Rock

REAL G'S MOVE IN SILENCE II

By Von Diesel

GRIMEY WAYS IV

By Ray Vinci

Available Now

RESTRAINING ORDER **I & II**

By **CA$H & Coffee**

LOVE KNOWS NO BOUNDARIES **I II & III**

By **Coffee**

RAISED AS A GOON I, II, III & IV

BRED BY THE SLUMS I, II, III

BLAST FOR ME I & II

ROTTEN TO THE CORE I II III

A BRONX TALE I, II, III

DUFFLE BAG CARTEL I II III IV V VI

Playa Ray

HEARTLESS GOON I II III IV V
A SAVAGE DOPEBOY I II
DRUG LORDS I II III
CUTTHROAT MAFIA I II
KING OF THE TRENCHES
By **Ghost**
LAY IT DOWN **I & II**
LAST OF A DYING BREED I II
BLOOD STAINS OF A SHOTTA I & II III
By **Jamaica**
LOYAL TO THE GAME I II III
LIFE OF SIN I, II III
By **TJ & Jelissa**
BLOODY COMMAS I & II
SKI MASK CARTEL I II & III
KING OF NEW YORK I II,III IV V
RISE TO POWER I II III
COKE KINGS I II III IV V
BORN HEARTLESS I II III IV
KING OF THE TRAP I II
By **T.J. Edwards**
IF LOVING HIM IS WRONG…I & II
LOVE ME EVEN WHEN IT HURTS I II III
By **Jelissa**
WHEN THE STREETS CLAP BACK I & II III
THE HEART OF A SAVAGE I II III IV
MONEY MAFIA I II
LOYAL TO THE SOIL I II III
By **Jibril Williams**
A DISTINGUISHED THUG STOLE MY HEART I II & III

232

LOVE SHOULDN'T HURT I II III IV

RENEGADE BOYS I II III IV

PAID IN KARMA I II III

SAVAGE STORMS I II III

AN UNFORESEEN LOVE I II III

BABY, I'M WINTERTIME COLD I II

By **Meesha**

A GANGSTER'S CODE I &, II III

A GANGSTER'S SYN I II III

THE SAVAGE LIFE I II III

CHAINED TO THE STREETS I II III

BLOOD ON THE MONEY I II III

A GANGSTA'S PAIN I II III

By J-Blunt

PUSH IT TO THE LIMIT

By **Bre' Hayes**

BLOOD OF A BOSS **I, II, III, IV, V**

SHADOWS OF THE GAME

TRAP BASTARD

By **Askari**

THE STREETS BLEED MURDER **I, II & III**

THE HEART OF A GANGSTA I II& III

By **Jerry Jackson**

CUM FOR ME I II III IV V VI VII VIII

An **LDP Erotica Collaboration**

BRIDE OF A HUSTLA **I II & II**

THE FETTI GIRLS **I, II& III**

CORRUPTED BY A GANGSTA I, II III, IV

BLINDED BY HIS LOVE

THE PRICE YOU PAY FOR LOVE I, II ,III

DOPE GIRL MAGIC I II III
By **Destiny Skai**
WHEN A GOOD GIRL GOES BAD
By **Adrienne**
THE COST OF LOYALTY I II III
By Kweli
A GANGSTER'S REVENGE **I II III & IV**
THE BOSS MAN'S DAUGHTERS I II III IV V
A SAVAGE LOVE **I & II**
BAE BELONGS TO ME I II
A HUSTLER'S DECEIT I, II, III
WHAT BAD BITCHES DO I, II, III
SOUL OF A MONSTER I II III
KILL ZONE
A DOPE BOY'S QUEEN I II III
TIL DEATH
By **Aryanna**
A KINGPIN'S AMBITON
A KINGPIN'S AMBITION **II**
I MURDER FOR THE DOUGH
By **Ambitious**
TRUE SAVAGE I II III IV V VI VII
DOPE BOY MAGIC I, II, III
MIDNIGHT CARTEL I II III
CITY OF KINGZ I II
NIGHTMARE ON SILENT AVE
THE PLUG OF LIL MEXICO II
CLASSIC CITY
By **Chris Green**
A DOPEBOY'S PRAYER

By **Eddie "Wolf" Lee**
THE KING CARTEL **I, II & III**
By **Frank Gresham**
THESE NIGGAS AIN'T LOYAL **I, II & III**
By **Nikki Tee**
GANGSTA SHYT **I II &III**
By **CATO**
THE ULTIMATE BETRAYAL
By **Phoenix**
BOSS'N UP **I , II & III**
By **Royal Nicole**
I LOVE YOU TO DEATH
By **Destiny J**
I RIDE FOR MY HITTA
I STILL RIDE FOR MY HITTA
By **Misty Holt**
LOVE & CHASIN' PAPER
By **Qay Crockett**
TO DIE IN VAIN
SINS OF A HUSTLA
By **ASAD**
BROOKLYN HUSTLAZ
By **Boogsy Morina**
BROOKLYN ON LOCK I & II
By **Sonovia**
GANGSTA CITY
By **Teddy Duke**
A DRUG KING AND HIS DIAMOND I & II III
A DOPEMAN'S RICHES
HER MAN, MINE'S TOO I, II

Playa Ray

CASH MONEY HO'S
THE WIFEY I USED TO BE I II
PRETTY GIRLS DO NASTY THINGS
By Nicole Goosby
TRAPHOUSE KING **I II & III**
KINGPIN KILLAZ I II III
STREET KINGS I II
PAID IN BLOOD **I II**
CARTEL KILLAZ I II III
DOPE GODS I II
By **Hood Rich**
LIPSTICK KILLAH **I, II, III**
CRIME OF PASSION I II & III
FRIEND OR FOE I II III
By **Mimi**
STEADY MOBBN' **I, II, III**
THE STREETS STAINED MY SOUL I II III
By **Marcellus Allen**
WHO SHOT YA **I, II, III**
SON OF A DOPE FIEND I II
HEAVEN GOT A GHETTO I II
SKI MASK MONEY
Renta
GORILLAZ IN THE BAY **I II III IV**
TEARS OF A GANGSTA I II
3X KRAZY I II
STRAIGHT BEAST MODE I II
DE'KARI
TRIGGADALE I II III
MURDAROBER WAS THE CASE I II

Elijah R. Freeman
GOD BLESS THE TRAPPERS I, II, III
THESE SCANDALOUS STREETS I, II, III
FEAR MY GANGSTA I, II, III IV, V
THESE STREETS DON'T LOVE NOBODY I, II
BURY ME A G I, II, III, IV, V
A GANGSTA'S EMPIRE I, II, III, IV
THE DOPEMAN'S BODYGAURD I II
THE REALEST KILLAZ I II III
THE LAST OF THE OGS I II III
Tranay Adams
THE STREETS ARE CALLING
Duquie Wilson
MARRIED TO A BOSS I II III
By Destiny Skai & Chris Green
KINGZ OF THE GAME I II III IV V VI VII
CRIME BOSS
Playa Ray
SLAUGHTER GANG I II III
RUTHLESS HEART I II III
By Willie Slaughter
FUK SHYT
By Blakk Diamond
DON'T F#CK WITH MY HEART I II
By Linnea
ADDICTED TO THE DRAMA I II III
IN THE ARM OF HIS BOSS II
By Jamila
YAYO I II III IV
A SHOOTER'S AMBITION I II

Playa Ray

BRED IN THE GAME
By S. Allen
TRAP GOD I II III
RICH $AVAGE I II III
MONEY IN THE GRAVE I II III
By Martell Troublesome Bolden
FOREVER GANGSTA I II
GLOCKS ON SATIN SHEETS I II
By Adrian Dulan
TOE TAGZ I II III IV
LEVELS TO THIS SHYT I II
IT'S JUST ME AND YOU
By Ah'Million
KINGPIN DREAMS I II III
RAN OFF ON DA PLUG
By Paper Boi Rari
CONFESSIONS OF A GANGSTA I II III IV
CONFESSIONS OF A JACKBOY I II
By Nicholas Lock
I'M NOTHING WITHOUT HIS LOVE
SINS OF A THUG
TO THE THUG I LOVED BEFORE
A GANGSTA SAVED XMAS
IN A HUSTLER I TRUST
By Monet Dragun
CAUGHT UP IN THE LIFE I II III
THE STREETS NEVER LET GO I II III
By Robert Baptiste
NEW TO THE GAME I II III
MONEY, MURDER & MEMORIES I II III

By **Malik D. Rice**
LIFE OF A SAVAGE I II III IV
A GANGSTA'S QUR'AN I II III IV
MURDA SEASON I II III
GANGLAND CARTEL I II III
CHI'RAQ GANGSTAS I II III IV
KILLERS ON ELM STREET I II III
JACK BOYZ N DA BRONX I II III
A DOPEBOY'S DREAM I II III
JACK BOYS VS DOPE BOYS I II III
COKE GIRLZ
COKE BOYS
SOSA GANG I II
BRONX SAVAGES
BODYMORE KINGPINS
By Romell Tukes
LOYALTY AIN'T PROMISED I II
By Keith Williams
QUIET MONEY I II III
THUG LIFE I II III
EXTENDED CLIP I II
A GANGSTA'S PARADISE
By **Trai'Quan**
THE STREETS MADE ME I II III
By **Larry D. Wright**
THE ULTIMATE SACRIFICE I, II, III, IV, V, VI
KHADIFI
IF YOU CROSS ME ONCE I II
ANGEL I II III IV
IN THE BLINK OF AN EYE

Playa Ray

By **Anthony Fields**
THE LIFE OF A HOOD STAR
By **Ca$h & Rashia Wilson**
THE STREETS WILL NEVER CLOSE I II III
By **K'ajji**
CREAM I II III
THE STREETS WILL TALK
By **Yolanda Moore**
NIGHTMARES OF A HUSTLA I II III
By **King Dream**
CONCRETE KILLA I II III
VICIOUS LOYALTY I II III
By **Kingpen**
HARD AND RUTHLESS I II
MOB TOWN 251
THE BILLIONAIRE BENTLEYS I II III
REAL G'S MOVE IN SILENCE
By **Von Diesel**
GHOST MOB
Stilloan Robinson
MOB TIES I II III IV V VI
SOUL OF A HUSTLER, HEART OF A KILLER I II
GORILLAZ IN THE TRENCHES
By **SayNoMore**
BODYMORE MURDERLAND I II III
THE BIRTH OF A GANGSTER I II
By **Delmont Player**
FOR THE LOVE OF A BOSS
By **C. D. Blue**
MOBBED UP I II III IV

240

THE BRICK MAN I II III IV V

THE COCAINE PRINCESS I II III IV V VI VII

By King Rio

KILLA KOUNTY I II III IV

By Khufu

MONEY GAME I II

By Smoove Dolla

A GANGSTA'S KARMA I II III

By FLAME

KING OF THE TRENCHES I II III

by **GHOST & TRANAY ADAMS**

QUEEN OF THE ZOO I II

By **Black Migo**

GRIMEY WAYS I II III

By Ray Vinci

XMAS WITH AN ATL SHOOTER

By Ca$h & Destiny Skai

KING KILLA

By Vincent "Vitto" Holloway

BETRAYAL OF A THUG I II

By Fre$h

THE MURDER QUEENS I II

By Michael Gallon

TREAL LOVE

By Le'Monica Jackson

FOR THE LOVE OF BLOOD I II

By Jamel Mitchell

HOOD CONSIGLIERE I II

By Keese

PROTÉGÉ OF A LEGEND I II

Playa Ray

LOVE IN THE TRENCHES
By Corey Robinson
BORN IN THE GRAVE I II
By Self Made Tay
MOAN IN MY MOUTH
By XTASY
TORN BETWEEN A GANGSTER AND A GENTLEMAN
By J-BLUNT & Miss Kim
LOYALTY IS EVERYTHING I II
Molotti
HERE TODAY GONE TOMORROW
By Fly Rock
PILLOW PRINCESS
By S. Hawkins

<u>BOOKS BY LDP'S CEO, CA$H</u>

TRUST IN NO MAN

TRUST IN NO MAN 2

TRUST IN NO MAN 3

BONDED BY BLOOD

SHORTY GOT A THUG

THUGS CRY

THUGS CRY 2

THUGS CRY 3

TRUST NO BITCH

TRUST NO BITCH 2

TRUST NO BITCH 3

TIL MY CASKET DROPS

RESTRAINING ORDER

RESTRAINING ORDER 2

IN LOVE WITH A CONVICT

LIFE OF A HOOD STAR

XMAS WITH AN ATL SHOOTER

Playa Ray

www.ingramcontent.com/pod-product-compliance
Lightning Source LLC
Chambersburg PA
CBHW071145260626
47162CB00003B/920